DEAD AND GONE

"Has anyone seen Sylar?" Ve asked. "He was supposed to walk back with us."

"He was here a minute ago," Gayle said.

Ve looked toward the back door. "He probably stepped outside for a moment. He wants me to think he quit smoking, but I know he still sneaks a few cigarettes a day."

"I'll check for him," I offered. I cut through the romance section and walked along a narrow hallway, past a restroom, a small kitchen, a storeroom, and an office.

I opened the back door and was surprised to find Sylar kneeling on the ground, an unlit cigarette hanging out of his mouth. Rain fell steadily.

Sylar's glasses wobbled on his nose as he looked up at me, his face drained of color. Rain dripped off his chin. It was then that I noticed that he was kneeling over someone.

I stepped forward. Alexandra Shively lay on the ground. My breath caught when I spotted Ve's beautiful turquoise scarf knotted tightly around Alexandra's neck.

"We need to call the paramedics," Sylar said in a small voice.

There was no use. Alexandra's face was swollen, blood trickled from her nose, and her eyes were wide open and bulging, but not seeing anything at all.

She was very clearly dead.

It Takes a Witch

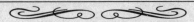

A WISHCRAFT MYSTERY

HEATHER BLAKE

AN OBSIDIAN MYSTERY

OBSIDIAN
Published by New American Library, a division of
Penguin Group (USA) Inc., 375 Hudson Street,
New York, New York 10014, USA
Penguin Group (Canada), 90 Eglinton Avenue East, Suite 700, Toronto,
Ontario M4P 2Y3, Canada (a division of Pearson Penguin Canada Inc.)
Penguin Books Ltd., 80 Strand, London WC2R 0RL, England
Penguin Ireland, 25 St. Stephen's Green, Dublin 2,
Ireland (a division of Penguin Books Ltd.)
Penguin Group (Australia), 250 Camberwell Road, Camberwell, Victoria 3124,
Australia (a division of Pearson Australia Group Pty. Ltd.)
Penguin Books India Pvt. Ltd., 11 Community Centre, Panchsheel Park,
New Delhi - 110 017, India
Penguin Group (NZ), 67 Apollo Drive, Rosedale, Auckland 0632,
New Zealand (a division of Pearson New Zealand Ltd.)
Penguin Books (South Africa) (Pty.) Ltd., 24 Sturdee Avenue,
Rosebank, Johannesburg 2196, South Africa

Penguin Books Ltd., Registered Offices:
80 Strand, London WC2R 0RL, England

First published by Obsidian, an imprint of New American Library,
a division of Penguin Group (USA) Inc.

First Printing, January 2012
10   9   8   7   6   5   4   3   2   1

Copyright © Heather Webber, 2012
All rights reserved

This one is for Jessica Faust.
Thank you for everything.

ACKNOWLEDGMENTS

I am beyond thankful for the wonderful editorial guidance of Sandy Harding. She not only took a chance on me (and Darcy), but also helped me shape this book into something I am incredibly proud of. A big thank-you also goes to Elizabeth Bistrow and everyone at NAL who had a hand in seeing this book come to life.

Endless gratitude goes to Sharon Short, who spent hours with me at a local Panera helping me flesh out Wishcraft rules. I can only imagine what eavesdroppers may have been thinking. Next time, Sharon, the green tea is on me.

To my critique partners, who always know just what to say (even when I might not want to hear it): You're the best friends a girl can have.

I'm so grateful for my family, who have always been incredibly supportive of me and my dreams. I couldn't do this without you. Much love.

Finally, to my readers who enthusiastically follow me—and my characters—wherever my books take us . . . I cannot express how grateful I am. Thank you.

Chapter One

Usually I'm not in the habit of tiptoeing through strange houses under the cover of darkness.

It was unsettling to say the least, and I felt completely out of sorts. My outfit only added to my discomfort. The flouncy, frilly pink satin bodysuit, tulle tutu, and pink ballet slippers were a far cry from my usual jeans and tee.

It didn't help that my every move was being watched closely.

As I crept up the aged wooden stairs of a large house along the coast of Salem, Massachusetts, Amanda Goodwin followed behind me with her mother-in-law, Cherise, bringing up the rear. They'd ushered me straight upstairs as soon as I'd arrived, their eyes lit like they were two little girls sneaking a peek at Santa. At the top of the steps, a long hallway branched into four bedrooms, one of which had its door closed. Pink and black polka-dotted block letters attached to the wood paneling declared it as my destination: Laurel Grace Goodwin's bedroom.

"Have you done this before, Ms. Merriweather?" Amanda asked softly, tugging on my gossamer wings. "Played the tooth fairy?"

I had sized up Amanda immediately as a hip suburban soccer mom, in her designer jeans, beaded tank top, and Grecian-inspired sandals. A natural blonde, she wore her hair long and straight, parted down the middle. Lots of lip gloss and mascara but not much else.

I smiled, trying to hide my nervousness. "Please call me Darcy, and this is my first time." I truly hoped it would be my last. Tulle and I didn't get along. My legs were itching something fierce, despite the thin protection of a pair of tights.

"Well"—Cherise had the strong Boston accent of someone who had been born and bred in this area—"your aunt Velma highly recommends you, and we trust her and As You Wish implicitly."

I had been working at my aunt Ve's business, As You Wish, for only two weeks. The company blended the tasks of a virtual personal assistant and a personal concierge service. Our clients' requests were diverse, often challenging, and sometimes just plain strange. They ranged from administrative tasks to running errands, to shopping for a gift, to providing an extra pair of hands to clean up a messy house, and much, much more. As You Wish's motto was that no request was too big or too small and no job impossible—as was proven by the fact that I was standing before the Goodwins looking like a character from a fairy tale.

I transferred my velvet drawstring purse from one hand to the other and noticed I was leaving a trail of glitter behind me. It sparkled on the rich dark oak floors.

Short and pleasantly plump with chin-length snow-white hair, heavily layered and teased, Cherise wore a bit too much makeup, and overaccessorized with several ropes of beaded necklaces and heavy chandelier earrings. "I was glad to hear of you and your sister moving in with Velma. I imagine she's been glad to share the *family business* with you?"

Ve had told me that she and Cherise were old friends, though they hadn't spoken in a while. Even still, I wasn't the least bit surprised Cherise knew of my arrival to the Enchanted Village, the unique Salem neighborhood where my aunt lived.

A new witch in town doesn't go unnoticed in these parts.

And two new witches? Rumors were flying faster than some broomsticks.

Cherise either was fishing for a little gossip or was genuinely curious to know if my sister, Harper, and I were aware that the *family business* she referred to wasn't the brick-and-mortar As You Wish, but the fact that we could actually grant wishes through a wishing spell.

It was a reasonable inquiry. Until three weeks ago, Harper and I were living in Ohio and dealing with lives that weren't what we'd imagined. When we received a note from Aunt Ve asking if she could visit because she had something important to tell us, we had no idea how our lives would change. Within a week we had packed up what little we had and moved to the Enchanted Village.

"We're glad to be here." Well, I was. Harper was still adjusting.

Putting my (disastrous) divorce and my inability to find a decent job behind me and getting Harper out of Ohio before she caused any more trouble may have been the perfect incentive to move, but learning about our heritage of the Craft, or in my family's case *Wish*-craft, was now a priority. I was still learning the Wishcraft Laws, and all the ins and outs that came along with the revelation that I was a witch.

Thankfully some of the laws were easy to remember. Like the fact that I can't wish death on anyone. Or prevent death. Or interfere with true love. Or that no Wishcrafter can grant her own wishes (or other Wishcrafters' wishes). I also can't solicit or refuse to grant a wish without severe consequence. However, the biggest rule of all was that I (or any Crafter for that matter) couldn't reveal to any mortal the truth about my powers or I risked losing my wish-granting abilities forever.

Unfortunately, some of the laws were a little fuzzy. Like the law about wishing for money—granting that wish meant the money would have to be *taken* from someone else. To follow the Crafters' basic principle of "Do no harm," the Wishcrafter Laws also required that only wishes made with motives pure of heart would be granted. How that was actually determined was still a mystery to me.

Cherise pressed. "How do you enjoy working for As You Wish?"

The Goodwins were Curecrafters, healing witches, and were apparently quite nosy to boot. "It's going well," I said. "So far this week I've tracked down sold-out tickets to tonight's Boston Pops performance, created a gift basket for a basset hound recovering from surgery, searched online for an out-of-print romance novel, and now this." I gestured to my costume. I didn't mention anything about the Wishcrafting, and how I'd been able to use a spell to help a client get last-minute tickets on a sold-out flight to Paris so he could surprise his girlfriend with a weekend getaway.

As You Wish was both popular and highly successful. Most of the requests received were accomplished through hard work and sheer determination. However, sometimes . . . sometimes magic was needed to get the job done right. Often, because of the name of the shop, people simply made wishes—which made our job a whole lot easier. Other times, seeking the help of other Crafters and *their* unique abilities gave us an edge.

But mortals, who were the majority of our clients, didn't know about the magic. And though the average customer wouldn't be surprised about something mystical happening in a place called the Enchanted Village, disclosing our family powers wasn't a risk Aunt Ve was willing to take, especially after having an ancestor nearly burned at the stake.

"Well, you make a lovely tooth fairy," Amanda said as a grandfather clock donged at the far end of the hallway.

It was nine. I had to hurry this along—or I'd be late for the emergency village meeting that was due to start at nine thirty. Ve had insisted Harper and I attend. Our aunt was still introducing us around the village and was eager for us to get acclimated. She wanted nothing more than for us to put down solid roots among the other Crafters. Well, that and take over As You Wish when she retired.

"Do you mind if I tape this?" Cherise asked, holding up a small video camera. "For my son? He couldn't be here tonight."

"I'm sorry," I said. "We don't allow videotaping of our services." For good reason. Wishcrafters emitted a blinding glow, a white aura, on camera. Which explained, after all these years, why there weren't any baby pictures of Harper and me, and why every picture we were in was always "overexposed."

I was surprised Cherise had asked. Didn't she know about the auras? I made a mental note to ask Ve how much Crafters knew about one another and their limitations. How secretive were Crafters with one another?

Cameras were definitely out. Not that I would even recognize myself right now, with all the costume makeup and glitter I was wearing. It took a lot of effort, and some amazing false eyelashes, to look fairylike.

"Dennis was welcome to be here tonight, Cherise." Amanda's cheeks flushed. "He declined. It's his loss."

"He's stubborn," Cherise said. "You know this."

I tried to blend into the woodwork—rather hard to do when one looked a lot like a giant glittery stick of pink cotton candy. The last thing I wanted was to get involved in the middle of a family dispute. Been there, done that.

Amanda must have sensed my unease. She said, "I'm sorry. My husband and I recently separated. I'm sure you don't need all the gory details. Suffice it to say that *he's* the one who moved out."

My heart ached for her. I was much better off without my ex, but it had taken me two years to realize that.

Cherise's eyebrow rose. "He's *very* stubborn."

Amanda flashed her an irritated look. "Besides, if you recall, it's his fault we had to contact As You Wish in the first place."

As You Wish had received a frantic call from Cherise this morning, needing to hire someone to play the tooth fairy. Amanda's daughter, five-year-old Laurel Grace, had lost her first tooth, and had been excited for the tooth fairy to come—until her father told her there was no such thing.

Aunt Ve, who had taken the call, had somehow deemed that this was the perfect job for me to take on. I had my doubts. Especially when I saw the gossamer wings and the pink tights. Not to mention the dreadful tulle.

Cherise looked pained. She explained, "He wasn't thinking. Once he realized what he'd said, he tried to convince Laurel Grace he'd been kidding, but the damage had been done."

"Not the first time," Amanda murmured.

"I just wish . . . ," Cherise began.

I sucked in a breath, waiting. My every nerve was on alert, standing on end, prickling, getting ready to react. Adrenaline surged, flowed.

"I just wish . . ." She shook her head. "Never mind."

I let out the breath I'd been holding.

Wringing her hands, Amanda said, "Five-year-olds shouldn't have to grow up so soon. Darcy, we need you to convince her that sometimes grown-ups can be wrong. The last thing we want her thinking is that magic doesn't exist, especially when she doesn't know about her Craft yet."

"I'll certainly do my best," I said. "Shall we give it a try?"

Aunt Ve had gone over exactly what I should do. I ran over the instructions in my head as I slowly turned the doorknob to Laurel Grace's bedroom. I held my breath and entered.

Moonbeams slipped through striped curtains, spreading muted light across the room. The walls were painted pastel pink and trimmed in creamy white. Touches of pale green were everywhere from the curtains to the overstuffed chair in the corner, to the duvet on the bed. Stuffed animals overflowed a toy chest, books were piled high on a corner bookshelf, and a dollhouse sat on a tiny table in the middle of the room, filled with delicate-looking miniatures.

I turned my attention to the four-poster bed. Tucked under a lightweight comforter, Laurel Grace slept on her side. I crept closer. Blond ringlets fell across a lace-trimmed pillowcase. Her little face, slack with sleep, was angelic and peaceful.

I was aware of Amanda and Cherise lurking in the doorway as I carefully slid my hand under Laurel Grace's pillow. I pulled out the little ribbon-edged, tooth-shaped pillow that had been delivered by courier earlier in the day for Laurel Grace to tuck her tooth into. I felt the lump of the tiny tooth under the fabric as I brought the keepsake over to Amanda and handed it to her.

I then walked back over to the bed, opened my purse, and pulled out a small satin pouch trimmed in white ostrich feathers. Laurel Grace's name had been embroidered in pink on the bag. Inside, two one-dollar gold pieces clinked together. I gently slid the pouch under the pillow.

I smiled in the twilight, thinking about how expensive that little tooth had been. Two dollars from the tooth fairy, fifty dollars for accessories, and one hundred dollars for a half hour of my time.

I bent my head close to Laurel Grace's and whispered the words Aunt Ve had me memorize.

"Hello, hello, little one,
A tooth you have lost,
More you will lose.
Put them under your pillow,
And take a sweet snooze.
For upon that eve,
You will receive
A visit from me,
If you just believe."

Laurel Grace's eyelids squeezed into a wince—I couldn't blame her—it was a horrible, horrible rhyme—then popped open.

Filled with a warmth that came from being part of such a special moment, I suddenly had visions of being the area's go-to tooth fairy, spreading love and happiness and gold coins across the state—heck, across all of New England. Even the tulle didn't seem so uncomfortable anymore.

Laurel Grace stared at me for a second, probably taking in the tiara, the eyelashes, the wings, the makeup and glitter. I kept quiet, giving her a moment for it all to sink in.

Abruptly, she sat upright, looked me straight in the eyes, and started screaming at the top of her lungs. Long, shrieking cries that hurt my ears. "Stranger danger! Stranger dan-ger!"

Startled, I screamed back.

Amanda rushed into the room, saying, "Shhh, shhh."

I wasn't sure if she was talking to me or her daughter.

Clamping my lips closed, I backed away as Amanda sat on the bed and gathered Laurel Grace close. "Shhh."

"Stranger danger! Stran-ger dan-ger!" Laurel Grace continued to howl.

"No, no," I said, gathering my wits. "I'm not a stranger! I'm the tooth fairy." Heaven help me, I even twirled. My skirt billowed out, raining sparkles on the carpet.

"No, you're not." Tears flowed from Laurel Grace's eyes.

Ve had not prepared me for *this* scenario.

"Yes, I am," I reassured, fluffing layers of tulle as though that would help my cause.

"She really is." Cherise sat on the other side of the bed, rubbing Laurel Grace's back.

"No, she's not," Laurel Grace insisted.

"Why isn't she?" Amanda asked her daughter.

"She's—she's ..." I was waiting for the words "a fraud" to fall from her lips, and was shocked when she said, "She's not blond!"

I held back a smile as I fingered my long dark hair, trying to think of what to do, what to say. I knelt by Laurel Grace's bed and improvised as best I could. "Fairies are just like people." *And Crafters,* I added silently. "We come in all different shapes, sizes, and colors."

She gazed at me with big blue eyes as though I wasn't even close to measuring up to her idea of a fairy. It was true I more resembled Esméralda from Disney's *The Hunchback of Notre Dame*, which might be a tad bit confusing to a five-year-old looking for the Tinkerbell sort, so I tried really hard not to be offended when she started wailing again.

I saw Cherise's lips moving but couldn't hear what she was saying, and then her left eye blinked twice. Laurel Grace immediately quieted but still wore a tremulous pout.

Cherise had used a curing spell to calm the little girl.

Amanda quickly said, "Why don't you look under your pillow, honey?"

I recognized a chance to escape when I saw one. "I should be going. Lots of stops to make tonight. Lots of teeth lost!" I backed out of the room as Laurel Grace pulled the satin pouch from beneath the pillow.

"How did she know my name, Mommy?" I heard from the safety of the hallway.

"Because she's magical," Amanda answered. "Do you believe now?"

"Maybe," Laurel Grace whispered.

I had to smile at her noncommitment.

Cherise had followed me out. "Thank you, Darcy," she said as we walked down the stairs. In the kitchen, she pressed a check into my hand. "I'll let Velma know what a great job you did."

I was ready to put this whole night behind me — and hang up my wings for good. I tucked the check into my purse. "You're welcome."

Cherise rubbed her ears as if they were still ringing. "She's tiny, but she has a pair of lungs that can rival an opera singer. Sometimes spells come in handy, don't you think?"

I fidgeted, not sure what to say.

Before I could come up with a response, she added, "I just wish Dennis could be here right now. He's really missing out on an important event in his daughter's life."

She stared expectantly at me.

She had me. As a Wishcrafter, I was obligated to grant the wish. However, if Cherise wasn't pure of heart in her motives for making the wish, my spell wouldn't work no matter how hard I tried to grant it. *Do no harm.*

My nerves tingled as I said softly, "Wish I might, wish I may, grant this wish without delay." I winked my left eye twice, which would look merely like a twitch to a mortal, but other Crafters would know my spell had been cast. "You're sneaky."

"I know. Sorry about that." She gave me a mischievous smile. "You just can't trust anyone these days."

Chapter Two

Ten minutes later, my cell phone, tucked into the car's cup holder, bayed like a bloodhound. The loud *arr-oooo* told me the caller was my sister, Harper, the tone chosen because of Harper's tendency to be all bark and no bite (most of the time). I answered.

"Where are you?" she asked in a tense whisper. "It's like I've been fed to the wolves. Questions are coming at me left and right."

Harper was being a bit melodramatic, especially since *she* was more of a wolf in sheep's clothing than anyone.

I said, "I'm in the car. I was waylaid by a wish."

"Did the wish come true?"

She was still skeptical about our talent and hadn't cast any spells since arriving in the village.

"It did."

A (justly) confused Dennis Goodwin had stormed into Amanda's house as I was on my way out. He took one look at me and started grumbling. Obviously, he hadn't been impressed with my glitter or my eyelashes, either. Like daughter, like father. He especially wasn't pleased to learn he'd been *wished* there.

I gave Harper the shorthand version of my night, and ignored her laughter at Laurel Grace's "stranger danger" reaction. "I'm almost to the village. Where are you now?" I'd expected to hear noise from the village meeting in the background, but there was only silence.

"I ducked into the back alley. I'm surprised someone hasn't followed me out. Vultures."

"I thought they were wolves?"

"Close enough. I'm still being picked apart, torn limb from limb."

I wasn't worried in the least about her being alone in a dark alley. Sure, she was tiny, but she was mighty and quite a fighter. Always had been, ever since she was born prematurely, twenty-three years ago. My chest tightened as it always did when I thought about Harper's birth. And how it had also been the day of our mother's death.

Besides, the Enchanted Village was about as scary as a baby duckling. Nothing bad ever happened here. That alleyway was as safe as safe could be.

"I'm still not sure this village is right for us. I sense some seriously bad juju at this meeting."

Lightning flashed in the distance, highlighting dark cloud cover. I shuddered. I hated electrical storms with every fiber of my being.

Focusing on what Harper had said, I knew I'd be a fool to ignore her instincts—they were finely tuned—but I thought this village was exactly where we needed to be. So much had gone wrong over the last few years in our lives, from my divorce to Harper's brushes with the law.

"It can't be worse than where we were, right?" I said.

"It was one little arrest, Darcy. Six months ago," she added impatiently. "Can we let it go now? I don't really want my arrest record to follow me around for the rest of my life."

She should have thought of that before she was caught shoplifting a puppy. Harper swore up and down it was the first and only time she'd ever stolen something, and I wanted to believe her, but didn't quite. Ever since she was little, she was always getting into some kind of trouble. In elementary school, it was writing on the bathroom walls about the injustices of processed cafeteria food (she was always too smart for her own good). In high school it was mostly silly pranks on the class bullies (sneaking into the locker room and putting itching powder in jockstraps). In college she'd been the lead suspect in setting free dozens of lab rats in a science lab (not enough evidence to file charges). As far as I knew, she was currently on a straight and narrow path, her misguided attempts at activism in check. Hopefully a change of scenery would keep her on that course. I really didn't want to see her go to jail.

"Hey, what's one more secret?" I completely agreed we should keep her past quiet. People could be terribly judgmental.

She laughed. "I think the witchy wish thing trumps my misdemeanor."

I smiled at the thought of Miss Demeanor, aka Missy, the gray and white Schnoodle (half Schnauzer, half Poodle) who was now part of our family. The dog was the only silver lining that had come out of Harper's arrest. Well, okay, all right. There had been the fact that Harper's arrest had sparked an investigation that led to the dreadful pet store and three puppy mills being closed down (which was why the judge was lenient with her, giving her community service instead of jail time). Be that as it may, Harper still didn't mind getting into all kinds of trouble if she believed she was fighting for a just cause.

I tried not to worry too much about Missy's slight personality change since our arrival to the village. She'd gone from a wild puppy with crazed frenetic energy to one who had more of a controlled enthusiasm. And one who had suddenly become an escape artist, running away as often as she could. Thankfully, she always returned, but it was exhausting searching for her, and for some reason, I couldn't figure out how she kept getting out of the yard. Was hers the normal progression of puppy behavior? Or was I just overreacting? After all, the move had been an adjustment for all of us. New house, new town, new everything. Even still, I wondered whether I should take her to a local vet for a checkup. Just to be sure.

I slowed and took a left turn down the road that led to the Enchanted Village. "I needed the change, too," I said so Harper wouldn't feel like this move had been all about her. "You know, because of the divorce." It was the truth. It was good to get away, to not have to see my ex with his brand-new family around town. The jab in my heart told me I still wasn't completely over what had happened, despite my attempts to convince myself otherwise.

An elaborate iron trellis covered in dripping vines and vibrant white night-blooming moonflowers marked the change from the paved road into a cobblestoned lane that twisted narrowly through the woods that surrounded the village.

As I drove along, the branches of mature yew trees stretched overhead, entwining to form a natural tunnel. The dark, shadowy passage stirred recollections of enchanted forests from old storybooks where pixies played and hollows hid mischievous trolls.

It was likely that in these particular woods pixies and trolls still played. I'd come to believe *anything* was possible in the Enchanted Village. After all, I was a witch.

Only four months had passed since my father's death, which had been the catalyst to my and Harper's lives changing drastically. Till that point, I'd been working at Dad's dental practice as an office manager. With his death the practice closed, and I lost my job—no more throwing myself into work to forget my painful divorce. No more pretending everything was just fine in my life.

Harper, a recent college graduate who hadn't had any job offers, had turned to activism to occupy her time.

Dad had left us a nice inheritance, sure, but we quickly found out that money didn't buy us the happiness we were sadly lacking or suddenly reveal our purposes in life. We were grieving, at loose ends. Not sure what to do with our lives. Until Aunt Ve visited us and made her big revelation. We were witches, something our father had known all along and hadn't told us. I was still trying to comprehend why he'd kept us in the dark, even going so far as to make Aunt Ve promise never to tell us while he was still alive.

Never in a million years would I have guessed I was a witch before Aunt Ve broke the news. I wondered how my life could have been different if I'd known about the wishing spells when I was growing up. How I would have been different . . .

I shook the thoughts aside. There was no use dwelling on what-could-have-beens. It was time to focus on our futures. "Has the meeting started?"

"Not yet. Everyone's waiting for the grand hoo-ha to arrive."

"Has there been any talk about why the meeting was called?"

"Not a peep—people are too busy interrogating me." Desperation caused a hitch in her voice as she added, "How soon will you get here?"

Harper had always preferred books to people, hated crowds, and, most of all, detested answering questions about herself. This meeting had to be torture for her.

"Another ten minutes or so. I need to stop at the house and change." I'd already shimmied out of the tutu and wings and put on a pair of jeans I'd had in the car. I used some wet wipes to take off the heaviest makeup, but I still wore the frilly pink bodysuit, and the glitter was being stubborn.

"What? No! You don't have time. I need you here, Darcy. Or there may be nothing left of me. Please?"

That was low. She knew I couldn't say no to her when she asked nicely. "Okay, fine. I'll be there in a couple of minutes."

I hung up as the natural tunnel widened, and I slowed at an ornate welcome sign at the side of the road, crowded with colorful flowers at its base.

WELCOME TO THE ENCHANTED VILLAGE,
WHERE MAGIC LIVES

I looked ahead, taken away by the beauty and charm before me. The village square was aglow in fairy lights and sparkling lanterns hanging from tree branches. Gaslights cast circles of light onto the stone sidewalks and threw shadows along the connected storefronts and individual shops that lined the main square.

Awnings shaded large plate-glass shop windows, and ivy trailed from flower boxes bursting with bold-hued annuals. A few tourists remained, walking hand in hand along the sidewalk, window-shopping—most of the shops closed at nine on weeknights. Windows glowed in the apartments above the storefronts, and specks of lights twinkled from the streetlamps along the lanes of the neighborhoods beyond the square.

Neighborhoods where magic lived.

The Enchanted Village had prospered by focusing on all things magical. Tourists loved it. But what the mortals didn't know was that magic was truly present here in the form of witches. From the time of the Salem Witch Trials in the late sixteen hundreds, this land had been a haven. A safe place for witches to hide until it was safe to practice their Crafts publicly once again.

That time had never come. There were still too many

who didn't understand the magic, the powers, and they feared what they didn't know.

So the decision was made to hide in plain sight. By creating the Enchanted Village as a tourist area, the Craft could be practiced under the guise of commercialism.

The Spellcrafters opened the Spellbound Bookshop — where I was headed for the meeting. The Herbcrafters opened Natural Magick Tea Shoppe. The Colorcrafters opened both the Magic Wand Salon and Just an Illusion Art Gallery.

Some of the shops in the village were owned by mortals, who had no idea they worked side by side with Crafters. To many, this was just a cute tourist destination and a quaint place to live. But to the Crafters, this village was their heritage — and a way to keep it alive.

Lightning lit the western sky as the road narrowed. At the center of the village, I slowed and turned right, heading toward the bookshop.

All the diagonal parking spots in front of the store were already taken, so I parked down the street, in the lot of the Pixie Cottage, a small B&B. Thunder rumbled in the distance as I hurried down the sidewalk, fighting against the strong breeze, fighting against the apprehension within me that arose with every storm. Across the village green, I spotted the brightly lit As You Wish sign swaying on the arched portico of a beautiful Victorian.

Home. I liked the calm and peaceful feeling the word created within me — serenity had been hard to come by since my divorce.

Smiling, I picked up my pace before the storm hit. Every shop I passed was closed up tight. The only businesses open this late were the Cauldron (the local pub) and the Sorcerer's Stove (a family restaurant with the best burgers in the village), but they were located on the other side of the square. I rushed past the Spinning Wheel and the Witch's Brew Coffee Shop, and paused ever so slightly at the Bewitching Boutique. Its window display highlighted a gorgeous blue flowing gown, perfect for a romantic night on the town.

Romance. It was a nice thought—for someone else. Though I'd come to fully believe in magic, to me love was a complete and total fairy tale. A bad one at that.

The sulfury scent of rain hung in the air, and lightning flashed brightly, a flickering warning to take cover. I was almost to the bookshop when I spotted a man approaching from the opposite direction, his gait sure and steady. Confident. Thunder echoed as we reached the door at the same time.

He was tall, dark, and dangerous with his don't-mess-with-me attitude. I'd never seen him before, though if he was attending the meeting, he must be a local.

Mortal or Crafter? I wondered.

No way to tell.

Even within the Craft world, there was no way to know unless the power was revealed through the eye twitch or through word of mouth between Crafter families. We all had to be very careful what we said. Revelation of our powers to a mortal, even accidentally, meant risking the loss of our gift forever.

I smiled politely and reached for the door handle. He beat me to it. My right hand landed on his left, and I felt a jolt of energy clear up to my shoulder. I dismissed it as a result of the electricity in the air and drew my hand back and waited.

But he didn't open the door. In fact, I was pretty sure he was holding it closed.

Great.

"I don't think I know you," he said, his voice deep, curt, and oddly mesmerizing. "Are you new in the village?"

"Fairly new." I glanced at the door, willed him to

open it. I wanted to *wish* it, but I couldn't grant my own wishes. Unfortunately.

He had a look about him—a keen, assessing dark gaze, the square of his shoulders—that screamed law enforcement of some kind. As far as I knew, I hadn't done anything wrong tonight—other than almost scaring a little girl to death—so I wasn't sure why I suddenly felt like a suspect.

"Nick Sawyer," he said, holding out his right hand, his left still firm on the damn door.

"Darcy Merriweather." I reluctantly held out my hand.

He surprised me by smiling. "Ve's niece?"

I nodded, hating what his smile was doing to my stomach. Making it feel all soft and gushy. I tugged my hand from his. Why was my mouth suddenly dry? And why did I suddenly notice his left ring finger was bare? "We should be getting inside, don't you think? We don't want to miss the meeting."

"No, we don't want to do that." He was blatantly staring at me, making no move to go inside.

"The door?" I resisted the urge to squirm under his scrutiny.

"Right." Again the smile. "Nice to meet you, Darcy Merriweather."

"You, too," I said as sweetly as I could muster. I couldn't remember the last time I'd felt so uncomfortable.

He (finally!) held open the door, and I rushed forward, so very glad to be free. But I suddenly ran into a solid wall of muscle. Nick had sidestepped in front of me, blocking my entrance. Surprised, I reached out before I fell backward.

Unfortunately, I latched on to *him*. Gripping his shirt, I could feel his muscled chest beneath my hands. His heartbeat, too. It was strong and steady, pulsing under my fingertips.

I backed off. Way off. I tucked my arms behind me, linking my fingers together tightly.

A sly smile pulled on his lips. "Just wanted to say . . ."

His gaze swept slowly over me, making me heat from the inside out. I didn't like it. Not one bit. I hadn't let myself get this close to a man since my divorce—when I'd sworn men off altogether. I couldn't let this instant attraction go any further than this doorway.

I didn't want to be hurt again.

"Yes?" I said with a hint of steel.

He held the door open wide. "I like your tiara."

Chapter Three

"Darcy, dear, this is Sylar Dewitt, owner of Third Eye Optometry and chairman of the village council." Aunt Ve linked arms with the man. Her cheeks colored as she added in a conspiratorial whisper, "He's also my beau."

Sylar shook my hand heartily, a wide grin splitting his doughy face. He was short and pudgy with kind blue eyes, a shock of spiky white hair, and a white mustache that curled upward at its ends. A pair of round glasses perched precariously on his bulbous nose. "Pleasure to meet you, Darcy. I've heard much about you from Ve."

I sensed a genuine fondness between the two of them, and it immediately relaxed me. They looked adorable together, a perfect pair of lovebirds.

"Hopefully not too much," I teased.

Sylar laughed and said, "Are you keeping secrets?"

Ve caught my eye and mouthed "Mortal." Ah. Okay. Sylar wasn't a Crafter and didn't know about the wishes.

"Doesn't everyone?" I countered. Maybe Harper was right about the wolves.

Ve's gaze swept over me, inspecting. Her thin eyebrows lifted and her smile broadened. "Did you come straight from the Goodwins'?"

I nodded. My cheeks were still burning after my doorway rendezvous with Nick Sawyer, but it was probably the glitter—or the eyelashes—that had captured her amusement. I'd already tucked the tiara into my handbag.

I glanced around. "It's crowded in here."

Sylar stuffed oversized hands into the pockets of pin-striped trousers, straining the expensive fabric. His red tie hung crookedly, and I wanted to reach out to straighten it and adjust the tails of the vest that clung to his big belly. "Most village meetings are usually well attended."

Bookshelves had been pushed aside to create a meeting space that was now filled with folding chairs. People were clustered in small groups, chatting. I saw a few familiar faces in the room. Mrs. Eugenia Pennywhistle, the feisty geriatric owner of the Pixie Cottage, who was known affectionately as Mrs. P, stood with Ramona Todd, a stylist at the Magic Wand Salon; Shea and Max Carling, who owned a jewelry shop named All That Glitters; and Marcus Debrowski, the village lawyer. I didn't know if any of them were Crafters—I was still learning my way around the village's magical residents.

Marcus said something, and Mrs. Pennywhistle threw her head back and laughed. I smiled—it reminded me of a Phyllis Diller cackle. Actually, now that I thought about it, Mrs. Pennywhistle looked a lot like Phyllis Diller, too. Outrageous strawberry blond hair had been teased sky-high and sprayed to look like she'd just come out of a wind tunnel. High cheekbones, long thin nose, pointed, painted-on eyebrows. She wore a pink velour tracksuit, and what looked to be brand-new hot-pink Nikes. We'd met a few times already, crossing paths on the green. She liked to power walk every morning, and Missy liked to see if she could trip her up.

A crack of thunder made me jump. Sylar squinted toward the front picture window. Rain slashed across the pane. He said, "I wish the rain would hold off until after the meeting."

My nerves tingled.

Ve patted my hand, indicating that she would grant this wish. She turned away from any onlookers. I saw her left eye twitch as her spell was cast.

No one but me seemed to notice that the rain had suddenly stopped.

At sixty-one, Velma was tiny, like Harper, but her eyes were a golden blue like my own. Tonight hers were skillfully made up with pink and purple shadows. Rosy blush made her cheeks glow, and soft gloss brightened her plump lips. Her coppery hair was worn off her face in a loose twist secured with a silver clip. I'd lived with her two weeks now and had never seen her hair down.

I looked around for Harper and found her with Vincent Paxton, Spellbound Bookshop's manager. She was smiling up at him as he pointed out reference books. Bookshops were Harper's nirvana, and she and Vince had become fast friends the day we arrived in the village. Apparently, his type of wolfishness was okay with my little sister.

"Is it hot in here?" Ve asked, drawing my attention back to her. She unwound a lightweight turquoise scarf from around her neck, then shimmied out of a cropped sweater and pushed both into Sylar's hands. The skin of her shoulders and chest glowed red above the neckline of her flowing sundress. The beautiful golden locket she never took off swayed from a long chain as she fanned herself.

"Very," I said in hormonal solidarity. I was lying through my teeth. It was actually chilly inside the airy shop.

Sylar dropped a kiss on Ve's forehead and said, "Why don't you get something cool to drink while I round up Gayle and get this meeting started."

Gayle Chastain owned the bookshop. I saw her standing off to the side, talking with a man at the snack table.

Sylar had to be the "grand hoo-ha" Harper had mentioned on the phone. "And I'll round up my sister," I said, looking around. She was no longer with Vince, who stood near the podium.

"The quicker the better," Sylar said darkly, his eyes narrowing on a spot across the room.

I followed his gaze. Harper was now cornered by a woman who looked to be in her midthirties. She was tall and slender, with crimped long blond hair that seemed to burst from her scalp like Medusa's snakes. She wore a striking blue one-shouldered dress, gold high heels, and the reddest lipstick I'd ever seen.

Harper caught my eye and mouthed "Help."

"Looks like Harper needs us," I whispered to Aunt Ve.

There was venom in Sylar's voice as he said, "That she does. Truly, I wish Alexandra Shively would just go away forever." He walked away.

I glanced at Ve. "Doesn't much sound like that wish was pure of heart. Though if she's evil or something, then maybe her being gone forever isn't a bad thing, right?"

"Alexandra is a complex person," Ve said. "She is a Seeker who publicly claims herself to be a Craft 'high priestess' and markets herself openly as a witch."

A Seeker was a mortal who sought to become a Crafter. "Does she realize she's making us look bad?"

Us. My transition into a life of a witch was happening so seamlessly I hardly noticed.

"Subtle warnings to cease go unheeded, and to openly discuss the matter, even in generalizations, would only fuel her fire. We all were hoping that once she realized she had no true powers, she'd simply go away. But she's convinced she is a Crafter."

The types of Craft native to this area were hereditary gifts, passed down from one generation to another. The only way a Seeker could become a true Crafter was if the Seeker had a Craft ancestor. However, there was a Craft law that allowed a mortal to become part of the Craft society through marriage, though that mortal wouldn't gain any power—just knowledge.

One thing for certain was that the Craft didn't have high priestesses. We had a secret Elder, the most powerful person in the village, the only witch who knew all of the Craft's laws, history, and secrets. The all-knowing Elder was the judge, jury, and disciplinarian for all Crafters. No one wanted to be summoned to see the Elder for breaking a Craft law. No one.

"Is it possible," I asked, "that she could be a Crafter?"

"Doubtful, though I don't know for sure. As far as I know, she has no family, no roots, here in the village. If there had been a Shively in the Craft ancestry, it would be known. The Elder keeps meticulous records."

Perhaps, but would she share them? Was she obligated to?

Ve turned and looked back at Sylar. "His wish about Alex going away forever worries me. He's been acting strangely lately, and I can't help but wonder if Alex is somehow connected to his troubles."

"Does he know her well?"

She hesitated before answering. "He's been quite vocal lately about how Alex's claims of being a witch might reflect badly on the village." She smiled. "He doesn't believe in witches."

"And that's okay with you?"

"Keeps things lively in my life. He's a sweet man. His thinking just needs a little adjustment. That, and his wish making as well."

His wish echoed in my head. "Maybe he meant nothing ominous by it. Maybe by 'go away forever' he simply meant that Alexandra moves away and never comes back."

I left out the other option. That it could mean *gone-*

gone, as in dead gone. Which certainly wasn't a wish that could be granted.

As if she knew the direction my thoughts had taken, Ve smiled wryly. "Only one way to find out." She cast the spell.

I looked toward Alexandra—she seemed unaffected, though Harper was glaring at me. I grabbed Ve's arm—I wasn't heading over there alone—and crossed the room.

"Alex! Darling, how are you?" Ve said sweetly. Too sweetly to be sincere. "Girls, this is Alexandra Shively, proprietress of Lotions and Potions."

Alexandra peered at Harper. "I would be better if I could get a straight answer from your niece."

Harper's arms were folded tightly over her small chest, and I could tell her patience was long gone. She stood at just over five feet, and with her short brown hair, delicate features, and big brown eyes, she looked—and sometimes acted—like a beautiful, impish woodland elf. I immediately went to her side. Power in numbers.

"What is it you wish to know?" Ve asked, all innocence and feigned candor.

"I simply asked your niece where she had been born and raised." Alexandra's eyebrows arched into sharp points. Her hair gave her an extra foot of height, what with the way the frizzy curls practically stood on end and all. She folded her arms over her chest, and I noticed the beautiful diamond watch she wore. If it was real, it had cost a small fortune. Alexandra said, "She refused to answer."

Harper's lips pursed. "Because it's none of your business."

"Very secretive," Alex said, eyeing us both.

A gavel banged down. Gayle stood at a podium set up in a spot normally reserved for the month's newest releases. Vince stood at her side. He was tall and lanky with curly brown hair. Black-rimmed glasses framed intelligent blue eyes. There were two pens in the pocket of his plaid shirt. He was definitely Harper's type — puppy-dog cute and smart.

"If everyone could find a seat," Gayle said loudly, "we'll get started in a couple of minutes."

She had a soft, mellifluous voice. She looked to be about fifty, with friendly blue eyes and honey blond hair. She'd bought the shop last year with her husband, who'd since passed away unexpectedly last winter from a heart attack. To hear Vince tell it, he'd been the bookshop's saving grace following the tragedy, keeping the shop afloat. He may be puppy-dog cute, but he had a West-minster ego.

Ve said brightly, "Let's grab some seats, girls. We'll have to continue this conversation another time, Alex."

"It's *Alexandra*. And trust me, we will continue this talk. After tonight, everyone will start taking me more seriously."

"What's that supposed to mean?" Harper asked with a who-do-you-think-you-are edge.

One sharply pointed eyebrow rose. With a note of tri-umph in her voice, Alex said, "It means that you'll finally have to accept that I'm one of you. I've finally learned the truth of my past."

Ve rolled her eyes, though I noticed the shadow of worry on her face. She said, "Have a nice night, Alex," and herded us toward the other side of the room, where I spotted Nick Sawyer leaning against a bookcase. He had been watching us.

Harper whispered, "What did she mean? She can't possibly know. . . ."

"Hush, now." Ve looked around. "She was fishing for information — that's all — hoping you'd slip up, since you're new in the village. You must be careful with Alex," Ve said in a fierce whisper as she claimed a seat and smoothed her dress. "She's so intent on learning the secrets of the Craft that she's not cognizant of those she hurts in the process. Now, I need a drink before I overheat." Her gaze settled on the refreshment table. "Punch will have to do until I can get my hands on something stronger."

Smiling, I said, "I'll get it for you."

Harper sat next to Ve as I headed for the punch bowl. A good-looking man stood at the refreshment table, fussing with miniature desserts laid out on a silver tray. Tiny cheesecakes, bite-sized cake balls, itty-bitty pies, and delicate baklava cups.

Suddenly, I was starving.

"Try one," the man said, holding up the tray.

I glanced at him and tried to hide my sudden shock at the sight of raised welts covering half his face.

Not soon enough, apparently, because the man sighed. "I'm not contagious. I let Alexandra try a new lotion on me. There was a bit of a reaction."

"A bit," I downplayed. Absently, I wondered what the plague looked like, and I fought the instinct to take a giant step backward. "Does it hurt?"

"It's itchy and burns a bit, but really it hurts only my vanity. I'm Evan Sullivan—I own the Gingerbread Shack. We specialize in miniature desserts." He held up the tray again. "Are you Darcy or Harper?"

I took a tiny cheesecake. "Darcy." I popped the cake in my mouth and moaned. "So good. Sullivan? Are you related to Starla?"

Perky blond-haired, blue-eyed Starla Sullivan was the owner of Hocus-Pocus Photography. I looked around but didn't see her. I did, however, spot village lawyer Marcus Debrowski in deep conversation with Alexandra across the room. Business or pleasure? I couldn't help wondering.

"Thank you," Evan said, tipping his head. "Starla's my twin. You've met, then?"

"Technically, our dogs met first."

"Have mercy, you met the beast."

The "beast" was a two-pound bichon frise mix named Twink. "He's ferocious." I ladled punch into two cups. "Is Starla here tonight?"

About my age, Evan was average height and slight in build. His blond wavy hair was cut short and gelled to stay in place. His clothes were impeccably pressed, his shoes shined, his tie neatly knotted. He was adorable.

"Working. She had an event to photograph. Ve's been talking about you nonstop for weeks now," he said. "I was beginning to think you and your sister were figments of her imagination."

"We've been lying low, trying to get adjusted. We're not exactly the social sort."

He grinned, his blue eyes sparkling. "That will change now that you're living here. I guarantee it. Starla will have you signed up on committees with her before you know it. The Midsummer Dance *is* coming up in a couple of weeks."

I thought about Harper at a village dance and knew she'd be suddenly sick as a dog that day to avoid going. "The dance is a big deal around here, then?"

"The biggest event of the year."

I thought of the beautiful blue dress in the Bewitching Boutique window. It would be perfect for a Midsummer Dance. I'd buy it in a heartbeat if I were going. Which I probably wasn't. Someone had to keep Harper company that night.

He winked. "I promise I'll save you a dance."

I smiled and played along. "You may regret that. I have two left feet." Flirting with Evan was easy and safe—because if my instincts were right, I wasn't his type. And my instincts were usually right.

"It's a risk I'm willing to take," he said solemnly.

I made no commitments as I grabbed a couple more cakes and two cups of punch, and headed back as everyone found seats and settled in. Unfortunately for me, Alexandra Shively had finished her conversation with Marcus and had taken a chair a few down from Ve and Harper. Her legs were blocking the path to my seat, and her curls were quivering menacingly, truly looking like snakes.

Great. Fantastic. Just what I needed. "Pardon me, please."

Nick Sawyer was but two feet away. I could feel his gaze on me, burning with its intensity.

"Healthy appetite you have there," Alexandra said loudly, eyeing my plate.

For a second I wondered what she'd look like with punch streaming down her face, then quickly tamped down my temper. I couldn't let this woman get to me. "The cakes are so delicious I couldn't help myself. Evan's poor face, though. I wonder what happened to him," I said innocently.

She arched a pointy eyebrow but didn't say anything.

I held firm on the cups so I wouldn't *accidentally* spill on her. "Would you excuse me, please? The meeting's about to start."

Her feet slowly drew back under her folding chair. "As you *wish*."

I rather wished at that point her foot had been sticking out so I could stomp on it as I passed. I was really beginning to resent my inability to grant my own wishes. I bit out a "thank you" and scooted past a few other people before finally sitting down.

I could still feel Nick watching me. Chancing it, I glanced his way. Our eyes locked, neither of us blinking. My heart beat so hard against my rib cage I thought for sure Aunt Ve could hear it.

I quickly looked away, feeling a blush again. Ve was smiling at me as I passed her a cup of punch. "Nick is cute, no?"

I handed the tasty goodies off to Harper, who had a

distraction of her own—Vince Paxton. She couldn't take her eyes off him.

"If you like that sort," I said.

"What, tall and gorgeous?"

"Men." Evan would have no competition from me.

She patted my hand. "You'll recover, Darcy."

I wasn't so sure about that. I stole another look at Nick, and found him still looking at me.

"Why is he still staring?" I whispered.

"It could be your sparkling personality."

"You're joking about the glitter at a time like this?"

She laughed. "How did everything go with the Goodwins?"

"There were a few issues, but overall, I think it went well."

"Issues? You should have called. Did you lose my number?"

She had made me memorize her three phone numbers (business, home, cell) and had written them on a sticky note and stuck it to my dashboard *and* programmed them into my cell phone. "No, Aunt Ve."

The gavel banged again and Sylar boomed, "Take your seats, everyone."

"You'll have to tell me about the issues later," Ve said.

I rubbed my temples, trying to ease a growing headache. I spared Nick another look and was surprised to see a young girl at his side, maybe eleven or twelve years old. She looked enough like him to suggest she might be his daughter.

He caught me watching him—again. His hard eyes softened just the smallest bit. My stomach got that gushy feeling again.

The gavel banged, distracting me, and I tried to stay focused on the proceedings. Ten minutes later, after roll call and the Pledge of Allegiance, my patience was rewarded—the reason the special meeting had been called was announced.

"Friends," Sylar said loudly, his thick eyebrows drawn downward. "I am truly disheartened to verify that the rumors are true." He paused dramatically, his gaze sweeping the room, lingering on a face here, there. "There is indeed a criminal among us."

Chapter Four

Whereas my heart was pounding earlier, it was barely beating now.

Had the village found out about Harper? Was it truly this big a deal that it needed a special meeting? It wasn't as if she were a violent felon. She had been charged with a misdemeanor. She hadn't even spent one day in jail!

The eruption that followed Sylar's announcement had died down. He said, "Two tourists filed claims with the Enchanted Village police today. Both had been pick-pocketed."

A gasp went through the crowd. I tried to think back to the afternoon—where had Harper been?

She certainly didn't need the money. My father had left us both good inheritances. But no, that didn't make sense. She broke laws only for what she deemed good causes. How would that principle relate to pickpocketing? Unless ... unless the tourists had gypped a server their tip ... or something along those lines that would cause Harper to seek retribution.

My stomach flipped. I glanced at Harper. She didn't look guilty. In fact, she seemed enraptured with what Sylar was saying, hanging on his every word.

"As you know," Sylar continued, "this is not an iso-lated incident. Over the past three weeks, nearly a half dozen claims have been filed. Last summer, we had three incidents in *total*. The reputation of our village is at risk, as are our livelihoods. If news of this spreads, our entire summer season will be affected. We must stop this crime spree and soon."

Three weeks? I let out a breath of relief. Harper couldn't possibly be involved. We hadn't arrived in the village until two weeks ago. How long before I started trusting she'd stay out of trouble, as promised?

Someone called out, "And how are we to do that, Sylar? Our police department is already understaffed and overworked." The Enchanted Village had only a tiny police force, staffed by four officers, including a decrepit police chief who, to hear Ve tell it, spent more time on the putting green than the village green.

Sylar said, "I've taken the liberty of bringing in a professional. Most of you have met Nick Sawyer, but few of you know that he has been in the military, worked for the Rhode Island State Police, and now freelances as a security expert. He's offered his services to the village to help catch our thief, free of charge. Nick, come on up here and tell us your plan."

It took all my effort to appear unaffected as my pulse started to pound as Nick strode to the podium. Military, state police, security? My instincts had been right about him being law enforcement.

Which also meant that I had to be very careful. Because my instincts also told me he was someone I could fall for.

And I couldn't let that happen.

An hour later the meeting had let out and I stood staring blindly at a row of cookbooks while nibbling on the rim of my paper cup. My cooking abilities were sadly mediocre—I knew enough not to starve—but I'd always wanted to widen my culinary horizons.

Nearby, Nick and Sylar were in a deep discussion of

what to do about the local thefts. I was doing my best not to eavesdrop, but it was too easy to listen in.

Nick hadn't really said much about his plans to catch the thief other than to claim he knew what he was doing.

Smart. If he said much more, he might tip off whoever was behind the crimes. Even if that person wasn't present at the meeting, word would spread. In a neighborhood this size, everyone would know by morning. He'd handed out business cards and asked everyone to be vigilant. The more people looking for the thief, the better.

Harper was helping Vince set the store back to rights, and Aunt Ve was fussing with the clasp of her locket after it had slipped from her neck during the meeting.

I was studying cookbook spines when I felt someone next to me. It was Marcus Debrowski, the town lawyer.

"Are you a good cook?" he asked.

"Not really. You?"

"Hardly. I'm a master at ordering takeout."

He wore a dark suit with a light pink shirt, no tie. There was the barest hint of scruff on his cheeks, not quite a five-o'clock shadow. I pegged him to be late twenties, maybe early thirties. Light green eyes, dark hair. He picked up a cookbook by a famous TV chef and flipped through it while also casting glances across the room. "I keep promising myself that one of these days I'm going to learn."

After the fourth time he looked past me, I followed his gaze. It seemed to be watching Harper and Vince. "I keep saying the same thing. I'm okay with basic recipes, but if it gets too complicated, I'm lost."

"Every now and again, the Sorcerer's Stove offers a cooking class. You may want to look into it if you're staying in the village." Again the glance past me. "You are staying in the village, right?"

I bit back a smile as he watched Harper. "Yes."

"Your, ah, sister, too?"

"Uh-huh."

He caught my knowing gaze and coughed. His cheeks pinkened. "That's good."

"Have you met Harper yet?" I asked.

He quickly shook his head. "No."

"Do you want to?" I asked, trying to help him along.

"I, ah—" His cell phone rang, cutting him off. He looked relieved. "If you'll excuse me?"

I nodded and watched him wander toward the back door of the shop. I spotted Evan cleaning up and went over.

"Saved you a cupcake." He handed me a perfect mini devil's food cupcake.

"Thank you." I ate it in one bite and wished I had ten more. I even whispered a spell out of pure hope that the Wishcraft Laws had been amended in the last few minutes, but no cupcakes appeared. For shame. "Do you need some help?"

"Sure. Starla usually helps me with the strike; it's a lot of work for one person."

"Strike?"

"Sorry. Theater term. Taking down the set after the show's over."

"Do you act?"

"I wish. Haven't been able to land a role quite yet, but I am the best stage manager around."

I was a bit sad that he hadn't phrased his wish properly so I could grant it. The person who makes a wish has to implicitly declare his wish, not just express a desire. So for Evan's wish to be granted, he would have to say, "I wish I would land a role." Of course, the more specific the wish, the better, but we Wishcrafters can work wonders with what we're given. "Modest, too," I said.

He laughed and bowed with a flourish.

I helped stack trays and fold tablecloths. Nick, I noticed, had moved to look at the gizmos and gadgets that hung on pegs at the register. He was clearly eavesdropping on our conversation and not being the least bit subtle about it.

"Where did you move from?" Evan asked, making conversation as we worked.

"Ohio," I said.

"Do you have family there?"

Suddenly uneasy, I said, "Not anymore."

Evan's face scrunched. "Sorry. Didn't mean to be so nosy."

"It's okay. How about you? Have you always lived here?" Most Crafters had lived in the village their whole lives, which would make it easier for me to determine if he was one.

"About four years," Evan said. "The bakery used to belong to our grandfather. Starla and I inherited it after he died, except Starla found out pretty fast that she can't bake, so she decided to take up photography. It all worked out. I need to rinse the punch bowl—I'll be right back," he said.

I spotted Nick headed toward me just as Sylar called out, "Nick, there's someone I want you to meet." He waved him over to where Harper stood with Vince.

I hoped Harper could hold her own against Nick. I was worrying about it when a young voice said, "Hi, I'm Mimi Sawyer. Well, it's Demetria, but everyone calls me Mimi. Are you Darcy or Harper?"

It was the girl who'd been standing with Nick earlier. "I'm Darcy."

"I'm twelve. How old are you?"

I couldn't help smiling. "Thirty. Are you Nick's daughter?" Might as well just ask since I was so curious.

"Yep." She leaned on the folding table. Her leg swung back and forth. "I heard you just moved here."

"Two weeks ago."

"We moved here two years ago from Providence after my mom died."

She spoke rapidly, and I was struggling to keep up.

"I'm sorry about your mom. Mine died when I was seven."

She looked up at me, the pain clear on her face. "It stinks, doesn't it?"

"Completely."

"Is your dad still alive?"

She asked in the way only a child could. Sincere yet without realizing how pushy she was being. "No. He died four months ago."

"Oh. That really stinks."

"Yeah, it kind of does." I thought about my dad. Patrick Merriweather had once been a doting father, but after my mother died, he'd become a workaholic who rarely spent any time at home. I suspected throwing himself into his work helped him avoid the two people who most reminded him of his greatest loss. So I, at seven years old, had pretty much taken over raising Harper. I liked to think I did a good job—if one didn't count all the trouble she gets into. I didn't.

It had been a bit of a blow to find out from Ve that Dad had known we were Wishcrafters and had chosen to keep it from us. My and Harper's lives might have been so different if we'd known about our heritage.

"Are you still in school?" I asked. It was mid-June and summer breaks were starting.

"I go to a private school, so I've been out for a few weeks. Did you know you're all glittery?" Mimi asked.

"I do. I had a job tonight playing the tooth fairy."

"No offense, but you don't really look like a fairy."

"My wings are in the car."

A tiny smile pulled on her lips. "That makes all the difference."

I laughed. She was a bright, funny kid, this girl, with her dark spiraling curls and inquisitive brown eyes.

"Do you live in the village?" I asked.

"At the end of Old Forest Lane. My dad's workshop is there, too."

"Workshop?" Thunder cracked along with my nerves. It had started raining again.

"He makes cabinets and furniture and all kinds of stuff when he's not doing the security thing. He calls it his passion." She rolled her eyes. "He's always in his shop."

I glanced over my shoulder. Nick was staring at us while Sylar talked and talked.

Mimi gave him a little finger wave. So did I. His features darkened.

"Dad has his *it's time to go* look on his face. I'll see you around, Darcy." She scampered off.

I was still looking at Nick when Evan came back.

He followed my gaze and whispered, "He's a bit easy on the eyes, isn't he?"

"A bit." I felt a blush rising.

He said, "He's single. Are you?"

"Technically, yes. But not looking."

"Too bad. He hasn't taken his eyes off you since you came in. I could feel the heat across the room." He fanned his face dramatically.

"It's the rash."

He laughed. "Where is Alexandra, anyway? She said she'd stick around to give me the antidote."

As we looked around, Mrs. Pennywhistle came tearing in from the back of the store, wild-eyed, with her hair more on end than usual. She raced past us and stiff-armed the front door. It thrust open, and she rushed into the dark rainy night, a fading pink blur.

I glanced at Evan. "What was that all about?"

His eyes were round with amazement. "I don't know, but she sure can hustle for an old lady."

Very strange. Mrs. P was about as outgoing as a person could get. It wasn't like her to storm out without so much as a good-bye. If the stricken look on her face was any indication, something had upset her greatly.

"Do you think we should go and check on her?"

"At that speed we'll never catch her." His eyes softened. "I'll go by the Pixie Cottage tomorrow morning with some scones and make sure she's okay." He looked around again. "I still don't see Alexandra."

"Do you really trust her to give you more lotion?"

"She's really very good at what she does. Just a bad batch this one time. She said she was staying late to talk to Sylar about something. Grab that side of the table, will you?" He made a flipping motion. We flipped the table over and folded in the legs.

"Meeting with Sylar? About what?" I couldn't imagine Sylar wanted anything to do with the woman—not after the way he reacted to seeing her, not to mention the wish he'd made.

Huh. Maybe it had been granted after all, since she was nowhere to be seen.

Evan's brow wrinkled. "Not sure."

Hopefully not for any face creams. "Well, I haven't seen her since the meeting ended."

I wish Alexandra Shively would go away forever.

A chill ran up my spine.

"I'm not sure how much longer I can deal with this rash." He scratched his cheek. "That antidote has to work."

"Have you thought about seeing a doctor?"

"I will if I have to. Hopefully Alexandra has the cure. She said she's been working on one."

He scratched some more, and I had to wonder just what had been in the lotion in the first place. If Alexandra considered herself a Crafter, she could have been toying with any number of herbs or extracts that would cause a reaction modern medicine wouldn't know how to treat. I made a mental note to talk to Ve about it—maybe she had some tips or tricks to help Evan.

Nick and Mimi left. Marcus, too—without an introduction to Harper, as far I knew—and just about everyone else had gone as well by the time I finished helping Evan load his van.

I met up with Ve and Harper at the register, where they were chatting with Gayle and Vince.

He was saying to Harper, "So we'll see you tomorrow morning?"

Harper's cheeks turned red. "Bright and early."

What was this about?

"What's this about?" Ve asked as if she had read my mind. "Did I miss something?"

Harper rocked on her heels. "I'm going to be working here at the bookstore part-time."

"We're glad to have her," Gayle said. "I've not met someone so knowledgeable in so many genres since my Russy died."

I noticed Vince's frown and wondered how he and Gayle got along. Was Harper about to become a pawn in some sort of power play they had going on?

Harper's vast knowledge came as no surprise to me. As an English lit major, she loved all books, all genres, and a bookstore was her kind of heaven—even if I thought it might not be the best use of her degree.

I opened my mouth to ask her if taking this job was such a good idea, but quickly snapped it closed. It wasn't my decision to make. I couldn't keep watching over her, trying to protect her, trying to make her decisions.

"If that's okay with you, Ve?" Harper added.

"Whatever makes you happy." She patted Harper's cheek. "We should get going home, though. Tilda shouldn't be left alone for so long with Missy."

Tilda was the family cat, who was none too pleased with a new dog in the house.

Ve looked around. "Has anyone seen my scarf? I found my sweater, but not my scarf."

"Not since you handed them both to Sylar," I said.

"Maybe he still has it," Ve said. "But has anyone seen *him*? He was supposed to walk back with us."

"He was here a minute ago," Gayle said.

Ve looked toward the back door. "He probably stepped outside for a moment. He wants me to think he quit smoking, but I know he still sneaks a few cigarettes a day."

"I'll check for him," I offered. I cut through the romance section and walked along a narrow hallway, past a restroom, a small kitchen, a storeroom, and an office.

I opened the back door and was surprised to find Sylar kneeling on the ground, an unlit cigarette hanging out of his mouth. Rain fell steadily.

Sylar's glasses wobbled on his nose as he looked up at me, his face drained of color. Rain dripped off his chin. It was then that I noticed that he was kneeling over someone.

I stepped forward. Alexandra Shively lay on the ground. My breath caught when I spotted Ve's beautiful turquoise scarf knotted tightly around Alexandra's neck.

"We need to call the paramedics," Sylar said in a small voice.

There was no use. Alexandra's face was swollen, blood trickled from her nose, and her eyes were wide-open and bulging, but not seeing anything at all.

She was very clearly dead.

Chapter Five

Fluffy white clouds hung low in the morning sky when I woke up to the *tap, tap, tap* of water dripping from the gutters. For a second I was disoriented, wondering where I was, where Troy was, and why his side of the bed was cold.

Then realization struck hard and fast, like a sucker punch in the gut. I rolled over, hoping the swift pain would subside quickly. It usually did. I came nose to nose with Tilda. The Himalayan's light blue eyes shone as she swiped a paw playfully at my cheek and flicked a whisker in my direction. She let me scratch behind her ears and reluctantly let out a soft purr.

It was progress. I was on a mission to win her over. If the fur balls hacked up on my bedspread every other day were any indication, Tilda wasn't happy I had moved in. Over the past few days, though, I felt more and more like she was coming around. She often followed me when she thought I wasn't looking, and now here she was purring in my bed.

I glanced around for Missy, who usually slept with me, but she must have cleared out when Tilda came in. Smart dog—Tilda's claws were sharp.

As I stretched and yawned, I squinted at the small digital alarm clock on the nightstand. It was just before seven. The storms had lasted most of the night, but today was supposed to be warm and sunny. A perfect June day.

I listened for sounds in the house—the perking of the coffeepot, Missy's toenails on the wooden floors, the soft drone of the morning news.

All was quiet except for the squeaking of the floorboards down the hall. Someone was awake. This early it had to be Aunt Ve. She was definitely an early riser, often up and about as early as five a.m. On the flip side, she was usually tucked into bed with a romance novel and a mug of peppermint tea by ten every night.

We were a lot alike. I was usually up bright and early and tucked into bed at a reasonable (well before midnight) hour, which might sound boring to some, but to me . . . it was comfort. I found reassurance in routines, in regularity.

When Troy and I first started dating, he said he found my quirks charming. By the time I kicked him out, my quirks had turned into excuses for his bad behaviors. I didn't like to travel, to entertain, to go out every night . . . to give up on a marriage because of a few difficulties. No, those were *his* specialties.

I rolled into the middle of the bed just because I could and tried to tell myself I enjoyed all the extra space. Scratching Tilda's head, I listened to her purr as I contemplated buying a twin mattress.

I tried to recall what time Aunt Ve had finally come in last night but realized I didn't know. I'd planned to wait up for her but had fallen asleep sometime around three. Last I'd seen of her, she was still at the bookstore and was waiting for Marcus Debrowski, whom she had retained on Sylar's behalf, to return. Turned out he was the best Lawcrafter around. From there, she planned to go to the village police station, where Sylar had been taken to be questioned more extensively by local detectives.

Things weren't looking too good for Sylar at this

point. I couldn't help but think back to the wish he had made about Alex. Had Sylar taken matters into his own hands? Hard to believe he would, especially since people knew of his intense dislike of Alex, but I didn't know him well enough to judge if he was capable of committing cold-blooded murder. I didn't want to think so. Didn't want to think someone I'd found likable and pleasant could have a darker side. But I also knew people were complex and complicated. Nothing was black-and-white. No one was perfect, and heaven knew we could make mistakes. And hide who we truly were, good or bad. Or both—I'd certainly been fooled before.

And well, wasn't I hiding, too? I was a witch. It had been almost too much to comprehend at first, but as the days slipped by and I used my powers more and more, the truth of who I really was had begun to slowly sink in. Not that I could tell many about it.

Tilda swatted my face again, this time with a bit of claw and a sharp *rrreow*.

Apparently I'd been fooled again, this time by a fluffy white and gray Himalayan in need of an attitude adjustment. "Just when I was beginning to like you," I said to her.

Tilda stared at me with an air of superiority before hopping off the bed. She pranced to the door, threw a look over her shoulder, and let out a sharp, insistent, thoroughly ticked-off *rrreow*.

It was a familiar meow. She was hungry. (She was always hungry.) Odd that Ve hadn't fed her already ... usually it was the first thing she did every morning.

I grabbed my glasses from the nightstand—I was in no mood to deal with my contacts—and pulled my hair into a loose ponytail. After slipping on a pair of shorts, I zipped up a sweatshirt, brushed my teeth, and finally followed a prissy Tilda along the upstairs hallway to Ve's room.

The door was open wide, and her bed hadn't been slept in, which meant she probably never came home last night.

The wood floor creaked under my feet, which roused Missy from Harper's room across the hall. Whereas Tilda was reserved, Missy was all enthusiasm. She charged through the doorway, her feet nearly flying out from under her, an out-of-control snowball. She lost her footing and slid straight into Tilda and both bumped into the wainscoting. Tilda shrieked and hissed and started swiping, claws fully extended. Missy, perpetually optimistic, licked Tilda's ear and then yelped as claws made contact with her nose. More hissing ensued before Tilda gave one final swipe and took off.

"You certainly know how to make an entrance." I rubbed Missy's curly-topped head and checked for damage. A small scratch ran across her nose, but it wasn't too bad. I was glad to see some of her former wild and crazy attitude come through. Maybe her shift in personality was just a result of growing up. I supposed that made perfect sense, and I felt no vet appointment was needed after all.

Harper stuck her head out the door. "Everything okay out here?"

I noticed her hair was wrapped in a towel—she'd been up for a while apparently. "Fine. Missy had a little run-in with Tilda. You're up early." She rarely woke up this early voluntarily.

"I start my new job this morning, remember?"

In the midst of all that had happened last night, I had forgotten. Harper had a new job at Spellbound Books. I opened my mouth, but before I could get a word out, she said, "And don't try to talk me out of it."

I snapped my mouth shut, reconsidered my choice of words, and said, "Is the bookshop even open today? After what happened last night?"

The murder. I didn't want to say the words aloud. I

didn't even like thinking them. My mind flashed to the image of Alexandra in the back alley, and my stomach rolled.

And to think that I had considered the Enchanted Village so safe. How wrong I'd been!

Harper leaned against the doorframe, her eyes filled with curiosity. "Did you get a really good look at the body?" She'd always had a morbid interest in forensics. "I've been thinking a lot about it, and maybe there's a clue on Alexandra's body as to who really killed her. Because it couldn't have been Sylar."

"No, I didn't get a good look," I lied, very clearly picturing Alex's lifeless body. Harper would be beside herself with the details of Alex's bulging eyes, swollen tongue, and bluish coloring. "Besides, I'm sure the police have it covered."

I also thought there was a reasonable chance Sylar had killed Alex, but I kept that opinion to myself. Last night, as soon as the police had taken Sylar away, Ve and Harper had gone back and forth about who the "real" killer could have been and had even started making a list of possible suspects. I thought of the two of them playing detective and almost groaned. Harper was all about a good cause, and if she felt Sylar was innocent, I could only imagine the lengths she'd go through to prove it.

And Ve. Poor Aunt Ve. She was as caught up in what happened as any person could be. Last night she had loudly and insistently proclaimed Sylar's innocence to anyone who would listen.

Harper lifted one eyebrow as though she thought I was crazy for putting all my trust in the police, but she didn't press for any gruesome details. "As far as I know, the store's open, and I'm due in at eight. I thought I'd get there early—it's important to make a good impression, don't you think?"

She wasn't fooling me. Getting to the shop early

meant she'd have more time to snoop in the back alley. Was crossing crime-scene tape punishable by law? I wondered. I could already imagine the phone call from the local police station to come bail her out.

I had a very good imagination.

"Try to stay out of trouble, okay?" I said as I headed for the stairs.

"You worry too much, Darcy," she called after me.

That was true. I was an excellent worrier, a trait that had kicked in right about the time my mother died.

As sunlight filtered through the picture window in the kitchen, there was no sign of a ticked-off Tilda. I filled her food bowl and gave her fresh water. When I reached for the coffee carafe to fill it, I found a note from Ve taped to the pot.

> *Darling girls,*
>
> *I didn't want to wake you when I came in for a change of clothes. Please cover for me today at As You Wish. My Day-Timer is on my desk with today's appointments. I am not sure when I'll be back, but I will check in as soon as I can. So far Sylar has not been charged; however, he is not being released. With hope we will both be home soon.*
>
> *Love, love, love,*
> *Auntie Ve*

She must have been in and out early this morning. I was surprised I hadn't heard her—usually I'm a light sleeper. After setting the coffee to perk, I slipped on a pair of sneakers and grabbed Missy's leash. We headed for the village green.

It was still too early in the day for tourists, but locals were already out and about. Several people were jogging, others walking their dogs, and there was a steady stream of customers headed into the Witch's Brew for their morning paper, coffee, and gossip.

There would be a lot of the last this morning, what with the murder and all. If Sylar had been concerned last night that the petty thefts were going to hurt tourism, I could only imagine what was going to happen now.

As Missy and I walked a lap around the green, I found myself drawn toward Alex's shop, Lotions and Potions. A village police cruiser and the police chief's unmarked vehicle were parked at the curb and people were moving around inside the shop and in Alexandra's second-floor apartment. I watched as a man in a tan suit came out carrying a bulging trash bag. I couldn't help but wonder what he'd found.

"What do you think they're looking for?" a voice asked from behind me.

I turned and found an out-of-breath Starla Sullivan holding a wriggling Twink. She set him down and Missy commenced in sniffing the littler dog.

"A signed confession from the murderer?" I joked.

Starla smiled, and it practically stretched from ear to ear. It lit her whole face, brightening her eyes and making her glow. Her name fit her perfectly. "That would be convenient," she puffed out.

"Are you okay?"

"Yeah. Just made a run for it when I saw you over here. Guess I'm a little out of shape. I need to add more cardio to my workouts." A runner jogged past us and gave a friendly nod. "Jogging," Starla said, lighting up again. "I should start jogging. No, *we* should start jogging. It's always more fun to run with a partner. What do you think?"

"Besides that you're crazy?"

Starla wasn't movie-star thin, but she wasn't heavy, either. I was naturally average bordering on the thin side (good genetics)—thank goodness, because I didn't have an athletic bone in my body.

She laughed. "Come on. Everyone can use a little toning."

"Why are you eyeing my triceps?"

"Well, now that you mention it"—she jiggled the loose skin on my upper arm—"it is kind of . . ."

"Be nice."

"Flaccid."

Flaccid. No one wanted to be *flaccid*, least of all me. "That's not nice."

"But honest. I'm always honest. I bet it jiggles when you wave. Go ahead, wave."

"I really don't think—"

"Just try it."

I figured it was easier to do what she asked than protest. I waved. Sure enough, my skin jiggled like Santa's belly.

An approaching jogger mistook my jiggle test as friendliness, waved back, and altered his course to head toward us.

As he neared, recognition hit fast and fierce and my heart started beating a crazy rhythm.

"Good morning," Nick Sawyer said as he slowed to a stop, his lean calves and upper arms glistening with an oddly appealing sheen of sweat.

"Good morning," Starla and I said in unison.

I fought the urge to hide my flaccid arms, and instead focused on keeping Missy from jumping all over him. I could completely understand why she wanted to, but it just wasn't polite. "Down, Missy!"

"She's all right," Nick said, squatting so Missy could have free access.

Lucky dog.

No. I gave myself a hard mental shake. No, no, no. He was just eye candy, and if my father, a dentist, had instilled in me one lesson, it was that sugar was bad for me. Very, very bad.

"Here comes the computer," Starla said, motioning

toward Alexandra's shop again. Her blond ponytail swung as her head turned.

Sure enough, a detective was carrying out a hard drive and a laptop.

"I can't believe I missed all the excitement last night," Starla added. "Alexandra wasn't the friendliest sort, but she was always nice to me, and Evan really adored her. I heard you found the body, Darcy. Do the police really think Sylar's guilty? How's Ve holding up?"

Her questions spun in my head, twisting and twining, making me a little dizzy. I noticed Nick looking up at me—he was still squatting, lavishing Missy with scratching and belly rubs. "I haven't seen her since last night. I found a note this morning that there haven't been any big changes. No news is good news?"

"What about Alexandra's watch?" Starla loosened Twink's lead and the dog bunny-hopped over to Nick to get his share of attention. "I'd say that's pretty big news."

Nick's brow furrowed and a bead of sweat slid down the side of his stubbled jaw. "What about her watch?"

I thought back to the night before, to the rain falling, to Sylar bending over Alex's body. I could see the puckering of her silk dress, the water beading on her legs, her arms. Her bare arms. Her fancy watch was gone.

"Whoever killed her stole it. It's all the talk over at the Witch's Brew," Starla said. "Speculation is running high that the local thief stepped up his game and killed Alexandra for her watch. According to Shea Carling at All That Glitters, that watch was worth almost fifty thousand dollars."

I gaped. "Fifty thousand?"

Starla tightened the band of her ponytail as she said, "She would know, too, since she sells Harry Winston pieces in her store." She dropped her voice. "Shea let it slip that Alexandra had come to her a few weeks ago to get an appraisal. She said Alexandra hinted that the watch had been a gift from a boyfriend, someone local, though Shea doesn't know who. There was an inscription on the watch, though. 'A Madness Most Discreet.' Sounds like a loving relationship, eh?"

"Shakespeare," Nick said. "Part of one of his more famous love quotations."

"Well, well," Starla teased. "Don't tell me you're a romantic at heart."

He didn't so much as blush. "I think I read it on a mug at the gift shop."

"Suuure," Starla said, drawing the word out.

I could tell she had a brother—I'd have a hard time joking with Nick like that without sounding like I was flirting outrageously. Somehow, Starla pulled it off.

Nick was probably right, though, about the quote being Shakespeare. Sounded like something he'd write.

Standing, Nick left Missy and Twink staring up adoringly at him. "Pickpocketing to murder is a big leap."

"It makes more sense than Sylar Dewitt killing her. He couldn't hurt a flea."

"Sometimes people are very good at hiding who they truly are." Nick reached out a hand, and I nearly jumped clear out of my flaccid skin when he brushed my cheek with his finger. At the tip, something sparkled. "Glitter," he said with a faint smile. "I need to get home. Good day, ladies." He bent and patted the dogs' heads before he broke into a sprint.

Starla stared at me.

"What?"

She laughed. "Oh, Darcy, you're going to be the envy of this village."

"What are you talking about?"

"Nick Sawyer is the village's most eligible bachelor. And it looks like he has his sights set on you."

I adjusted my glasses. "Have I told you that you're crazy?"

"Only once so far today."

"Is that watch really worth fifty thousand?"

Starla accepted the change of subject. "Yes, but what's got my curiosity up is who gave it to her in the first place. No one in the village knows of Alex having any kind of boyfriend."

It made me wonder what other secrets Alexandra Shively was keeping.

And if those secrets were why she was killed.

Chapter Six

As You Wish's phone was ringing when I pushed open the kitchen door. I dropped Missy's leash and made a run for the handset in our private office off the first-floor hallway. The room was tight with two desks, overflowing bookshelves, filing cabinets, and enough clutter to make me feel claustrophobic. I had yet to convince Ve to let me tidy the place and create some form of order. Thank goodness the clients never saw this space, or they might question our organizational skills.

Sunlight splashed off pretty light green walls as I grabbed the phone. "As You Wish, this is Darcy. What is the wish you wish today?"

There was no chance of any wish being spoken over the phone being granted. Another of the Wishcraft Laws was that the wisher had to be present for the wish to be fulfilled.

"Darcy, I'm so glad you're there. This is Cherise Goodwin, and I need your help."

I sank into the upholstered desk chair and looked around for a pad of paper. A pile of invoices toppled before I finally found some sticky notes. "What can I do for you? Laurel Grace didn't have nightmares about sparkly pink strangers, did she?" My glasses slid down my nose as I searched for a pen. I finally found one under Ve's day planner.

Missy had followed me in, and I unhooked her leash and rubbed under her chin. She trotted out of the room, probably on a Tilda hunt.

Cherise laughed, then cleared her throat. "No, no, nothing like that. Apparently you made quite an impression on Laurel Grace after she had time to think about it—a good impression. So much so that suddenly she's lost another tooth this morning. One that was wiggly but probably not quite ready to come out."

I winced.

"She wants to see you again. Tonight. Please tell me it's possible. Whatever the cost, I will cover it."

I heard Missy let out two excited barks, but then she quieted right down. I thought she'd probably found Tilda, until I heard footsteps. I craned my head to see who it was—had Harper come back?—and, off-balance, nearly fell off the chair. "Are you sure?" I said absently to Cherise.

I jumped when a head poked into the office. Ve looked drawn and tired, but I was glad to see her. I covered the phone's mouthpiece. "Are you okay?"

Ve nodded. "You finish up—I'll be in the kitchen."

I tuned back in to what Cherise was saying, all the while worrying about Ve. I had a feeling things were going to get much worse for her before they got better.

"Trust me." Cherise sounded worn down. "It will be worth it if Laurel Grace gets what she wants. Otherwise we'll never hear the end of it. And I mean never."

I tapped the end of the pencil on the sticky notes, leaving a pattern of polka dots. "Does she have any other loose teeth?"

"Dear Lord, I hadn't thought of that. This can go on and on until all her permanent teeth come in."

"I was thinking more about how far Laurel Grace would go to forcefully remove her teeth just to get a tooth fairy visit."

There was silence on the line for a second while

Cherise contemplated what I'd said and its ramifications. Cherise was a Curecrafter, but I didn't know if that covered dental work.

Finally, she said, "We have to come up with something to tell her, Darcy. She can't keep yanking out teeth just to see you. Can you think of anything?"

I had a few ideas. "I'll take care of it. What time would you like me to be there?" I was already dreading putting on the tulle again. This time, however, I'd go easy on the glitter.

"Same time as last night?"

"I'll be there."

I hung up and put a call in to Laurissa Hale at the Spinning Wheel and left a message on her machine (the shop didn't open till nine) that I needed another embroidered tooth fairy pillow for Laurel Grace, to be picked up this afternoon.

As I jotted the appointment into Ve's day planner, I noticed a notation for this afternoon. ****_Find wombat._****

Why would someone want a wombat? A wombat of all things. I racked my brain trying to come up with any wombat facts I had stashed in the cobwebby corners. Australia popped right up along with a fuzzy image of an oversized groundhog-type critter. I could only imagine how Ve had planned to find one. I took the day planner with me into the kitchen. It was empty.

I heard hushed voices coming from upstairs. I stood at the bottom of the back staircase and listened. Sure enough, Ve was in the midst of a heated conversation with another woman whose voice I didn't recognize. I noted that Ve's cell phone was on the counter next to her purse and keys. The house phone didn't have a speakerphone option. Had she brought someone home with her?

I could hear only bits of the conversation. Something about someone being naive, and something about it being dangerous, foolish, and familiar. I had no idea what "it" was. When I heard the unknown woman tell Ve she was making a "foolhardy decision," I debated whether to check on Ve and finally decided to give her some privacy. I looked in Tilda's food bowls (the food hadn't been touched) and filled Missy's bowl. I washed my hands and finally—finally!—poured a cup of coffee.

I'd just added creamer when Ve came down the stairs with Missy following behind her.

"Please pour me some also. I'm going to need all the caffeine I can get." Color was high in her cheeks as she pulled herself up onto a counter stool and whisked imaginary crumbs from the quartz countertop. "Who was on the phone, dear? A client?"

Missy made a beeline for her food dish, and I watched the stairs as I poured coffee, but saw only Tilda staring down at us from the top step, her tail curled around her body.

Sliding a mug in front of Ve, I said, "Cherise Goodwin," and explained the situation.

Ve took a sip of her coffee and frowned. Abruptly, she stood up, went into the butler's pantry, and rooted around. She came out with a bottle of Grand Marnier and poured a generous amount into her coffee. She sipped, smiled, and said, "That's better."

She left the bottle on the counter, one hand resting on it as if she'd rather be drinking straight from its glass neck.

"Long night?" I asked with a smile.

She grinned. "How'd you guess?"

I didn't want to push for details on Sylar right off the bat. A little bit of decompression time was probably needed after what she'd been through.

I listened for footsteps upstairs, but heard nothing. Finally, my curiosity got the best of me. "Aunt Ve?"

Gripping her mug like a lifeline, she said, "Yes, dear?"

"Who were you speaking with upstairs just a few minutes ago?"

"Speaking with? Why, no one. No one else is here."
She drained her mug and motioned for a refill.

I brought the coffeepot over. "I definitely heard
voices."

"I must have been talking to myself. I do that often—I
should have warned you."

"But—"

"You're sure you can handle running As You Wish on
your own today?" Ve smiled tightly as she added a
healthy amount of liquor to her mug.

Her swift change of subject didn't go unnoticed. "I'm
sure."

"You need to use extra caution. You're still new to
your powers. You have no idea of what you're capable."

"If I have any questions, I can call you."

Ve worried her lip. "You can also contact—" With a
shake of her head, she cut herself off. "Never mind.
Call me."

"Who else is there?"

She sighed, drank, and said, "The Elder, but let's not
bother her today."

"The Elder is a she?"

Smiling, Velma said, "Always. Crafters are matriar-
chal."

I leaned down on my elbows. "Is it someone I've
met?"

She wagged a finger. "The identity of the Elder is
held in the highest of confidence. Her powers are great,
Darcy. Very few know her identity as a matter of her
protection, and we're all bound to silence on the matter.
You'll find out in due time. Have patience, child."

"How does a Crafter make contact with the Elder?"

"It's a conversation for another day, Darcy."

Hearing the weariness in her tone, I decided not to
push the matter. "I did have one question." I slid the day
planner toward her. "Why do we need to find a wombat?" I left off the "how." I figured she had a plan.

She groaned. "I completely forgot, and the party is tomorrow."

"What party?"

"Jake Carey's seventh birthday. He's crazy for wombats and is having a marsupial-themed birthday party. His mother hired As You Wish to find a wombat piñata. So far, I've had no luck, but where there's a will, there's a way. Unfortunately for you, it has to be your will and your way. I need to leave soon. Sylar is due in court in two hours. I need to bring him a suit."

"Court? Why?"

She let out a heavy sigh. "He's been arrested and will be arraigned for Alexandra's murder later today."

By noon, anxiety was building, slow and steady. I could feel it pulsing in my hands, throbbing in my neck. I took a few deep breaths, and shut down my laptop before I had a full-blown panic attack.

I wasn't one to have so many things out of my control at once.

Missy lifted her head as I backed away from the desk, stretching sore neck muscles. I couldn't help but notice that Starla was right—my upper arms did jiggle. I frowned at them and wished for toned muscle.

I wasn't the least bit surprised when nothing happened.

Didn't matter. I could fix a jiggly muscle. It might take some time, but it could be done. I was going to take Starla up on her offer to go jogging and get in shape. What were a few more changes after the upheaval of moving here?

Glancing at the phone, I hoped it would ring. Ve said she'd call as soon as she had word about Sylar. The police were convinced he had killed Alexandra. Motive was still a little fuzzy, but he had been the last one to have possession of Ve's scarf, and Evan Sullivan had told the police about Alexandra's plans to talk to Sylar after the meeting—not to mention that he was found hovering over the body. It was enough for the overeager prosecutor to take immediate action. Ve was most incensed with the village's police chief, Martin Leighton, who'd pretty much turned the case over to the state police so he could get back to his golf game. I had a feeling that once this case was all said and done, Ve would find a way to get Chief Leighton to retire.

I drummed my fingers on my laptop. Should I do another round of online searches for wombat piñatas? I'd already spent close to three hours searching with no luck whatsoever. The closest I could find was a piglet piñata that I might be able to doctor a bit, but that idea fell through when I called the store and found out the piñata wasn't in stock and would take three weeks to arrive.

That wouldn't work so well for a birthday party late tomorrow afternoon.

Which meant I had only one option, since Mrs. Carey hadn't implicitly wished for a wombat piñata. I was going to have to dig deep into memories of art class papier-mâché and make one myself. Time was of the essence—I had lots of shopping to get done. I made sure the front door was locked, and the BE RIGHT BACK sign was in place on the door. We didn't get many walk-in clients, but occasionally people happened inside just to see what the business was about.

I glanced around. Everything was neat and in its place. The spacious front room, the main meeting space for As You Wish, held a sofa, several chairs, and a small conference table. An area rug covered dark floors, and warm blues and greens made the large parlor feel a lot smaller and cozier. Fresh-cut hydrangeas floated in a bowl on the coffee table, and antique glass vases decorated the mantel. Silvery blue wallpaper with a playful faded curlicue design covered the walls, and sunlight slipped in through the gauzy curtain panels. The room was light and airy and welcoming. And yet, the room also brought out another feeling. A notion that there was something more going on in here. Something unseen. Something magical.

Which, of course, there was.

And then there was my favorite thing about the whole house. Above the mantel hung a large rectangular watercolor of a magic wand. The golden colors ebbed and flowed, swirled and twirled. It was perfect.

In the mudroom off the kitchen, I tugged on my sneakers, noticing that the tread was worn. If I was going to start jogging, I'd need a new pair. More shopping.

Missy bounded over, jumping and prancing.

Take her? Leave her? "You may have to wait outside some of the shops." Most of the village shops allowed dogs inside, but some held fast to the rule that pets remained out of doors.

She turned in a circle, her tail wagging.

I reached for her leash and snapped it on. Grabbing my wallet from my purse, I headed out the door.

Apparently there had been no need to worry about tourism. The square was packed. Alexandra's murder had people flocking to the village. I spotted Starla with her camera. One source of her income was taking random pictures of the tourists, and then selling them the prints.

I headed her way, Missy bouncing along next to me. Starla was just handing a couple a claim ticket when she saw me.

"Want a picture done?" she asked, steadying her lens.

"No, no!"

"Don't tell me you're camera shy?"

"Isn't everyone?"

"No, thank goodness, or I'd be out of business." She slipped a pad of claim tickets into one of the many pockets of a lime green work apron (the kind a construction worker might use for nails and screwdrivers) embroidered with "Hocus-Pocus Photography." "I hate to say it, but murder is good for business. The village is hopping."

We both turned toward Lotions and Potions. It was deserted. There wasn't even any crime-scene tape to indicate something terrible had happened. Just a cardboard CLOSED sign taped to the door.

"I heard Sylar was arrested," she said. "I just can't believe it."

Abruptly, Starla tipped her head, looking at something over my shoulder. She quickly switched lenses, adjusted her zoom, and took aim. I turned to see the object of her attention. Mrs. Pennywhistle sat on a hand-hewn log bench in front of a multitrunked birch tree, its branches heavy with new leaves.

She looked in a daze, staring ahead at nothing in particular. If I wasn't mistaken, she was wearing the same pink tracksuit she'd worn the night before at the village meeting. Her hair was deflated, and her hands stayed in constant motion, twisting and turning over themselves. "She looks like something's very wrong. Did she know Alexandra?"

Starla lowered her camera. "Everyone here knows everyone. But if Mrs. P and Alex had a special friendship, I didn't know of it."

"Did Alexandra have many friends?"

Missy, who had been sweeping the area for any interesting smells, settled at my feet and seemed to be looking at Mrs. Pennywhistle, too.

"A few. She and Evan were friends. They'd hang out and watch movies and hit the pub now and again."

Starla didn't mention anything about Alex's forays into Crafting, and I wasn't going to bring it up.

"She wasn't the easiest to get along with. Very . . . intense. I sensed a loneliness in her. I thought it was because she never dated, but apparently she did. Secretly."

"Why would she keep it secret, do you think?"

"Maybe her boyfriend was married?"

If he was, and his wife found out about the affair, that would be good motive for murder. Maybe Harper and Ve were right. Maybe Sylar was innocent. . . .

"I have to get these images back to the shop and get them uploaded. Are we on for running tomorrow morning?"

I nodded. "You'll be sure to bring the defibrillator paddles?"

"Never leave home without them," she called over her shoulder as she walked away.

I looked down at Missy. "I hope she knows I wasn't joking."

Missy thumped her tail.

Inwardly, I debated whether to go over and see if Mrs. Pennywhistle was okay, but when I glanced her way, she had her head down as if she was praying. I decided to check back with her on my way home.

Looking around the square, I wondered where I could pick up wombat supplies. First and foremost, I needed balloons. And newspapers—lots of them. And glue. I started for the village's general store, the Crone's Cupboard. When I passed the bookshop, I paused. Was Harper behaving herself? I peeked in the window and saw her shoulder to shoulder with Vince, arranging a display.

She spotted me and motioned for me to keep on moving. I'd just decided to go in and give her a good teasing when a raised voice turned my attention. Missy started yapping and tugging on her leash, wanting to see what all the excitement was about.

Down the street a bit, I spotted a man in front of Lotions and Potions, beating on its door. I moved a little closer. It was a man I didn't recognize at all. Tall, fit, and completely bald.

A good-sized crowd had gathered round. I looked for any familiar faces to see if they knew the man, but I didn't recognize anyone. Sirens screamed as a police cruiser pulled to the curb. The man wasn't the least bit fazed by the approaching patrolmen.

"Come out of there, you witch!" he shouted. The glass door panes rattled under his fists. "You're nothing but a phony! You'll pay for what you've done to me! Mark my words! I'll make you pay!"

Apparently, Alexandra had made many more enemies than friends in this village.

Then I remembered a mournful Mrs. Pennywhistle sitting on the bench. I turned to see if she was still there, but she was gone.

Chapter Seven

"His name is Griffin Huntley," Harper said as she stirred sugar into a glass of iced tea. "He's a local car salesman. You've probably seen his commercials. They certainly run often enough."

It had been a few hours since I'd seen Griffin beating on the door to Lotions and Potions. I'd stuck around just long enough for the village police to stuff him into the cruiser. Elbow-deep in flour, glue, and newspaper strips, I tried to recall if I knew the name. "Wait. The used-car dealer with the bad dye job and cut?" His hair was an unnatural ebony and always slicked back in a pompadour.

"That's him. The Elvis wannabe." Harper dropped a straw into her glass. Her first day on the job at the bookstore had gone well, and she'd come home all smiles with stories to tell. "Vince told me Griffin was a client of Alex's. He wanted to be handsomer, richer, and desperately wanted his hair to stop falling out. He thought Alex's potions could work miracles. He was wrong. The crème she gave him made all his hair fall out."

My papier-mâché skills were lacking. I was having a hard time keeping strips of newspaper from sliding off the balloons I'd rigged together to look like a wombat. "Did Griffin really think Alex was a witch? That she had powers?"

Harper nodded. "He's not the only one. Vince thought so, too. She had a lot of people convinced."

Tilda hopped up on the counter, sniffed at the wombat, and hopped down again, her tail in the air as she sashayed away. Missy rose from her doggy bed, yawned, stretched, and headed toward the doggy door. The tiny fenced-in backyard was perfect for her to roam on her own, though she'd managed to escape a time or three over the last couple of weeks.

"How much did she charge for her potions?"

"Not much. According to Vince, she really just wanted to help people."

"Like Evan and Griffin? That's help I think I'd pass on."

Harper rummaged through the cabinets. She pulled out a sleeve of crackers and grabbed a tub of garlic-and-herb cheese from the fridge. "If you ask me, Griffin was plenty handsome before. You know, if you didn't count his hair. At least now he doesn't have to worry about that. He should be grateful to Alex."

I pasted on two tiny wombat ears and tried to figure out how I was going to rig a marsupial pouch on its back. Would birthday boy Jake notice if it was missing? "No wonder I didn't recognize him. His pompadour was gone. *Completely* gone."

Smiling, Harper nodded. "Every last strand fell out after he used the phony potion."

Her face glowed with happiness—it had been a long time since I'd seen her this way. She obviously liked her new job—and all the information she could get from Vince about Alex. If she was on a quest to clear Sylar's name, she'd be eager to fill in the blanks about Alex's life. I also suspected she liked Vince. She had that falling-for-someone look about her.

She reached into a quilted tote bag and pulled out a reporter's notebook. "I ran into Ramona Todd from the Magic Wand Salon on the way home, and she said Griffin—"

"You know Ramona?"

"I met her last night at the meeting. She's nice. Suggested you get some hip and chic blue highlights and a more flattering cut. Your hair is too blah and too long."

"She did not."

"You're right. That was me."

I stuck out my tongue. Harper had been on me to get a mini makeover since my divorce. I happened to like the way I looked just fine, with the exception of that flaccidness. "I'm not one of your pet projects."

"Don't get cranky with me. You're the one who taught me that first impressions count, and to always look well put together and respectable."

"Hey, I look respectable!"

"For an old maid. You've let yourself go. A lot."

"I'm not old."

"Thirty. Soon it will be thirty-one. Then thirt—"

"I can count."

"Old."

"What did Ramona say?" A change of topic was desperately needed or Harper would, well, harp. What was the point of getting my hair and nails done? I had no one to impress—most of all there was no one I *wanted* to impress. I pushed the sudden flash of Nick Sawyer's face straight out of my mind. Men were heartbreakers, every last one of them.

Harper grinned like the little mischief-maker she was. "She said Griffin bought the potion Wednesday afternoon."

"Ramona knows Griffin?"

"He's one of her clients at the salon," she said at a snail's pace, as if I were slow on the uptake. "Anyway, Ramona tried to talk him into seeing a dermatologist about his hair loss, but he trusted Alex." She made a notation in her notebook.

"What is that?" I asked, laying the last strip of papier-mâché onto the balloons. My version of a wombat wasn't too bad, if I said so myself. A little paint and it would be perfect. I just hoped the piñata dried in time. I had to deliver it to Jake Carey's birthday party tomorrow at four. Not a lot of time, but what's a witch to do?

"What's what?"

"That notebook."

"I'm keeping track of suspects."

I rolled my eyes as I picked up the wombat. It was bound to dry faster outside in the sunshine. "Can you open the back door for me, please?"

"Did you just roll your eyes at me?" She headed for the door.

"I really don't think it's a good idea if you get involved in a murder investigation." I set the wombat on the back porch. Inside, I washed my hands.

"Too late. There are a lot of suspects, Darcy. The police have hardly looked at them."

"A lot like who?"

"Well, the unknown pickpocket for one. Griffin is another. Evan Sullivan."

"Evan?"

"Have you seen his face?"

"They were friends, Evan and Alex."

"Still, have you seen his face?"

She had a point. I didn't like it much, though.

"Also, there's the whole secret-boyfriend angle. He's a suspect. And if he's married, his wife is a suspect, too. We have to find out who they are."

"You've been talking to Starla."

"She stopped in the bookshop." Her voice cracked into a giggle. "I hear you're taking up running."

"Why are you laughing?"

"You, running?"

"How hard can it be? It's essentially fast walking, right? I can walk fast. Really fast."

"You can also twist an ankle walking down the hallway," Harper pointed out.

I can. And had. "Your point?"

"How is As You Wish's medical plan?"

I tossed a cracker at her. She picked it up and lathered it with cheese. "Although the more I think about it, we can probably rule out Griffin as Alex's killer."

"Why?" I wiped down the kitchen counter and left the bowl of papier-mâché mixture in the sink to soak.

"Darcy, if he was banging on Alex's door this morning demanding she come out, he obviously didn't know she was already dead."

I carried leftover newspapers to the recycling bin in the mudroom. "Or did he just want everyone to *think* he didn't know she was dead?"

Harper's brows dipped like they always did when she was in deep concentration, and then she frowned. She hated when she hadn't thought things all the way through. "Good point. It would explain the huge scene this morning, too. The more people who think he had no clue Alex was dead, the more people might actually believe it. Okay, then. He goes back on the list. We need to find out if he had an alibi for last night."

"We?"

"Of course 'we.' Ve's too busy to do any snooping. Someone has to clear Sylar before they lock him away forever. I, for one, can't let an innocent man go to jail."

I agreed, but I didn't think those people should be us. And said so.

"If not us, then who?" Harper asked. "Don't say the police, either, because we know what side they're on. That Chief Leighton is virtually useless. So is the whole village police department at that. Vince said that Sylar's been trying to get Leighton fired ever since he became chairman of the village council, but no one likes the idea of change."

Probably Chief Leighton most of all, especially if he was getting paid to improve his golf swing. This tidbit might explain why he hadn't gone out of his way to find other suspects in Alex's murder: Leighton wanted Sylar gone.

"Okay," I said, remembering how devastated Ve was. Truthfully, I didn't know Sylar well enough to judge if he was guilty or innocent, but I loved Ve, and I'd do anything for her. Even if it meant sticking my nose where it didn't belong. If Sylar was cleared, Ve would be happy. It was good enough motivation for me to get involved. "But only a little snooping. Nothing dangerous or anything. Promise."

"Cross my heart." She crossed with a cracker in hand. "I'll see what I can find out about Griffin, and you need to check and see if Evan has an alibi. And we both need to keep an ear to the ground for news about Alex's secret boyfriend, and more about her life in general, because one thing became clear today—no one really knows who she is or where she came from. Gossip is flying right now, but some of it is bound to be true."

My stomach fell. I didn't much like the idea of snooping into Evan's life but realized it was necessary. "I have to run over to the Spinning Wheel to pick up the tooth pillow for tonight. I can stop by the bakery and see if Evan's there on my way." I grabbed the leash from the hook by the back door. But when I whistled for Missy, she didn't bound up the steps like she normally did.

And after a quick search of the backyard, I realized she was nowhere to be found.

I couldn't figure out how she escaped. The gate was closed and there were no escape tunnels I could see. After much debate, Harper agreed to pick up Laurel Grace's pillow and deliver it while I searched for Missy. How far could she have gone? I didn't have much time to search, and honestly, I wasn't too worried about her. She always managed to find her way home.

I walked the perimeter of the square, whistling and calling her name. When I passed the Gingerbread Shack,

I doubled back. Going inside to see if Evan had heard about someone finding a lost dog might be the perfect chance to talk to him and discover his alibi.

A bell on the door jangled as I pulled it open. The sweet scent of bakery made my mouth water. Vanilla, buttercream, a hint of cinnamon. I didn't know how Evan wasn't three hundred pounds.

As if drawn by an invisible force, I walked directly over to the display case. One side held regular-sized cakes, cupcakes, cookies, cream puffs . . . and the other held miniature versions.

"May I help you? Miss?"

I realized the clerk behind the counter was talking to me. "Sorry." I laughed. "I was a little distracted."

"Happens all the time." He was a good-looking guy, maybe late twenties, with bright blue eyes and a wide smile. His name tag read MICHAEL.

"I actually came in to see Evan. Is he here?"

The bakery was small, light, and bright. There was just enough room for a couple of pub-style tables, the display case, and a beverage bar. I adored the white beadboard walls, the dark bamboo floors, and the oversized photos of cake close-ups. Starla's work, I was sure.

Michael shook his head. "Called in sick today."

"Oh." I was oddly relieved that I wouldn't have to pry, but I was worried about his rash. Had it spread? Or had he called in because he was heartbroken over the loss of his friend? Either way, I felt the need to check on him. One problem, though. I didn't know where he lived.

I eyed Michael. He'd probably think I was a nut job if I asked for Evan's address. Besides, it didn't much matter—I had a better source.

"Thanks anyway. You, uh, didn't happen to see a lost dog, did you? Or hear of anyone who found one?"

Michael shook his head. "Sorry."

Five minutes later, I left the shop with a bagful of treats. I had no willpower whatsoever when it came to chocolate. I had bought several of the mini devil's food cupcakes and also a couple of chocolate-filled cream puffs.

I found Starla on the green and headed her way. She smiled when she spotted the bag. "Good thing you're going to start running tomorrow."

"You don't have to keep reminding me."

"I think I do. I'm afraid you're going to back out."

Truth was, I'd been thinking about doing just that. But I wasn't about to confess. "I noticed Evan wasn't at the bakery. Is he okay?"

Her eyes grew wide and her voice dropped. "His rash is covering his whole face now. He's afraid it's going to scare away customers."

"How's he handling Alex's death?"

"Sad, but I think he'd be more so if he wasn't so worried about himself."

"It's too bad he didn't get the antidote cream from Alex before . . ." There was just no way to properly end that sentence.

"I know. He was devastated last night when I came in. He'd been calling and calling her. He didn't hear the news about her death until this morning."

It was strange he hadn't heard the sirens. It seemed like most of the village had been on the green last night, trying to see what was going on. Had he gone straight home after the village meeting?

If Evan had killed Alex, he would have had to have done it at the meeting sometime. Maybe when he'd gone back to rinse his platters? But no, Mrs. P had emerged from the hallway after Evan—surely, she would have seen something amiss.

Shaking my head, I couldn't believe I was thinking such things. This was what hanging around with Harper did to me. If I could get Evan's alibi, maybe it would put my mind at ease. "Did he say if he saw anything last night? Anything out of the ordinary?"

"Nothing. He feels terrible about what happened to Alexandra. He thinks he should have somehow prevented it. How, I have no idea."

I felt awful prying this way, and I didn't want Starla to get suspicious of my questions, so I let the rest go. For now. I was going to have to learn some sleuthing skills fast. "I'd love to stop by and see him. Maybe bring him a bowl of soup or something."

"He'd love that! Maybe tomorrow, though? I don't think he's up for company today." She took a pad of paper out of her apron and jotted down an address. "We share a brownstone on Fairy Hollow, just around the corner."

I tucked the address into my pocket. "You haven't seen Missy anywhere, have you?"

"She's missing again?"

"A regular escape artist."

"I'll help you look."

We split up. Half an hour later, I was just about ready to give up and wait for her to come home on her own when I heard a familiar bark. I looked ahead and my breath caught when I saw whom she was with.

Chapter Eight

"We were just at your place," Nick said, "but no one was home, so we decided to wait here until someone came back."

I glanced at As You Wish, just across the street. I could still see the BE RIGHT BACK sign in the window, which meant that Harper was still making her delivery of the tooth pillow for me.

As the As You Wish sign swayed in the soft breeze, a sense of pride came over me. The house was picture-perfect, elaborately painted with various purples and a soft green trim. Clapboard siding, detailed millwork, a high hip roof with several smaller roofs slanting downward and stunning corner tower. It looked like something out of a fairy tale, which was how it had been intended when it was designed. It was home, and oddly, it felt like it always had been.

Nick was sitting next to Mrs. Pennywhistle on the log bench while Mimi and Missy played in the grass.

"Thank you. I've been looking all over for her."

"At the Gingerbread Shack?" Nick asked drily, eyeing the bag I was holding.

I smiled. "I dare you to walk past that shop without going in. Anyone want a mini cupcake?"

Mimi's hand shot up. As she relieved the cupcake from its wrapper, she nodded to Missy. "We found her at our house. She was barking at the gate. At first I didn't know who she belonged to, but then Dad saw her and knew right away that she was your dog."

"She should wear a collar," Nick said.

"She does." I bent down to attach her leash, but realized quickly her collar was missing. Heat filled my cheeks. "Well, normally she does. I don't know where she lost it." Somewhere between As You Wish and Nick's place.

Missy looked up at me and wagged her tail. I knew she'd taken a liking to Nick that morning, but to have tracked him to his house? That was taking her adoration a little too far. "I'm not sure how she got out. I hope she wasn't too much trouble."

Nick said, "None at all. And it's been nice visiting with Mrs. Pennywhistle, too. Do you two know each other?"

Nodding, I said, "Are you feeling well, Mrs. P?" Sure enough, she wore the same tracksuit as last night, and her usually sky-high teased hair was flat on one side. Day-old eyeliner smudged the wrinkles under her eyes, and mascara flaked on her cheeks, looking like dark freckles, and one of her painted eyebrows had worn off. My guess was that she hadn't slept a wink last night.

"Just a tad under the weather, dearie." Sadness filled her normally vibrant blue eyes as she looked at Lotions and Potions.

Though it was fairly obvious the murder was the source of her grief, I didn't want to press my luck to ask about Alex.

"Are you sad about Miss Alexandra?" Mimi asked.

Out of the corner of my eye, I saw Nick wince at his daughter's frankness. If she had been in foot range, she may have gotten a tiny warning kick from him not to be so nosy.

Me? I was glad she had asked—because I had wanted to know, too.

Mimi added, "I'm sad, too. She was my friend."

Nick's forehead dipped a little bit at that. Had he not known?

"I cannot say we were friends, little one, for I hardly knew her," Mrs. P answered, "but I am quite sad about what happened to Alexandra. No one deserves such a fate."

Who was Alexandra Shively? On one hand, it seemed most of the Crafters thought she was a nuisance and Sylar openly disliked her, yet both Evan and Mimi considered her a friend.

As *I* considered both Evan and Mimi friends, I trusted their judgment. So what was I missing about Alex? Did she have a split personality? Because what I'd seen of her last night hadn't left a good impression on me.

Complex, as Velma had described her. It was turning out to be a fitting term.

"Did you know her well?" I asked Mimi.

"Sure! She always let me hang around her shop and gave me lots of samples of her lotions and sprays."

I thought about Griffin Huntley's hair and Evan's face and hoped Mimi had none of those lotions. A quick look at Nick, and I could tell he was thinking along the same lines. His eyes had darkened and his whole body tensed.

"That was nice of her," I said. Missy barked as if in agreement.

Mimi nodded. "She was always talking about how she was a witch, and once she even wore a pink pointy hat around the store as a joke, and she had loads and loads of books about potions and witchcraft and stuff." Her voice trailed off as she looked toward Alex's store. "What's going to happen to all her stuff, Dad?"

"I'm not sure." Nick bent to pat Missy. She had nuzzled up against his leg. "Once the police are done going through it, the rest will probably go to her next of kin — her relatives."

Mimi's nose wrinkled. "But she doesn't have any fam-

ily. It was just her." As if telling a story she'd heard re-
peatedly, she continued. "Her dad died when she was
just a baby, and then her mom died when Miss Alexandra was my age—just like me. She didn't have brothers
or sisters, and she didn't have any other family. She lived
at an orphanage, and all the stuff she owned fit into one
little suitcase." Her brown eyes had grown wide with the
telling of the tale.

I suddenly recalled what Harper had said earlier,
about some bits of gossip proving true. I wondered what,
if any, information was accurate in the rundown Mimi
had given.

Nick seemed shocked that Mimi knew so much about
Alex, and Mrs. P had her eyes closed. I wasn't sure
whether she was dozing or praying or making silent
wishes that we'd all go away and leave her in peace.

It was strange and unsettling seeing her so quiet.
Usually she was a chatterbox, an elderly firecracker.

Missy was oblivious to the tension in the air. She was
too busy snuggling with Nick.

The lucky dog.

No, no, no! I had to stop thinking like that.

I'd sworn off men. If only I could remember that
when he was around. It continually slipped my mind
when he was nearby—a bad habit I was going to have to
break.

"So where does her stuff go?" Mimi asked Nick again.

Mrs. P's eyes popped open—too alert to have been
asleep. Praying or wishing? Hard to tell.

He said tightly, "I don't know."

"Do you think the police would let me have her pink
pointy hat? I really liked that hat, and Miss Alexandra
always said it looked good on me."

"I don't know. . . . I can ask, I suppose." Nick gave me
a pleading look, and I realized he wanted me to change
the subject.

Mrs. P's hands were in motion again. I checked to see

what she was holding and was a bit surprised that her fingers clutched a tiny green leaf. "Is that a four-leaf clover?"

"We've been hunting for them while we waited for you to come home," Mimi said brightly. "I have one, too. See?" She held it out to me, and I gave it a good inspection.

"It's perfect. How lucky you found it. And you?" I asked Nick. "Did you find one?"

"Not so lucky." He stood and stretched. Now that the subject had been changed away from Alexandra, I noticed a shift in him as well. His body had relaxed, but his eyes were in constant motion, sweeping across the village green. Looking. Searching. He was working, I suddenly realized. Working to find the pickpocket.

I wished he'd work a foot farther away from me. He stood a little too close for my liking. I could feel his body heat. As if he sensed that he was making me uncomfortable, he looked my way. Moved just a hair closer.

I had the feeling he liked making me uncomfortable. I took a tiny step away from him under the pretense of shifting my weight.

"We're still looking, though, aren't we, Missy?" Mimi said as she rubbed the dog's head.

"Did you make wishes?" I asked, holding my breath as I waited for the answers.

"Yes! Mine was for—" Mimi cut herself off abruptly. "I don't want to say. I want it to come true, and doesn't saying it out loud jinx it?"

"Not always," I said softly.

Mrs. P looked up at me and winked.

I blinked. What did that wink mean? Was she a Crafter? Did she know I was a Wishcrafter?

I certainly couldn't ask *her*. But I could ask Ve. Maybe she'd give me a list of who's who in this village. It would make my life a little easier.

Mimi finger-combed through a patch of clover. "Well, I don't want to chance it, but Mrs. P wished she had enough money to do something nice for her grand-daughter."

Since Mrs. Pennywhistle hadn't made the wish aloud to me, I had no obligation to fulfill it.

Mrs. P rose from the bench. "Just wishful musings of an poor old woman."

I frowned. I thought the Pixie Cottage was doing well. It always seemed to have a NO VACANCY sign hanging out front.

"I'll be going now, dearies." She patted my cheek. "Give Ve my best, now, won't you? And Sylar, too. I'm not sure what that idiot prosecutor is thinking." She pressed her eyes closed and more mascara flakes fluttered to her cheeks. "I'm not sure what this village is coming to."

She waved and speed-walked off, leaving me standing oh-so-close to Nick, while Mimi sat at our feet, searching through clover. Missy had settled down after her long adventure, but still kept a watchful eye on Mimi.

"Darcy! You found her!" Starla headed toward us. Suddenly she stopped, raised her lens, and snapped my and Nick's picture. I hadn't even had time to put my hand in front of my face.

She was grinning as she handed me a claim ticket. "It should be ready in an hour." Bending, she patted Missy on her curly-topped head, and spoke in baby talk to the dog. "I'm so glad you're safe and sound. Yes, I am. Yes, I am."

Nick smiled at me, and I felt a flutter of warmth in my chest.

I chose to think of igloos and Eskimos and frozen tundra to counteract it.

"Okay, gotta run," Starla said. "It's the busiest day of the season so far."

I thought about what she said earlier.

I hate to say it, but murder is good for business. The village is hopping.

If that was true, how far would someone with a failing business go to drum up customers?

I looked at the pink blur in the distance. How badly was the Pixie Cottage doing? What *had* upset Mrs. P the night before?

It was yet another thing to look into, to test my non-existent sleuthing skills.

Starla hurried off, her camera lens at the ready. Leaving me alone with Mimi and Nick.

I checked my watch. It was getting late. "I should be going. I have to work tonight."

Mimi said, "Another fairy job?"

"As a matter of fact, yes."

Her eyes lit. "Will you show me your wings one of these days?"

"Absolutely."

"Wings?" Nick asked.

There was a spark in his eye that went beyond simple curiosity, a light that made me feel that damn warmth again.

"Gossamer, about this big," I said, stretching my arms. He smiled.

I scooped up Missy and started for As You Wish. "Thanks again for bringing her home. I'll, uh, see you around."

"Wait!" Mimi cried.

I turned. Mimi held up a four-leaf clover. "I found one!" She brought it over to me. "Here. It's for you, Darcy."

"For me?" I gently took it. "Thank you."

Mimi said, "Now you have to make a wish."

I looked between her and Nick, down at Missy, and back to Nick again, who was staring at me intently. I closed my eyes and wished.

"Well?" Mimi asked. "What did you wish for?"

I smiled. "I can't say. Or it might not come true, right?"

I waved and headed off toward As You Wish, already putting my wish out of my mind. My thoughts had already turned to tonight. I hoped all would go well at the Goodwins', and that there wouldn't be any surprises.

And I tried really hard not to think about the photo Starla had taken.

And how it was going to be overexposed.

Chapter Nine

I vowed never to wear tulle again. There had to be a suitable substitution. If I was going to keep up the fairy work, I needed to make an appointment at the Bewitching Boutique to have some sort of an original design created—a sign in the window touted the shop as a custom clothier.

Moonlight cast my winged shadow across the Goodwins' front door as I knocked softly. Cherise opened the door with gusto, and ushered me inside. Color was high on her cheeks as she led me into the kitchen. "We're glad you're here."

Amanda stood on one side of the granite island with her arms crossed, and Dennis stood on the other, in the exact same pose. Their backs were to each other.

With more enthusiasm than a whole cheerleading squad, Cherise's voice rose, and she clapped her hands. "I said, we're so glad you're here, Darcy! Aren't we glad?"

Neither Amanda nor Dennis said a word. In fact, neither looked at me at all. Tear tracks stained Amanda's cheeks.

I frowned at Dennis, suddenly wishing I could turn him into a toad or something. He was medium height, average-sized, not handsome—but not unfortunate looking, either. He wore a tight, fancy T-shirt tucked into belted black trousers and dark loafers. He looked like the type to cart around a big ego that probably had more to do with his successful medical practice than any kind of winning personality. Frankly, I wondered what Amanda saw in him.

"I don't know what I ever saw in you," Amanda said.

My jaw dropped. Could she read my mind? I contemplated whether Amanda was a type of Crafter I hadn't heard of yet, one who could read people's thoughts. Which was much too scary to contemplate, so I turned my attention to the kitchen's flowered wallpaper and wished I were somewhere else. Anywhere else.

"Now, now," Cherise said with a skittish laugh. "Darcy came all this way—"

"Dollar signs," Dennis answered dully.

Amanda spun on him, and sputtered, "Oh! Oh! How *dare* you! You're just such a—"

"Now, now!" Cherise slammed her hand on the countertop. "I *said*, Darcy came all this way."

Her voice hadn't risen, but the tone had changed drastically. It was enough to make me glad she wasn't my mother.

Both snapped their mouths closed and looked at me, as if only just realizing I was standing there. "Hello." I finger-waved and watched glitter fall to the floor.

Color flooded Amanda's cheeks. "Hello."

Dennis nodded.

"Now, then," Cherise said, "let's remember tonight is about Laurel Grace. Not about petty squabbles."

Amanda opened her mouth, but Cherise wagged her finger. "Nuh-uh. Not a word."

At this point I just wanted to dissolve into the woodwork—or, better yet, make a run for the door. But my work ethic held strong, and I decided I'd better get this done and over with so I could go home. Consoling an inconsolable Ve was much better than being in the crosshairs of a marital spat.

My heart twisted at the thought of my aunt. Sylar's lawyer, Marcus, had dropped her off at the house just before I headed out. They'd already been to the Cauldron, and Aunt Ve had had one too many gin and tonics to be coherent. But Marcus had explained everything, and it all boiled down to Sylar being denied bail.

Harper and I had managed to get a sobbing Ve into bed, where she promptly passed out.

It was probably best that way for her. I'd left Harper at Ve's bedside. She was reading a forensics manual to pass the time while she kept an eye on snoring Ve. Now, more than ever, Harper wanted to clear Sylar's name.

Heaven help us all.

"Shall we?" Cherise asked me.

Grateful, I nodded. In a repeat of the night before, I carefully climbed the wooden steps. Only this time, three people looked on. Two of whom wanted to kill each other.

I opened Laurel Grace's door and crept inside. Tiptoeing to the bed, I thought carefully about what I was going to say.

As I bent over her, Laurel Grace suddenly popped up. Our foreheads slammed together, and pain radiated down the back of my head, down my jaw. Stars swam in my eyes, and my vision narrowed. I glanced quickly at Cherise; then everything went dark.

I woke to a small voice asking, "Did she die, Mommy?"

"No, no." That was Amanda. She didn't sound convinced.

I winced as I opened my eyes. Dennis was kneeling over me, his eyes intent on my face. They were nice eyes, I decided. Kind. Maybe there was more to him than an egomaniacal jerk.

"Hold still," he said smoothly.

He needn't have worried. My head hurt so bad that I

didn't want to move. Lord, I hoped there wasn't any blood. I couldn't stand the sight of blood. I usually fainted if it amounted to more than a nick.

Over his shoulder, he said, "I told you having her here was a bad idea."

I winced in pain.

"Now is not the time, Dennis," Cherise chastised.

Dennis rubbed his hands together and slowly lowered one palm to my forehead. His lips moved, and his left eye twitched twice. Warmth flowed across my forehead, fizzing its way over my head, down my face, through my whole body.

"Is the pain gone?" he asked.

I nodded. Suddenly, I liked him a whole lot better.

"Good. Now it's time for you to go."

And just like that, he was a jerk again.

"No!" Laurel Grace cried. "I need to give her my tooth!"

Cherise helped me stand up (the wings were a little unwieldly), and I realized I felt better than I had in a long time. No wonder Dennis's medical practice was doing so well. I wondered if he could cure broken hearts, and if he could, maybe I should make an appointment with him for Ve.

Dennis rolled his eyes and motioned me over to the bed. Laurel Grace was fairly bouncing with glee. If she'd been affected by the head bumping, she showed no signs of it—or she'd been healed before me, when I was out cold. "I lost another tooth!"

"So I heard." Turning to face my audience, I said to them, "May I have a few moments alone with Laurel Grace?"

"I don't think—," Dennis began before Amanda took hold of his arm and forcibly pulled him from the room.

I had a little chat with Laurel Grace, explaining how from now on, I (as the tooth fairy) would visit her only when she was asleep, and that even though she wouldn't

see me, she'd know I had been there when she woke up
and found her special coin pouch. And that I wouldn't
visit at *all* if I suspected she was pulling her teeth on
purpose just for a visit. I stressed the importance of that
last fact, and how fairies *always* knew the truth.

She looked at me solemnly, her eyes wide with wonder.

"Now it's time for you to go back to sleep," I said
softly.

Snuggling under the covers, she said, "I'm glad I
didn't make you dead."

I smiled. "I'm glad, too."

From beneath her pillow, I removed the tooth-shaped
pillow, and I pulled from my velvet pouch the special
coin pouch embroidered with Laurel Grace's name. I
handed it to her. "Remember what I said."

She nodded and clutched the pouch, her tiny fingers
gripping the fabric tightly.

Glitter rained down on the carpet as I waved good-bye
and backed out of the room, closing the door behind me.
In the hallway, Amanda and Cherise awaited. Dennis was
gone, but I could hear him downstairs, moving around.

Quietly I explained what I'd told Laurel Grace. I
handed Amanda the tooth pillow and a small bottle of
glitter. "For more coin pouches, just call Laurissa at the
Spinning Wheel. You might want to have several tucked
away." From now on, Amanda would be taking over my
duties.

"I'm going to hide these and then go check on Laurel
Grace. Thank you so much, Darcy, for everything."

I said, "You're welcome."

I couldn't say I'd miss the tulle. Or the tights. But I'd
definitely miss Laurel Grace's smile.

"Come," Cherise said, leading me downstairs.

Dennis sat sullenly at the kitchen table, his hands
wrapped around a steaming mug. Dunking a tea bag, he
gave me a sideways glance and scowled.

Cherise frowned at him as she reached for her checkbook.

His petulant scowl was unnerving, so I turned my back to him. "Can I ask you a question, Cherise?"

She searched a drawer for a pen. "Sure thing."

"Can Curecrafters heal broken hearts?"

Her gaze drifted over my wings and settled on, I assumed, her son. "Unfortunately, no. Only true medical ailments."

I wanted to argue her point, because there was nothing more painful than heartache, but I knew it was useless. The Curecrafters had to abide by their own laws, and if it said no healing broken hearts, then there would be no healing of broken hearts.

"Whose? Yours?" Cherise asked, an empathetic warmth in her eyes.

Though my heart was still bruised, it was nothing like what my aunt was going through. "Ve."

Her forehead dipped into a deep frown. "This business with Sylar?"

I nodded. "He was arraigned this afternoon."

Letting out a breath, she said, "It's terrible. Just terrible."

"For me, too," Dennis said.

I turned to face him as Cherise said, "Not everything is about you."

He scowled at her, too. Glad his bad attitude wasn't reserved just for me.

"A good portion of my clients are Alexandra Shively victims," he said. "My practice is going to see a loss of profit now that she's gone."

Victims. Such a strong word. It reminded me of Griffin Huntley, the car salesman who lost his hair. How many others were there? And had any of them sought revenge?

I heard footsteps on the stairs as Cherise said to her son, "Only you would turn a woman's death into a tragedy for yourself. You didn't even know her."

Dennis stood. "It would be a tragedy if my practice failed. How would I pay for this house, this mug, *her*?" He pointed at me.

Hmm. Seemed to me, Cherise had paid for As You Wish's services.

"Please," Cherise countered. "You have a waiting list three months long for new patients. Your profits won't wane in the least. You're missing the bigger point. Life is not about money, Dennis. It's about family. It's about *love*."

He was scoffing as Amanda came into the kitchen. She'd obviously heard what he said. The naked hurt on her face made my chest tight.

"Is that so?" Amanda asked him, her voice cracking.

Dennis pulled his shoulders back. "I don't see you cutting up your credit cards."

Tears filled her eyes.

Cherise said, "That's enough. You're never going to learn what love is until it's gone." She faced me. "I wish Dennis would learn exactly what it's like not to have Amanda and Laurel Grace in his life for a while."

My heart pounded. I looked between the three of them and winced as I said, "I wish I might, I wish I may, grant this wish without delay." I blinked twice.

Amanda vanished. I spun around, looking for her. "Where'd she go?" My hands started to shake.

"You don't know?" Dennis demanded.

I shook my head. She'd been standing there within arm's reach; then she was gone. Just. Like. That.

Panic seeped in. Where had she gone?

Cherise, I noticed, was smiling. How could she be *smiling*?

Dennis ran for the stairs, took them up two at a time. A second later he was back, out of breath. He got right in my face. "Laurel Grace is gone, too."

My stomach cramped.

"Bring them back, right now." Fury shone in his eyes.

"I c-can't." How could I? I didn't know where they went.

He closed his eyes tightly; then they popped open. "I *wish* they'd come back. Right this minute," he said through tightly clenched teeth.

Absolutely, this was the last fairy job ever. How did I get myself into this position?

Quickly, I said, "Wish I might, wish I may, grant this wish without delay."

Nothing happened.

Dennis took a step back, looked around. "Where are they?"

I shrugged. I had no earthly idea.

"Why didn't the wish work?" he demanded to know.

My guess was because it wasn't pure of heart. I glanced at Cherise. I had a feeling she knew it, too.

And I wasn't surprised to see her still smiling, not the least bit worried.

I, on the other hand, was scared to death. Because I had no idea if I could ever wish the mother and daughter back.

Chapter Ten

White twinkle lights lit the front porch as I pulled into As You Wish's driveway and cut the engine.

It was a little past ten, the village green was quiet, and I was still shaken. Dennis had stormed out of the Goodwin house when his wish hadn't worked, and Cherise had simply handed me a check and bidden me a good night.

Moonlight guided me up the walkway toward the back of the house, through the small picket gate, and up the steps and into the mudroom. I hung my wings on a hook by the back door, and greeted a sleepy Missy, who gave two halfhearted barks when I came in.

Tilda sat on the kitchen counter, eyeing me warily. I cupped her face and scratched behind her ears. She pushed her head into my palm and a purr vibrated against my hand. I couldn't help but smile.

Hearing steps on the back staircase, I turned and found Harper coming down. She wore long loose lounge pants and a T-shirt as pajamas—with her short stature and delicate features, she looked about fifteen years old, not twenty-three, a fact I knew she detested. In her hand was the forensics book, which had been copiously dog-eared.

"Whoa," she said when she saw me. "You look like someone stole your magic wand."

I pulled the tiara off my head and picked out a few long dark strands of my hair stuck in its combs. "Worse."

"What happened?"

Ve's snores drifted down the stairs. I motioned upward. "Has she been out this whole time?"

Harper lifted herself onto a counter stool. "Completely. I don't think she's even rolled over."

It had been a long twenty-four hours for Ve. Rest could only be good for her.

"I can't imagine what she's going through," I murmured. I went to Ve's liquor cabinet and looked inside. I didn't see anything that looked the least bit good.

Harper hopped off the stool, went to the freezer, and pulled out a York Peppermint Patty and handed it to me. I set my elbows on the counter and leaned on them as I peeled the wrapper and nibbled on frozen chocolate.

"Are you going to tell me?" Harper asked.

My eyes drifted shut and I groaned. "It's bad."

"How bad?"

"Bad bad."

There was lightness in her tone as she said, "Did the little girl get tangled in your tulle?"

"You're making fun, but this isn't amusing. I think . . . I, well—"

"What?"

"I made Amanda and Laurel Grace Goodwin disappear."

Her dark eyebrows dipped as she frowned. "Disappear?"

"Vanish."

"No one just vanishes."

"Into thin air. Right before my very eyes. Well, Amanda at least." Tilda came over and sniffed around the peppermint patty. I explained about Cherise's wish.

Harper's eyes grew wide. "Where did they go?"

"I don't have a clue. I need to talk to Ve."

Tilda *rreow*ed, and nudged my chin with the top of

her head. I scratched under her chin, wondering if she was lulling me into a false sense of security. Again.

"I don't think Ve's going to be coherent until morning."

My stomach churned. I was afraid of that. "I don't know what else to do. Who else to talk to. I suppose the Elder would know. . . ."

"Do you know how to reach the Elder?"

"No."

"Marcus Debrowski came back after you left for the Goodwins'. He's a Lawcrafter, so he might know something, right?"

"I don't know. Maybe. Why'd he stop by?"

"He wanted to make sure Ve was okay. And he dropped off some papers for her."

"What kind of papers?"

She shrugged. "They're in a sealed envelope. He stayed for coffee." She rubbed the countertop. "He seems nice."

I studied her carefully. "How nice?"

"He asked me out for coffee."

I smiled. "And you said?"

"I'd think about it. I'm not sure he's my type."

"Only one way to find out."

She shrugged. "I suppose."

I couldn't help but get the feeling she was disappointed that Vince hadn't been the one to ask her out.

"What are you going to do about the Goodwins?"

I shook my head, feeling fairly useless. Taking a deep breath, I said, "Cherise didn't seem the least bit worried. Maybe I should take that as a consolation. If something bad was happening, she'd be worried, right?"

"You're asking the wrong person. I don't know the first thing about all this witch stuff. Honestly, I don't think I want to know and be the cause of people disappearing."

I narrowed my eyes at her.

"Sorry," she said, shrugging.

Missy let out a little yap. She sat in the doorway of the mudroom. I'd closed off her doggy door for the time being, until I could figure out how she kept escaping.

"I can take her," Harper said.

"No, no. I'll go. The fresh air will help clear my head."

Running upstairs, I peeked at Ve as I passed her room. Sure enough, she hadn't moved. I shimmied out of my tutu and into a pair of jeans.

I hadn't found Missy's collar yet, so I rigged a temporary slipknot with her leash, making sure I left enough slack so she wouldn't choke. Tomorrow I'd go to the pet shop, the Furry Toadstool, and buy her a new collar.

It was a gorgeous night, warm and breezy, and I wished I could enjoy it. My chest was tight, and I could feel anxiety thrumming below the surface. I hadn't felt this way since Troy had walked out. No, scratch that. Not since I found out he had remarried and his new bride was pregnant.

I took deep, even breaths, and tried to tell myself everything would be okay. If I could get through my divorce, I could survive just about anything.

I hoped.

Missy trotted along. She stopped to sniff anything that interested her—plants, park benches, trees, a stray piece of litter. She hadn't seemed the least bit affected by her adventure this afternoon.

I tried not to worry about the Goodwins. Once Ve woke up, I'd find out what I could do to bring the pair home. I thought about calling Cherise to see if she knew how to contact the Elder, but my gut instinct told me that she wouldn't tell me. Cherise was happy about this turn of events. And apparently *her* wish had been pure of heart. I thought about that for a moment.

Do no harm.

If the wish had been granted—and it had—that meant there had been no harm done.

Immediately, I felt better. Amanda and Laurel Grace would not be harmed. I was still left to wonder if they'd be *returned*.

Ve would know.

She had to know.

I recalled what she'd said earlier. *You need to use extra caution. You're still new to your powers. You have no idea of what you're capable.*

Her words had obviously been proven true. There was so much I still had to learn.

A dog started barking, a loud vibrating *woof, woof*, and I turned around to find Gayle Chastain being walked by a Saint Bernard.

"Shush, Higgins," she was saying. "You'll wake everyone within three blocks."

I slowed and let her catch up. Missy started sniffing the bigger dog as if she had no clue that one of his paws was bigger than her.

"Who's walking who?" I joked with Gayle.

She smiled. "Do you have to ask?"

"He's huge."

"I know. Practically breaks my arm every night on these long walks. Russy used to do the leash holding."

Russ—her husband who had passed away.

"Just one of the many reasons I still miss him," she said, her heartache plain.

"Losing someone you love never gets easier."

She glanced at me. "That's right. Both your parents have passed?"

Had to love small towns and how fast gossip spread. "My mom from a car accident when I was seven; my dad four months ago from a heart attack."

I was grateful the green was well lit at night as we walked along.

"That's what Russ died from, too. A heart attack. So young. So preventable." She shook her head, sadness emanating from her every pore.

"How old was he?"

"Just fifty-three."

My dad had been almost sixty, and the heart failure hadn't been a surprise. He'd purposely avoided the surgery that could have cured him. He'd wanted to die. He'd wanted to for twenty-three years.

Gayle sighed. "He knew he had heart problems, but they weren't anything major, which was good, because he hated doctors. But then last December he caught the flu, and it was just too much for his heart to bear. If only he'd seen a doctor early on . . ."

The flu had been particularly nasty last year. "How are you coping?"

Higgins barked again, and she shushed him. "Some days are good; some bad. The bookshop helps. Keeps me busy. Harper's been a great addition."

We passed in front of the bookshop and Higgins pulled hard left, taking Gayle with him.

Missy tried to follow, but she was a little easier to control.

Gayle laughed. "I guess he's ready to go home." She lived in the apartment above the bookshop. "See you later, Darcy!"

I glanced down at Missy. "I'm glad Harper didn't shoplift a Saint Bernard."

She barked, as if in agreement. We'd done two more laps around the green when I suddenly stopped, having spotted something unusual. A light flashing up and down.

It was coming from inside Lotions and Potions.

As if pulled by an unknown force, I walked toward the shop, not sure what to do. Someone was inside, searching around with a flashlight. Every once in a while, the thin beam of light would stop, focused on something in particular.

I didn't have my cell phone on me, and there wasn't a

pay phone in sight. I was afraid to dash back to As You Wish, afraid that if I did, whoever was inside would get away scot-free.

Was it a scavenger? Someone who read about Alexandra's death and came to rob the place? I'd heard about people like that, burglars who read obituaries in search of their next mark.

Was it the person who killed her? Looking for something left behind? A clue missed by the police?

I looked down at Missy. "What would you do?"

She stared back at me, then headed toward the shop, her nose to the ground.

I didn't want to yank her back, because of the slip-knot. I hurried behind her. She stopped abruptly at the edge of the green. From here I could see a shadowy figure moving about the shop. I had a clear view of the front door, but not the back. If someone headed out that way, it would be easy to escape.

Scooping up Missy, I sat on a bench, pretending to stargaze. My plan was that I'd stay put and wait for someone to happen past. It wasn't terribly late. There was a chance I could flag down a car, or come across another dog walker. Hopefully someone would have a cell phone and could call the police.

My leg jiggled as my gaze darted back and forth down the street and then back to the shop window. I wanted to move closer, peek in. See if I recognized the intruder. But I'd seen enough horror movies to keep my distance.

"Boo!" someone whispered in my ear.

"Eeee!" I screamed, jumping up.

I clutched my heart and turned to find Nick Sawyer holding in a laugh. I punched his arm.

"Hey," he protested. Then, when he got a good look at me, he said, "The sparkles suit you. But where are the wings?"

"Hung up for the night." I grabbed his arm and yanked him down onto the bench. Missy immediately climbed into his lap and lavished his jaw with kisses. I frowned at her and said, "Do you have your cell phone?"

"No, why?"

I pointed to the now dark shop. "We need to call the police."

"Why?"

"Watch."

After a second, the dot of light reappeared, making sweeping passes. Nick stood up. I pulled him back down. He stared at my hand on his arm. I quickly removed it.

"Stay here," he said, moving toward the shop.

I went after him, Missy trailing after me. "You can't go in there alone. That could be the killer in there."

"All the more reason for you to stay here." He stopped and I bumped into him. Reaching out, he steadied me. His hands lingered on my arms. "Stay here."

I shook my head. "We need to call someone."

In the moonlight, I saw him roll his eyes. "Did you forget I used to be a state trooper?"

I had, but still. "You're not one anymore."

"I'm not going to argue with you." He broke into a jog, heading toward the back door of the store.

Missy followed him, and I followed her. Okay, I was more than willing to follow him, too. Abruptly, he stopped again. "I told you to stay back there."

"I thought you weren't going to argue with me. I'm coming along." Partly because there was power in numbers, partly because I was dying to know who was in the shop. Was it someone I knew? Why was the person in there? What, exactly, was the intruder looking for?

The back alley was dimly lit, with a tall wooden fence separating it from the neighborhood behind the shops. Hulking Dumpsters sat every few yards. Wind whistled down the narrow lane, bringing with it foreign noises — a scattering of leaves, rustling of branches, the movement of nighttime critters. I scooped up Missy and edged closer to Nick as he crept along the back of the building.

Suddenly there was a loud noise a few yards away, and I jumped. "What was that?" I whispered to Nick.

"Probably raccoons," he answered, looking toward where the noise had come from. "I don't see anything."

His explanation didn't settle my nerves. Bricks scraped my shoulders as we neared the back door of Lotions and Potions. The jamb was splintered where someone had taken a crowbar—which lay on the ground—to the frame.

He held up an arm and nudged the door. It swung open into a dark hallway. We stepped inside. Missy sniffed the air and wiggled, but I held her tightly. An office was to my right, a storeroom to my left. I tapped Nick's shoulder. He turned. I could barely make out his features in the darkness, but I could feel how tense he was.

"Phone," I mouthed. There was one sitting on the desk inside the office.

Nodding, he motioned me to go in, but he kept moving toward the front of the shop.

I took a step into the office. Moonbeams streamed in through a high window, lighting a space that was small and tidy with a desk, a filing cabinet, and some shelves. There wasn't much personality that I could see. No pictures, no knickknacks, no clutter. I removed the phone from its base and punched in 911. I left it off the hook, knowing that the operator would trace the number while I darted back into the hallway. To borrow one of Harper's phrases, I was feeling some seriously bad juju.

The musky scent of herbs mixed with sweet perfumy undertones filled the air as I caught up with Nick at the end of the hallway. He held a finger to his lips. Missy, normally a yapper, was quiet as could be, as if she could sense the danger.

The shop's layout was a smaller version of the bookstore's: Narrow floor-to-ceiling shelving lined one whole wall, and the shelves were filled with glass bottles tiny, large, thin, and wide. There were three rows of shelves directly in front of us, neatly stocked with bottles of lotions, bath scrubs, and beauty supplies. To our right was the cash register area, a horseshoe-shaped counter that had a large chest of drawers behind it. This was where the burglar was rummaging, bent over, back to us. It was hard to tell whether the person was a man or a woman. All I could see was that the person wore a long flowing black satin cape, hood up. The counter concealed the burglar's lower half.

The person obviously hadn't heard us come in, as he or she continued to rummage through the chest of drawers. Stacks of papers sat on its top, tossed aside after a quick scanning. The burglar was apparently looking for something specific.

A beautiful wooden box sat on the counter next to the cash register, and atop that, the pink pointy hat Mimi admired. I wanted to snatch it for her, and wondered if Nick would care.

He looked at me over his shoulder and nodded downward—telling me with his eyes to stay right where I was. I was already thinking ahead, to if the burglar somehow got away from Nick and came my way. Being hidden had its advantages. All I'd have to do was stick out my foot, and the thief would go sprawling face-first.

Keeping low, and out of sight beneath the countertop, Nick crept closer to the intruder. Closer and closer. My heart was pounding so hard I could feel my pulse beating near my ear. Missy's heart, too, was working overtime. I could feel it thumping against my palm.

In the distance, I could hear the faint bleat of an approaching siren. Nick had reached the opening leading behind the counter. There was really no escape for the burglar unless the person scaled the counter—and I was ready if that happened. Nick slowly rose from his crouch.

Missy barked.

The intruder jerked upward, and suddenly there was a puff of sparkling bright light.

Nick lunged forward and grabbed . . . nothing at all.

The intruder had vanished.

Just. Like. That.

Chapter Eleven

The next morning, I propped one foot on the bench beneath the birch tree in a pose I'd seen other runners strike and fought back a yawn as I waited for Starla Sullivan. It was early, just after six. The green was quiet, eerily still, with an early-morning haze that would be sure to burn off as the sun rose higher in the sky.

Across the green, I studied Lotions and Potions. There was nothing out of place, no reminder of what had happened last night.

Maybe because what *had* happened wasn't clear.

By the time the police arrived, Nick and I had agreed to lie and say the intruder had evaded both of us and escaped out the back door. Our statements were taken and we had been sent on our way.

Neither of us had really talked about what had happened, what we'd seen.

He'd been stunned. I'd been left wondering what kind of Crafter had been at work. I didn't know of a Craft family that could make themselves disappear. I hadn't known what to say, or how to explain. All I could do was act as baffled as he was—which wasn't much of a stretch.

If it was indeed a Crafter in the shop, what was he or she looking for? Had Alex really known something about the Craft, as she had intimated at the bookshop the night she died? Was it possible she *had* been a Crafter?

I glanced over at As You Wish, looking spectral in the spooky light. I'd been eager to talk to Ve this morning, but I had been quite surprised to find her room empty. Missy and her leash were gone, too, so I figured they were out on a morning walk, but I hadn't seen them on the green.

I was trying my best to ignore the little knot of worry in the pit of my stomach. I really needed to talk to Ve about the Goodwins. And how I could bring them home.

Harper had been sleeping when I left, but she had plans to work in the bookshop today. I was curious to see what she would learn about the latest incident at Lotions and Potions, Alex's life, and Griffin Huntley after another day on the job.

I had my own sleuthing to do—namely, get Evan's alibi and find out what was bothering Mrs. Pennywhistle. Whatever it was had to be related to Alex Shively.

I switched legs, stretching my muscles. Hearing footsteps, I turned to find Starla jogging toward me, a bright spot in the murky morning. She wore a bright blue T-shirt, matching shorts, and neon green sneakers. Her blond ponytail swung wildly as she bounded up and jogged in place. Beads of sweat pearled along her hairline, and I noticed she was huffing and puffing just a bit.

"Are you okay?" I asked.

"Fine! Great! I love running! Ready?"

I was as ready as I'd ever be. I hadn't had a chance to get new running shoes yesterday, and I wasn't nearly as color-coordinated as Starla. I wore an old pair of black gym shorts, a vintage *Tom and Jerry* T-shirt, and my old sneakers. My hair was pulled high atop my head and coiled into a sloppy bun. My face had been scrubbed clean of any glitter.

We started at a slow pace along the path that wound

around the green. "How's Evan?" I probed. "Is his face any better?"

"I haven't seen him this morning, but he looked terrible last night." She breathed hard. "We're not sure what to do."

I reached up and rubbed the spot on my forehead where Dennis Goodwin's hands had cured my headache the night before. Would he—or Cherise—be able to help Evan?

Carefully watching my words, I said, "I've heard of a local doctor, Dennis Goodwin, who comes highly recommended. Maybe Evan should try and see him."

Starla gave me a sideways look, one full of curiosity. "You've heard of Dr. Goodwin?"

I left out the part about how I made his wife and daughter disappear, and tried to sound casual. "Aunt Ve mentioned something about him. Apparently, he's popular around here?"

We had slowed to the pace of a fast walk. Starla's fair skin had flushed a bright pink. "Very popular, and therefore booked up for the foreseeable future. Evan tried to get an appointment, but because he's a new patient, it will be three months."

"Even for an emergency?"

Starla rolled her eyes. "The receptionist said if it was an emergency to go to the emergency room."

My heart was starting to beat harder. I successfully veered around a foraging squirrel. "That might not be a bad idea."

"Trust me, I've suggested it. Boston has some of the best doctors in the world. But Evan is being stubborn—he keeps hoping his skin will clear on its own. Maybe he'll listen to you. Are you still coming by today to see him?"

I nodded, although I felt guilty that I also needed to see if he had an alibi for the time of Alex's death.

"Good. I really hope you can talk some sense into

him and get him to a doctor." Huff, puff. "I hate to see him suffering."

Maybe I could ask Cherise for a favor. After all, I knew she was a Curecrafter and I figured she owed me, using me the way she did to get her wishes granted.

There were no Craft laws against what Cherise had done other than ethical ones. Crafters were very aware that they shouldn't take advantage of one another or their powers. I could only figure that Cherise was really desperate to piece her family back together to abuse my powers like she had.

Starla and I jog-walked in silence for a little bit before passing in front of Lotions and Potions. Starla craned her neck as we went by. "Did you hear about the break-in last night?" She glanced my way. "Evan and I were watching a movie, and heard all the hubbub."

A cramp was starting somewhere near my liver. I pressed my hand into it and forced a wry smile. "A little bit. I was there."

She came to a sudden stop, and her jaw dropped. "Details!"

I explained what had happened and hoped she didn't notice the gaping holes in my story.

It didn't escape my notice that she had specifically mentioned that she and Evan had been watching a movie when the burglar hit. Had mentioning it just been her being her normal friendly self? Or had it been because she wanted to give herself and Evan an alibi?

I hoped I wasn't being too obvious when I asked, "Which movie were you watching? Anything good?"

She stumbled a bit, tripping over a crack in the sidewalk, then righted herself. Her blond eyebrows rose, and a bead of sweat slid down the side of her face. "Something with Denzel Washington. Evan has a crush."

"Don't we all?"

She laughed. "Guns, running, shouting." She shrugged as she trotted along. "I get all the titles mixed up."

It sounded plausible, especially since I couldn't keep those movies straight, either. Even still, something wasn't sitting right. I didn't quite trust what she was saying.

Had Evan been the intruder? I supposed it was possible. Though neither Nick nor I saw a face, the burglar had been on the small side, and thin. It could have been Evan. If I were in his shoes, I might have broken into the shop, too.

Which also made me think about the way the intruder had disappeared in a dazzling cloud of smoke. If it was Evan, did that mean he was a Crafter? Was it possible? And if he was a Crafter, was Starla?

I glanced at her. Her pink cheeks had turned red with exertion. She didn't appear to be trying to pull one over on me.

"So you didn't see who it was?" Starla asked.

"It was too dark, and the intruder was wearing a hooded cape."

"A cape? How dramatic."

Dramatic. The word reminded me of Evan's mention that he was involved in theater. He might have access to a cape from the wardrobe department.

"Very." I'd try to get more out of Evan today instead of pushing Starla. The cramp in my side was subsiding as we passed a crowded Witch's Brew. A nice scone sounded good right about now, but I figured Starla might notice if I suddenly steered off course and headed straight for the baked goods. My flaccid arms might notice, too.

Most of the haze had burned off as we rounded a curve. Birds chirped happily, the green grass glistened with dew, and the sun warmed my face. "It's bound to be another busy day here," I said, my words coming out in staccato bursts. My chest was burning, tight with the strain of exercise, a foreign concept to my body. Summer weekends were the village's busiest time. Tourists came in droves to soak in the enchantment.

"I hope so," Starla puffed. "The green cleared out

pretty fast yesterday after those police reports were filed."

I slowed to a stop. "Police reports?"

Starla bent at the waist and tried to take in gulping lungfuls of air. "You didn't hear?"

I shook my head. "What happened?"

"The pickpocket struck again." She sank into a crouch.

I sank down next to her and we both plopped to the ground, sitting on the grass, off the pathway. "How many times?"

"Five, to the tune of about two hundred dollars each, give or take."

A thousand dollars. I could feel my eyes widen.

"Yeah," Starla said. "It's a little shocking."

"I hadn't heard a thing."

"It happened during the late-afternoon, early-evening hours. The green was a ghost town by eight."

I'd been too wrapped up with Aunt Ve and then the Goodwins to notice.

"It's not going to be too long before the media catches wind and descends full force—they're already sniffing around Alexandra's death. This could be disastrous for the upcoming dance—and the village itself. I'm not sure this is a job Nick Sawyer can handle on his own." Her eyes brightened. "Maybe we should help him. Form a task force or something." She gestured with excitement. "I'm on the green most of the day with my camera, anyway. I can be a lookout or something."

What was with the people in my life willingly jumping into the thick of things? Wasn't anyone content with minding their own business anymore?

Then a little stab of guilt pricked my conscience. Hadn't I thought about going into Lotions and Potions alone last night? And been more than willing to when Nick arrived? That wasn't exactly minding my own business.

So why was a cringe my first reaction to Starla's plan? Nick, I realized.

Somehow in the past two days, he'd been shoehorned into my life. I wasn't sure how I felt about that. Or him. He stirred things in me that I'd rather leave covered in emotional dust.

I had to be careful around him. Not just to guard my feelings, but to protect my heritage as well. He was bound to question what he'd seen last night, and because I'd seen it, too, it seemed reasonable that he'd come to me with questions and theories.

"I can take Missy for more walks than normal," I said, pushing Nick out of my thoughts, "and also ask Harper to keep an eye out for anyone suspicious, even couples and families."

Starla's color was slowly returning to normal. "You don't think the pickpocket is working alone?"

I picked at some grass. "It seems like someone working alone would stand out around here. But if there's a pair, or even someone using kids as a distraction, then they might be easy to overlook."

Starla was nodding as she stood up, dusting herself off. "I'm still not convinced that whoever is stealing from the tourists didn't kill Alex, too. That watch was worth a fortune."

True, which made me think just the opposite—the pickpocket would be long gone if he was sitting on a fifty-thousand-dollar watch.

"I'm not sure how much Nick would like us helping him out," I said. In fact, I was pretty sure he'd hate it. "So maybe we shouldn't tell him just yet?"

Starla nodded. "Good point. We'll keep it on the down low for now. I need to head off and check on the bakery—Evan's going to miss another day of work. I'll see you later?"

"Noontime sound okay?" It would give me enough time to paint the wombat piñata this morning.

"Perfect," she said. "I might be a little late, but don't leave without seeing me." Her tone shifted, turning serious. "There's something I want to show you."

"What?" I asked.

"You'll see. Something illuminating." She waved and ran off, heading toward the Gingerbread Shack.

Something illuminating.

It didn't sound bad, but for some reason my stomach was now full of dread.

Chapter Twelve

After scooping up the wombat from the back porch, I made my way into the kitchen, where I found Aunt Ve at the stove, scrambling eggs and frying bacon. I set the wombat on the counter. It wobbled, then steadied. The scent of coffee hung alluringly in the air, and though I was sorely tempted, I went straight for the fridge and a cup of filtered water.

Ve eyed the wombat. "What's that?"

"The wombat piñata."

A thin eyebrow slowly rose. "It's very . . . artsy."

She was trying to be nice. Behind the rim of my glass, I smiled. "It's not done yet."

"Oh, thank God."

I didn't take any offense. Right now it looked rather unfortunate, a newspapery blob. But in my mind's eye, I could see the outcome and it was going to be wonderful.

Missy snoozed in her bed by the door, and Tilda watched us with feigned disinterest from the top of the steps. I could hear Harper upstairs, singing.

Singing.

At seven in the morning.

Something was wrong. Very wrong.

I frowned.

Ve said, "She's been like that since she woke up. I think she likes that new job of hers."

Undoubtedly, but I think she also liked her new boss.
I kept that bit to myself and took a good look at my
aunt. She looked none the worse for wear after all those
gin and tonics—for all she'd been through, for that matter. Her coppery hair was pulled back in a tidy twist; her
makeup was flawless.

"Some breakfast?" Ve asked.

"Sure. You're chipper this morning. Considering all
that's happened."

She shook a spatula at me. "I'm a woman on a mission."

"Oh?"

"I've decided to be proactive about Sylar's predicament." The red rising in her cheeks matched the vibrant
scarlet tunic she wore, paired with pristine white capri
pants. "I'm going to offer a reward for Alexandra Shively's watch. Whoever has that watch holds the key to this
whole case. If I know one thing for certain, it's that Sylar
is not a killer. The police need a little more proof, however."

It wasn't a bad plan. I pulled a mug from the cabinet
and filled it with coffee. "How much of a reward?"

"Ten thousand dollars."

I almost dropped the mug. "Do you have that kind of
money?" I really didn't know. Though we always knew
we had an aunt—she sent us birthday and Christmas
cards every year—before she had come to visit Harper
and me, I had met her only once before. At my mother's
funeral. My father had done his best to keep Harper and
me separated from this part of our family tree. Aunt Ve
had honored his wishes to raise us as mortals and promised to keep her distance from us until the time was
right. It was a decision, on both their parts, that I wasn't
sure I agreed with. Harper and I should have had a say,
made the choice ourselves.

Ve smiled as she removed bacon from the frying pan
and set it on a plate covered in paper towels. "My fourth

husband, God rest his soul, was very sweet, very generous."

Fourth husband? This was the first I'd heard about any marriages. "How many times were you married?"

She slid a plate over to me. "Just the four."

Just.

"The first one, I was madly in love, but too young to know what I really wanted, or how to make a relationship work. He had no clue, either, and eventually left me for greener pastures." The eyebrow arched again. "Cherise."

I choked on a piece of egg. "Goodwin?"

She smiled a sneaky smile. "None other."

As I let that sink in, my appetite vanished. I suddenly remembered how I had made Amanda and Laurel Grace disappear. I pushed my plate away.

"Husband number two was"—she shook her head—"a huge mistake. A rebound, if you will. Number three I prefer not to discuss, the rat, toad, bottom dweller. Thankfully, number four restored my faith in men." She chomped on a piece of bacon.

"Were they Crafters?"

"The first and the third."

I tipped my head. "If you've married mortals, how come you still have your power to grant wishes? I thought all Crafters lost their gift if they married a mortal."

Ve wagged a finger. "Only if you tell the mortal you're a witch."

Seemed like going into a marriage with such a huge secret would doom the union from the start. It might explain Ve's marital track record. "Isn't that kind of secret hard to keep?"

"Not as hard as you may think, but it does begin to take a toll on the marriage."

As I thought about that, my conscience nagged. It was time to fess up about what had happened to Laurel Grace and Amanda. "About the Goodwins . . . there's something I need to tell you."

"Darling, so serious all of a sudden! What happened?"

There was no way to sugarcoat the situation. I explained everything, from the marital squabble to the vanishing act in the kitchen.

"Do no harm, right?" I said to Ve.

"This is quite the unusual situation, I admit, but you're absolutely correct. The wish would not have been granted if Laurel Grace and her mother were put in harm's way. Undoubtedly, they're at a vacation hot spot, relaxing. No matter where you wished them, Darcy, rest assured they still have free will to call home, to come back."

"I don't have to wish them back?"

"Oh no. Unless someone else makes the wish, and their motives are pure of heart." She set the empty skillet into the sink. "You may want to contact Cherise and ask her about wishing the pair back."

Maybe I should. It would be nice to not worry about the two of them. "I'm surprised you and Cherise are still friends."

"Misery loves company, dear."

I pushed cold eggs around my plate. "Are they divorced, then? Cherise and ex number one?"

Ve nodded. "It didn't last long at all. Just long enough to produce Dennis. He's a lot like his father."

"Are you sure the 'rat, toad, bottom dweller' wasn't in reference to him?"

She laughed. "Terry Goodwin is an interesting man. He lives next door, you know."

"No!"

"Yes."

I hadn't met the next-door neighbor yet, though my first night in the village I'd almost called the police to his house. I'd woken up in the middle of the night to loud shouting, then screaming.

Turned out the ruckus had been perpetrated by Archie, a loudmouthed macaw. Apparently our neighbor liked to watch a lot of TV and DVDs and Archie picked up a few sounds and phrases. Like a shoot-out from *Scarface* and the Janet Leigh shower scene from *Psycho*.

"He's a CPA; perhaps you've seen his shingle in the front yard? These days he's very reclusive, so you won't see him much about the village. He's actually a nice man," she said. "Just . . . interesting."

"What's so interesting about him?"

"You'll see eventually."

"Dennis does have nice eyes," I said, trying to find something nice to say about him.

She wagged a finger at me. "I thought you were smarter than to fall for a nice pair of eyes."

I suddenly thought of Nick's brown eyes and shook the image free.

"Let's just call it a momentary lapse of judgment." And consciousness, but there was no need to tell Ve about that little mishap.

"Was ex number one, Terry Goodwin, a Curecrafter, then?"

Ve spooned scrambled eggs onto the corner of a piece of toast. "No, he's actually a Numbercrafter."

"But Dennis is a Curecrafter?"

"His powers come from Cherise."

"Do all powers come only from mothers?"

Ve shook her head. "If two different types of Crafters have a child together—a Curecrafter and a Numbercrafter, for example—the child is considered a Cross-Crafter." She smiled. "Kind of like a hybrid. One power will be dominant over the other. For Dennis, his strength is as a Curecrafter, though make no doubt about it, he's also good with numbers."

Right. So much to learn. So much to remember.

"Terry thinks he can win me back," Ve said, motioning with her head to the house next door. "He's been thinking that for over twenty years."

I had to give him credit for hanging in for the long haul.

"Cherise is just happy it's me he's chosen to live next to. She rubs it in every chance she gets."

I laughed. "What kind of crazy town did I move to?"

"Never a dull moment," she said.

No. Not yet at least. "Where's Mr. Rat Toad Bottom Dweller now? Does he live around here?"

Her eyebrows rose again. "Indeed he does. I'm sure you'll meet him soon."

"But you're not going to tell me who it is?"

"I prefer you learn the village on your own, form your own opinions. You'll be amazed how quickly you'll start picking up on who's a Crafter and who isn't. My guess is, they'll start introducing themselves to you because they already know you're a Crafter and will have no fear of losing their powers. Be alert."

"So, you're not going to give me a list of who's who?"

She took a sip of her coffee. "Where's the fun in that?"

"Fun would be nice." I thought about Amanda and Laurel Grace. "I was so worried I'd done something wrong last night. . . ."

She turned and faced me, her expression serious and guarded. "You didn't, but you must remember my warning from yesterday. Your powers are great—you must be careful. If there is something you do not understand, you should call me."

I didn't mention how futile that would have been last night, but apparently she must have been thinking along the same lines.

"Or perhaps it is time I show you how to contact the Elder. She knows all the answers you'll ever need."

Harper hurried down the stairs, a pep in her step. She slung a small backpack on the counter, nearly knocking the wombat onto the floor. "Did I hear you say 'the Elder'?"

"Does she live around here?" I asked.

Aunt Ve smiled. "Hers is not a door on which you can knock."

"What does that mean?" I asked.

Harper eyed my plate, and I slid it her way. She zapped it in the microwave for twenty seconds to warm up the now cold eggs.

"There are steps in place to contact her. Take with you your message on a piece of paper. There is a well-worn path in the woods behind the house. Follow it along until you cross a small creek, and farther still until the path curves around a large boulder in the shape of a piece of cake—aptly called Cake Rock. Over rocks and roots and past mossy meadows and clovered hollows. In the middle of a small clearing there is a tree. In its trunk there is a small hole. Insert your message there, and go home. Wait for a reply."

"Holy *Mission: Impossible*," Harper said. She hadn't taken a bite of the food, so enraptured was she in Ve's directions.

Ve smiled. "It is a bit convoluted, but that is the process, and it must be followed."

I should have taken notes. There was no way I was going to remember all that.

"You will need to memorize the directions," Ve added, "for it is forbidden to write them down."

There went that plan.

"Crafters are very secretive about our society and how it's run. We have to be. Even in this day and age."

She reached for the bacon pan, and as she leaned forward, her locket came off and bounced with a loud clatter on the range top. Ve picked it up and looked at the clasp. "I need to get this fixed at All That Glitters—my little slapdash quickie fix didn't hold." She slipped it in her pocket. "Now, tell me. What else did I miss last night?"

Harper glanced at me. "Did you tell her about the disappearing act?"

"The Goodwins?" Ve said. "Yes."

"No, no. Even better. Tell her, Darcy."

"Yes, tell me," Ve said.

I found myself retelling my experience from the night before. I finished by saying, "And suddenly there was this puff of smoke and the person was gone."

"Just like that," Harper added.

"Just like that," I echoed.

Tilda hopped up onto the counter, and I noticed even Missy had come closer, sitting at Harper's feet. It was as if they sensed the importance of this conversation.

Ve's face had gone pale. "Describe the smoke to me."

I thought back. "It was bright at first, like a quick explosion, but without the noise. Then smoke formed in a pluming cloud, but it looked almost like the remnants of Fourth of July fireworks—it had a touch of something sparkly in the fading fog. Within another minute, the room had cleared completely and it was as if nothing ever happened. But the intruder was gone. Vanished."

Ve chewed her lip, then said, "It couldn't be."

"Couldn't be what?" I asked.

"A Vaporcrafter. There hasn't been one in these parts in decades."

"Are they evil or something?" Harper asked.

Ve laughed. "Not at all, Harper, dear. But until now . . . everyone thought they were extinct."

"That can happen?" I asked.

"The Craft is hereditary, Darcy, dear. If there are no heirs, the line will die out. It's unfortunate, but it happens from time to time."

Die out. I shuddered at the phrase and wondered, if that was the case, what was one doing in Alexandra Shively's shop?

And what, exactly, had that Vaporcrafter been looking for?

*   *   *

Harper left, Aunt Ve disappeared into the office, and I beelined for the shower.

My head was spinning as I thought about what had been going on the last couple of days. Between the pick-pocketing and Alexandra's death and the Goodwins' disappearance ... never mind the whole Wishcrafter thing. As I wrapped myself in a towel and wiped steam from the mirror, I caught myself smiling. I hardly thought Troy could call my life—call *me*—boring now.

My smile faded as a familiar pain thrummed in my chest, and I sagged a bit. It had been two years since the divorce was final. When would the ache go away and never come back? How long did it take to fall out of love with someone? To evict him from a heart for-ever?

I glanced at the mirror.

You've let yourself go. A lot.

I was embarrassed to admit how much so. Or why.

That I hadn't cut my hair or bought new clothes since the day I kicked Troy out. Because a tiny part of me had wished, had hoped, that he'd come back, begging me for another chance. That he'd see I'd been perfect the way I was. That I hadn't needed a change.

Standing here, the tiles cold under my feet, I suddenly realized something.

Troy had been right.

To a point. I had led a boring—safe—life, but I'd been perfectly happy. Or so I thought. Turns out I just didn't know better. Now I knew that back in Ohio I'd been *content*. Content to let life live me, instead of me living life.

It wasn't until I made the momentous decision to move here that I started to realize how much happier I could be. This village, this house, my heritage ... these things made me truly happy.

Two years had been too long to live in the past. It was

time to take control of my life again. And there was no
better time to start.

In the mirror, I saw a smile start to curl the corners of
my lips. I fumbled around in the vanity drawers and
found what I was looking for. A nice sharp pair of scissors.

I set them on the edge of the sink, picked up my
comb, and ran it through my long hair. I pulled a section forward and lifted the scissors. Held them there.
Then put them back down. Not because I'd changed
my mind, but because I'd really come to love my long
hair.

Biting my lip, I knew I had to do something, anything,
to mark this turning point. Taking a deep breath, I
combed the hair along my forehead forward, and picked
up the scissors again.

The first cut was the hardest.

By the time I was done, I felt a little freer. The last
time I'd had bangs was when I was a just a small thing,
maybe four or five.

I liked them. True, they were a little lopsided, but not
terribly noticeable. And perhaps a few chic highlights
wouldn't hurt. Maybe I'd stop by the salon later on and
make an appointment.

Until then I had work to do. I had a wombat to finish,
soup to make, a sick friend to visit, and, in between, a
little snooping to do.

I set my laptop up on the kitchen countertop as I
set about making chicken and rice soup for Evan and
searched online for Alexandra Shively. Harper was right—
we needed to learn more about Alexandra if we were
going to solve her murder. Her shop was one of the first
hits. I browsed the site as I shredded chicken breasts and
chopped carrots.

I couldn't find anything unusual, except for the contact form for scheduling personal consultations. Since
the police had confiscated her computer, they'd have the

information of who had set up appointments with Alex—and if they were potential suspects.

Another person who might have a list of Alex's clients, at least a partial list, was Dr. Dennis Goodwin. Not that he'd share that information with me. Even if he wasn't bound by legal and ethical laws, the man hated me. And I couldn't say I blamed him.

I glanced at the phone. After wiping my hands, I picked it up and, taking Ve's advice, dialed Cherise Goodwin.

"Darcy, what a surprise! What can I do for you?" She sounded like she hadn't a care in the world.

"I've been thinking a lot about Laurel Grace and Amanda. Have you heard from them?"

"Last night—Amanda needed a credit card number to secure her room at the resort. They're in Disney World of all places. Laurel Grace is beside herself with happiness and is lunching with some princesses today."

I bit the inside of my cheek. "Do you think I could stop by later? It might be time to wish them back, don't you think?"

"Not really. Dennis has hardly learned his lesson after only half a day."

"It's just that I'm not really comfortable with making people disappear. I'd really like to bring them back."

There was a stretch of silence before she said, "How about this? Why don't you come over tonight and we can discuss it. If your argument is convincing, I'll wish them back. And if it's not, then I'll let you call and talk to Amanda so you can have some peace of mind."

I agreed and hung up, but as I stared at the phone, I had the feeling Cherise was up to something. I just didn't know what. Or how I played into it.

While the soup simmered, I mixed paints to use on the wombat piñata. Once upon a time, I went through a Martha Stewart phase and became quite crafty. It just about drove Troy nuts when he came home to find the hall mirror suddenly turned into a mosaic or the house stinking of lye because I'd decided to try my hand at making homemade candles. He wasn't one to appreciate homemade creativity.

I went about painting the wombat, and have to say I was quite pleased with the results. It really looked like a wombat. I tipped my head. Well, it was close enough. I set it aside to dry and looked at the clock. There was just enough time to run out and shop for a pick-me-up for Evan, a little something to brighten his day.

Aunt Ve was in the office, working on a press release about the reward for the missing watch—Marcus had dropped off a template the night before. She was bent over the computer, pencil perched between her teeth. A stack of flyers, hot off the copier, sat on the edge of the desk.

"I'm going to run a few errands," I said. "Do you need anything?"

She took the pencil out of her mouth, tucked it behind her ear, and tapped the flyers. "Can you start handing these out around the village?"

The flyers were printed on bright green paper with the words "REWARD $10,000" emblazoned across the top of the page. There was a picture of a replica of Alex's watch underneath, with a giant-fonted "LOST" below that, along with Aunt Ve's cell phone number.

There was no mention of Alex, or of the murder, or of Sylar. To any tourist, it would seem as though someone were simply anxious to have an heirloom returned.

"Just be sure not to tack them anywhere, especially light poles and trees—the village council frowns upon signage of that nature. I'll be going to visit Sylar soon."

"How's he doing?" I asked.

"As well as can be expected. He's hopeful he'll be exonerated soon." A frown crossed her lips. "The evidence against him is pretty damning, but it's only a matter of time before he's freed."

"You're so sure?"

An eyebrow lifted. "Of course. He's not a violent man. He's sweet . . . and kind. He collects eyeglasses for the needy and then funds trips to third world countries to distribute them. He sponsors a scholarship in his late wife's name at the local high school."

I held my tongue from asking about his late wife—now probably wasn't the best time.

"He loves this village, and the people of this village, and we all love him. His arrest is an outrage, an abomination. He's a scapegoat, plain and simple." She took a deep breath. "The whole reason he's behind bars is because of Chief Leighton and his grudge against Sylar. After this incident, I think the village council will be in favor of removing the chief from his position, don't you?"

I agreed. If Sylar was cleared of murder, then the chief was probably playing his last game of golf on the village's dime. And honestly, from all I'd heard, it was time the chief retired. Hopefully, whoever took his place would do a better job. I knew I'd appreciate knowing the village had more of an involved police presence. Especially after what had happened to poor Alex.

The trouble was that Sylar had to be cleared first for any changes to be made. I felt my eyebrows dip as I scrounged for some courage. "Why didn't Sylar like Alex? Do you know for certain?"

She waved a hand in dismissal, but said, "Alex was difficult to like. It was as if she went out of her way to grate on people, to bring turmoil to the village. Sylar is a peaceful man. He doesn't like turmoil, which is why he didn't care for Alex. It's as simple as that. Nothing nefarious."

"You really love him, don't you?"

She shrugged and smiled coyly. "I'm rather hoping he might be husband number five."

Fussing with the flyers, I said, "Even though he doesn't believe in witches?"

"Everyone has their flaws." She winked.

"Do you want me to come with you to visit him?" Rearranging my day would take some doing, but if she wanted my support, I'd be there in a flash.

"You're sweet for offering, but he's only allowed one visitor a day. But you can help me find that watch."

Which would hopefully lead to the real killer. Because Ve had convinced me of Sylar's innocence. Someone else had hated Alex enough to kill her. Had found Ve's scarf at the bookshop and taken the opportunity at hand to kill Alex. But who? Obviously someone who'd been at the village meeting . . . I had to find out. And soon. Before Sylar was convicted of a crime he didn't commit.

"Can you handle delivering the piñata on your own?" Ve asked.

"No problem." Though, after working so hard on the piece, I hoped I wouldn't have to see it smashed to smithereens.

"Oh, Darcy?"

"Yes?"

"The bangs are adorable."

Smiling, I took a handful of flyers. Missy was curled at Ve's feet, sleeping, so I decided against bringing her out with me. Which also reminded me that I needed to pick up a new collar for her. Maybe one with a GPS tracker.

Unfortunately, Starla had been right about the village's thinning crowd. Normally by this time the sightseeing buses had arrived, and tourists were out in full force. But I saw only one flock of little old ladies shuffling along the sidewalk. A news crew had set up in the middle of the green, so I took the scenic route to the Ye Olde Village Gift Shop to find a gift for Evan.

It was the first time I'd been in the store and I could hardly believe my eyes at all the witchcraft paraphernalia. Pointy hats, warty noses, magic wands, even cooking pots and planters in the shape of cauldrons. Black cats, snakes, goats, rabbits, and toads as cute stuffed animals. There was the usual assortment of souvenir items like magnets, shot glasses, key chains, and spoons. Mixed in were all kinds of touristy kitsch from sunscreen to sweat-shirts. I wasn't sure what I was looking for to bring to Evan, but I was beginning to think I wasn't going to find it here.

A display of mugs caught my eye, and remembering the conversation with Nick yesterday morning, I wan-dered closer. A tall swivel display stand held hundreds of mugs. Many with the witch theme, including one with a pointy nose jutting off the ceramic, one a tankard in the shape of a witch hat (the point was hinged), and oth-ers with quotes from the Wicked Witch of the West, from *The Wizard of Oz*. I turned the rack. Sure enough, there were more quotation mugs. Mostly ones quoting from *Macbeth*, but I did spot "A Madness Most Discreet." I scanned the others. "When I saw you, I fell in love, and you smiled because you knew." "Journeys end in lovers meeting." "Love is a familiar. Love is a devil. There is no evil angel but Love."

My gaze lingered on that last quote. The first line in particular. "Love is a familiar." *Familiar*. The word was sticking like a thorn in my subconscious. I knew I'd heard it recently, and suddenly I recalled that it was also connected to witchcraft. I couldn't for the life of me re-member when I'd heard it—or what it meant in terms of the Craft.

Looking around, I spotted a bookshelf filled with books on witchcraft. I found a book that had a terminol-ogy chapter and ran my finger down the page until I found a listing for "familiar." My eyes widened as I read. A familiar, also called an imp, is basically a supernatural spirit disguised as an animal, one who aids witches with their magic. If what I read was true, history and litera-ture are full of familiars, from *Macbeth* to *Harry Potter*. Cats, spiders, owls, birds. Chickens, dogs, mice, toads.

Were there really such things? Would Ve tell me? Or wait for me to figure it out on my own?

I roamed around the gift shop, taking everything in, trying to spot one item that screamed Evan's name. I wound my way to the back of the shop and stopped dead in my tracks. On a rack near the back wall hung a row of capes. Just like the one the intruder had been wearing last night.

But as I drew closer, I saw these capes were made of paper-thin material. Nothing like the dreamy satin cape from the night before.

"May I help you?" a woman asked. She was midforties, with short shaggy dark hair and green eyes behind a pair of rectangular glasses.

"Maybe," I said. "I'm looking for a cape just like this, but a little fancier. Maybe satin. Do you carry those?"

The woman's eyes narrowed on me. "Aren't you one of Velma's nieces?"

I smiled and nodded. "I'm Darcy Merriweather."

"Jeannette Dorsey," she said, shaking my hand. "I've heard so much about you. Nice to finally meet you. So you're looking for a cape?"

I nodded but didn't explain why. I could tell by the look in the woman's eye that she suspected—or knew—I was a Crafter. Which probably made her one, too.

"I'm surprised Velma didn't tell you that for special-order capes you need to go see Godfrey at the Bewitching Boutique." She leaned in and dropped her voice. "All the Crafters in the village get their capes from him."

I thanked her, handed her one of Ve's flyers, and ten minutes later left the shop with a fancy chocolate bar, a thousand-piece puzzle of *Wicked*'s playbill, and the question of whether the Vaporcrafter in Lotions and Potions had special ordered a cape through the Bewitching Boutique. . . .

Chapter Thirteen

On my way to purchase a new collar for Missy at the Furry Toadstool, which was next on my to-do list, I decided to pop in on Harper. The bell on the Spellbound Bookshop's door jingled as I went inside. Harper and Vince Paxton were standing elbow to elbow at the cash register counter. Not a soul other than us was in the store.

"Darcy, good. Maybe you can help your sister out," Vince said. He had a book open on the counter.

Harper rolled her eyes. "Oh, for the love. Don't drag Darcy into this."

"Into what?" I asked, intrigued by their playful tone.

Vince cleared his throat and read from the book. " 'What happens twice in a week, and once in a year, but never in a day?' "

Harper groaned.

"Slow day at work?" I asked her.

"Make him stop." She grabbed for the riddle book.

"The letter *e*," Vince said, eyes bright behind his glasses. He snapped the book closed and held it out for Harper to take. "It's deathly slow, to answer your question." He winced. "Bad choice of words."

My gaze immediately went to the back of the shop. The crime-scene tape had been taken off the back door, but the bad-juju feeling lingered.

"I like the bangs," Harper said. "It's a start."

"What is?" Vince asked.

I waved off his question. "Nothing. Just Harper being silly."

"Not silly. I just think— Oh no," Harper said. "Look." She pointed out the picture window.

The news reporter had moved her location to the front of the shop. The camera lights turned on and Harper and I looked at each other and darted out of the shot in case we could be seen through the glass.

I pretended to look at a rack of bookmarks while Harper took the riddle book and put it back on the shelf in the humor section.

"I heard a report on the news this morning about the murder, and it seemed like the network has decided to play up the witch angle of Alexandra's death," Vince said. "Apparently they don't care about setting the witchcraft movement back two hundred years. They're all about the sensationalism." He shook his head in disappointment.

My gaze shot to Harper. She was shaking her head without trying to appear obvious. To anyone watching, it looked like she had a tic.

Because saying nothing would seem a little strange, I opted for, "Witchcraft movement? You believe in witches?"

I noticed Harper hung her head.

His eyes widened. "You don't?"

I shrugged noncommittally and picked up a penguin bookmark and studied it like my life depended on it.

"Darcy!" Vince enthused. "History books are filled with accounts of witchcraft, dating back centuries. Witchcraft is still strong in this day and age. Alive and well, even in this village. I can go on and on with accounts and depictions and—"

I cut him off. "So you think Alexandra was a witch?" I asked. No wonder Harper had hung her head. He didn't appear to have an off switch. "Do you think that might be why she was killed?"

"I didn't know her well," he said just as the door opened, the bell jingling. The reporter strolled in.

That was my cue to leave. I handed Harper one of Aunt Ve's flyers and told her I'd talk to her later.

I shimmied around the cameraman and out the door as fast as I could. Once outside I blinked against the bright sunshine, seeing spots, and ran smack-dab into someone who'd been lurking at the front of the shop, peeking in the window.

"I'm sorry!" I cried. "So sorry." I reached out to steady the woman. It was Ramona Todd from the Magic Wand Salon.

"It's my fault, standing there like that," Ramona said, straightening her skirt; then she gave me a quick look. "Bangs! I love them!" She came a little closer and inspected. "They're a little uneven—a do-it-yourself job?"

"Spur of the moment."

"Most do-it-yourself jobs are." She handed me her card. "Come over to the salon sometime, and I'll even them out."

"I will," I promised. Then I noticed how she kept looking in the window with a pained expression on her face. "Are you worried about the news crew? The bad press?"

"The what? Oh, no. This will all blow over."

I stepped up behind her to see what she was staring at. Or whom, rather. Her gaze was intent on Vince. Ah. "You and Vince?" I asked. This would be good information to have so Harper didn't get too attached.

Ramona quickly shook her head. Color faded from her cheeks. "I have to go, Darcy. I'll see you soon?"

I didn't get a chance to reply as she hurried off.

Strange.

With one last glance at Vince talking the reporter's ear off, I headed on my way.

I had a collar to buy, a rashy man to question, something illuminating to see, and a wombat to deliver.

*   *   *

As I walked, I tried to calculate exactly how far Starla and I had run that morning, and I figured it to be about a lowly quarter mile. Feeling a little pathetic, I upped my pace just a bit and stole a page out of Mrs. Pennywhistle's speed-walking book.

I scanned the green, looking for her, but her bench, as I'd started calling it in my head, was empty. I made a mental note to check on her, make sure she was okay. She'd been acting so strangely yesterday.

About a block from the Furry Toadstool, I heard hurried footsteps coming up behind me, and suddenly had crazy thoughts that the town pickpocket may have turned into a mugger. I held tightly on to my wristlet and looked back over my shoulder.

Unsteady, my feet tangled together, and I felt myself pitching forward. I let out a yelp and flailed my arms to keep from falling on my face.

Next thing I knew, a pair of strong arms were wrapped around me, holding me tightly.

"I've got you," Nick said as he pulled me backward, upright.

My cheeks heated as I stepped out of his arms. "Thank you."

"For making you fall?"

It *had* been his fault, but as his touch lingered on my arms, I let the blame slide. "For catching me."

The bright sunshine made his brown eyes seem more golden. "Anytime."

I took another step back and told myself to stop smiling. Really, it was downright embarrassing, my natural reaction to him. The last thing I wanted was to give him the wrong impression.

Dark circles colored the skin beneath his eyes. It looked like he hadn't slept much at all last night. Small wonder after what we'd seen in Lotions and Potions.

"I was just heading to your house when I spotted you

zipping past," he said. "I was going to leave this on the back porch, but since you're here . . ." He pulled forth Missy's collar and handed it to me. "I found it in my yard, in a hole under the fence. 'Missy' is a cute name."

I didn't dare tell him what it stood for—"Miss Demeanor"—especially as he was trying to track down a thief. No need to offer Harper up as a suspect on a silver platter.

Curling my hand around the linked chain, I said, "You just saved me a trip to the Furry Toadstool. Thank you."

He was wearing a pair of dark jeans, and a button-down shirt with the sleeves rolled. I tried not to notice how great his jeans fit, his strong hands, the small scar near his left eyebrow, or the appealing stubble along his jaw. I tried—but it was impossible not to.

"You're welcome."

I wondered if I should mention something about last night, about what we'd seen. I didn't know how to broach the topic. He was mortal. I couldn't tell him about the capes or the Vaporcrafter.

I was surprised, however, that he didn't say anything. It's not often a person vanishes in front of your eyes.

Unless you're me. And it happens twice in the same day.

Nick, though, probably had dozens of questions. But he wasn't asking them. He was just looking at me as though he wanted to say something. Yet he kept quiet.

I rocked on my heels. Then said, "Well, I should get back. Oh! Here, take one of these." I handed him a flyer.

He scanned it. "This is going to bring the kooks out of the woodwork."

"Do you think it will help get the watch back?"

"It might. But probably not. If the pickpocket took the watch and killed Alex in a struggle, then that watch isn't going to surface for a long, long time. It's too recognizable. If Alex was killed for another reason and the watch taken to throw suspicion on the pickpocket, then that watch is never going to surface. It's probably at the bottom of the Charles." He shrugged, his eyes sparkling. "But it can't hurt to try."

I laughed.

He smiled.

A second passed. Two. The stretches of silence were becoming a habit. They weren't uncomfortable. Instead, they were filled with a tension that hummed between us. Of wanting to say something, but not knowing what. It was the getting-to-know-you dance. He gives a little; I give a little.

It was exciting.

And terrifying.

"I like what you did," he said, motioning to my hair.

My cheeks suddenly burned. "Thanks. It was time for a change."

"Change is hard." He sounded like he knew from experience.

"The first cut was the hardest," I shared, wondering why I couldn't keep my mouth shut. "The fear of not knowing how it would look . . ."

"Fear of the unknown is even harder than change. I—," he began, then stopped. "I mean, Mimi . . ." He shook his head, cut himself off.

"Is Mimi okay?"

"She's fine. Great. Busy running around here somewhere." He glanced around. "Camp starts next week. . . ."

A second passed. Two.

"I guess I'll see you later," I said. I moved to leave and his voice stopped me.

"Darcy? I do have a piece of interesting news."

"Oh?" I asked. I could tell he was warring with whether to tell me.

"Do you remember how Mimi was asking about Alexandra's belongings yesterday afternoon?"

I nodded.

A smile ghosted across his lips. "She didn't exactly let up on the topic once we went home."

I imagined not. Mimi didn't seem like one to let things go easily.

"She kept going on and on about Alexandra not having any family, and what was going to happen to her possessions . . ."

There was such tenderness in his voice that it caught me off guard. The love he had for his daughter was obvious. And endearing. And attractive. I stepped a little bit farther away.

". . . and then one thing led to another and she was talking about what was going to happen to Alexandra. What was going to happen to her body? Would there be a memorial? A funeral? It was upsetting her that Alexandra might not have those things."

Exasperation had entered his tone. I smiled. "What did you do?" Because I knew, just knew, he'd done something. I could tell he'd do anything for his daughter.

There was that faint smile again. "I figured if Alexandra meant that much to Mimi, then the least we could do was see that she was buried properly. I made some calls, and eventually discovered Alexandra's body was still at the medical examiner's office. I went down there this morning to find out what I had to do to claim the body, since she had no relatives."

Again his forehead wrinkled. I was beginning to recognize that he did this when he was disturbed. "Did they let you claim her?"

"No," he said.

"Why not? Is there some sort of legal process that has to happen?" I couldn't imagine the medical examiner just gave bodies away to anyone who asked.

"There is, but, Darcy, this is the strangest part. Her body had already been claimed. By her next of kin."

Chapter Fourteen

With a Tupperware full of soup in one hand, and a gift bag in the other, I hurried down Fairy Hollow Lane as I searched for Evan and Starla's address along the charming row of brownstones.

I could hardly believe what Nick had told me. Alexandra had a next of kin. Her story about being an orphan was just that—a story.

Unfortunately, the attendants at the medical examiner's office would not give Nick the name of the person. I doubted he'd let the matter drop until he found out exactly who it had been who claimed the body. I also suspected he'd let the police know of this latest development.

The sudden appearance of Alex's next of kin and my cynical side had me wondering if the ME's office went through an extensive process to verify that sort of thing. If it was anything like what I went through after my father died, it would be easy to deceive the ME's office. They probably had a similar form to the one I'd filled out and signed, having me verify only through my signature that I was, in fact, the next of kin. No ID check.

So, in fact, anyone could have claimed Alex's body, by simply claiming to be a relative. Especially if the person knew Alex was alone in the world. I wondered how much money she had. Or if she had a will. Or like Mimi wondered as well—what happened to all the stock in her storeroom? Would all those things go to this new-found relative?

If so, that might be motivation for murder.

There had to be a way to find out who the person was who claimed the body.

A thought struck. When I claimed my father's body, I had to list what funeral home to have him taken to. Alexandra's next of kin would probably have had to do the same. It was another thing to look into.

I found Evan's address and followed a walkway lined on each side with flowers bursting with color toward the door. Before I could even ring the doorbell, the red front door swung open and a hand reached out and grabbed me, pulling me inside.

"Darcy, you have to help me. I'm desperate. I'm a Man on the Edge." Evan hid in the shadows behind the door. Twink pranced around my feet, and I reached down and gave his head a pat.

I tugged Evan forward into the light and gasped at what I saw. Chicken soup was not going to help him in the least.

Huge welts covered his face. His eyes were almost swollen closed. Chipmunk cheeks puffed out, and worst of all, the rash looked to be spreading down his neck.

"You have to go to the ER," I proclaimed.

"I can't. I don't think modern medicine can help me. I don't even know what was in Alexandra's lotion—how can it be counteracted? I need to find her formula."

It pained me to look at him. "How are you going to do that?"

"Break into her shop, that's how. Will you help me? I can barely see."

I set the gift bag and soup onto a console table by the door. "Was it you in the shop last night?"

He looked down at his feet. My heartbeat kicked up a notch. Was Evan the Vaporcrafter?

"I know Starla told you we were watching a movie, but she was covering for me." He smiled. At least I thought it was a smile. It was hard to tell with all the swelling. "She was trying to protect me."

I understood the need, the overwhelming need, to protect a sibling.

"But she didn't have to worry. It wasn't me in the shop last night. Someone beat me to it."

I must have had a "Please explain" look on my face because he went on.

"I'd planned to break in and search Alexandra's files. I dressed all in black, stuck to the shadows in the alley. By the time I reached Lotions and Potions, I saw someone there, using a crowbar to crack open the back door."

"Did you see who it was?" Twink barked, which was more like a squeak, and I picked him up.

Evan shook his head. "It was too far away, it was too dark, and like I said, I can't see very well right now. The person wore a cloak with a hood and was short. Shorter than me."

He was about five feet eight or so, give or take an inch. I filed that away.

"I waited in the shadows for the person to leave. Then I saw you and Nick Sawyer creeping around the building. I didn't wait around. I accidentally kicked an aluminum can and thought I'd die right on the spot. I ran all the way home."

That noise I'd heard in the alley last night had been Evan. It made sense, and his story held a ring of truth.

"So, will you please help me, Darcy?"

I was trying my best to think of a way to get into the shop without actually breaking and entering. Was there any way to gain access? Who could let us in? Alex's landlord, perhaps, though I doubted that was legal—and most people, including me, frowned on breaking the law. But as I looked at Evan's face, I knew I had to do something. Fast. If the swelling reached his throat, he could possibly die.

"Why me?" I asked. I barely knew him.

He glanced at me, a guilty look in his eye. "I can't ask Starla. I'd never forgive myself if she got into trouble."

I raised my eyebrows. "But you're willing to risk *me* getting into trouble?"

"That sounds harsh, doesn't it?"

"A tad," I said, trying not to laugh.

"I'm desperate, remember? Honestly, Darcy, from the moment I met you, I knew you to be someone who goes out of her way to help others. You're a nurturer. I need nurturing."

He blinked at me, trying to be charming. The welts made it look more pathetic than anything.

Truth was, I did want to help him. My heart broke for him, this situation he was in. It seemed so unfair. He was suffering, his business was suffering, and his life was potentially in danger.

"Do you still have the lotion?" I asked. "Maybe we can get it analyzed. What did it look like?"

He fidgeted. "It was pink. Smelled good. I'd show it to you, but I don't have the tube anymore. I, ah, lost it."

I narrowed my eyes on him. "Lost it? Where?"

"I don't know. If I did, it wouldn't be lost."

He had a point.

"Why do I feel like you're not telling me everything?" Scratching, he said, "I don't know. Will you help?"

I knew I had to try. Could I possibly get him to wish himself well? There had to be a way around the law that governed against soliciting wishes, a sneaky way of coercing him to say what I wanted.

I thought about it for a second and finally said, "I bet you wish you hadn't used that lotion."

He sat on the bottom step of a wooden staircase. He gave me a look I had trouble deciphering—it looked a lot like sympathy for some reason. "I wish a lot of things. I wish my face didn't look like this. I wish I hadn't used that lotion. At this point, I wish I'd never met Alexandra Shively."

Relief flowed through me. I turned my head and mouthed "I wish I might, I wish I may, grant these wishes without delay." I blinked twice. Expectantly, I turned to Evan.

Nothing had happened.

In fact, he looked worse.

Twink licked my hand, as if offering condolences.

Why hadn't the wish worked? Evan's wishes had to have been pure of heart—the kind of passion in his voice when he made them couldn't be faked.

Had the wishes not been granted because I'd tricked him into making them?

Guilt flowed and a knot twisted in my stomach as I sat down next to him on the step.

"I have to get into that shop, Darcy."

I bit my lip. "There might be another way."

"What?" he asked, hope in his eyes.

"What are you doing later on?"

"Hiding in the house."

Smiling, I said, "I have to run errands now, but I'll pick you up at three thirty." He'd have to stay in the car when I dropped the wombat off at Jake's party, but we could go straight to Cherise Goodwin's afterward. I couldn't imagine Cherise would deny my request to cure Evan—especially after she saw him.

"Where are we going?" he asked.

"To drop off a wombat and then beg a favor."

He smiled (I think), and said, "You lead an interesting life, Darcy Merriweather."

I reached for his hand and squeezed it. I was slightly embarrassed at the tears filling my eyes. "That's one of the nicest things anyone has ever said to me."

"Honey, you need to get out more."

I was laughing as the front door flew open. Starla burst in, breathing hard. "Oh, thank goodness you're still here, Darcy! I thought I'd missed you."

Twink barked and I set him on the floor. He hopped over to Starla, who hung her camera on a coatrack, kicked off her shoes, and rubbed her hands together eagerly.

"Are you ready?" she asked me as she scooped up Twink.

She was scaring me. "Ready for what?"

"Oh, you'll see. You'll *really* see. It really is illuminating."

I wasn't sure what to expect as we followed Starla up the stairs and into a spare bedroom that had been turned into an office.

Starla gestured me inside. I looked back at Evan, who leaned against the doorway, grinning (I think).

"This is my studio." Starla dropped into her leather desk chair, set Twink on her lap, and cleared a screen saver from the computer on the desk.

The room was warm and inviting, decorated in light blues. Framed photos covered the walls. People, flowers, architecture. Starla had a great eye for capturing an intriguing shot.

On the desk sat a stack of photos. The picture Starla had taken of Mrs. Pennywhistle yesterday sat on the top. I picked it up as Starla clicked through folders on her PC.

The photo was striking, captivating. Mrs. P was clearly lost in her thoughts, and the camera captured sheer anguish in her eyes. My heart broke just looking at her, and I decided a quick trip to the Pixie Cottage on the way home was in need, even though it would throw my schedule out of whack.

Starla was humming as she clicked away.

A sudden thought hit. "Did you get a picture of the

pickpocket?" Maybe after our talk this morning, she'd gone through her shots from yesterday and found an image with the pickpocket in action.

"Nope. Here. Look at this." She clicked a few buttons and the image on the screen enlarged.

I blinked. It was the shot, a close-up, she'd taken of me and Nick yesterday afternoon. Nick looked gorgeous as usual and as he stared my way, I saw a softness in his eyes that I'd never noticed before. The image of me was simply a white starburst.

"I've never looked better," I joked, my palms starting to sweat.

"I was quite surprised when I loaded this image," Starla said. "This kind of result doesn't happen often."

"Maybe the sun was hitting me wrong?" I tried.

Starla looked at Evan, happiness surrounding her like a glow. "She's cute. Isn't she cute?"

My palms really started to sweat. What was going on? And how did I get out of it?

"Adorable," Evan said, nodding.

Starla opened a desk drawer and pulled out a photo album. "Here."

I took it.

"Open it," Starla urged.

I opened it. Mesmerized, I flipped page after page. A crib with a sunburst in the middle. A prom picture with a line of dolled-up girls, except for a starburst to the right of the frame. A group shot on the green, a sunburst catching a Frisbee.

Starla stood. "I imagine you have a lot of similar pictures. You and Harper."

I glanced at her, then Evan, as realization dawned. And I suddenly also knew why Evan's wish hadn't been granted. Because Wishcrafters can't grant each other's wishes.

"I— You—" I couldn't say it aloud. If I did, and I was wrong, I'd lose my powers forever.

Starla nodded, but she wasn't talking, either.

"Oh, for Pete's sake, I'll say it. Hello," he said, dipping his head. "I'm Evan Sullivan, and I'm a Cross-Crafter, half Bakecrafter . . . and half Wishcrafter."

"Wishcrafter just like you," Starla added, her smile dazzling.

Chapter Fifteen

Mrs. P's picture haunted me as I hurried through the back alley that ran behind Spellbound and Lotions and Potions on my way to the Pixie Cottage. I felt an overwhelming need to make sure Mrs. Pennywhistle was okay.

I emerged from the alley on the other side of the square. The Pixie Cottage took up a corner lot and looked like it had been plucked out of a Grimm's fairy tale and set in the village. "Charming" wasn't strong enough a word. It was a large stone bungalow with lush gardens, an inviting wraparound porch, and beautiful ivy creeping up the chimney.

A whimsical sign with *Pixie Cottage* written in a looping font hung from a post in front of a white picket fence. A NO VACANCY notice dangled from a hook beneath the sign. The gate squeaked as I pushed it open. Butterflies flitted about, and a bee buzzed by my ear.

My step was light as I followed the flagstone path to the arched wooden door. I pushed down on the handle and went inside. A woman I didn't recognize was on the phone behind a whitewashed registration desk. She smiled when she saw me and held up an I'll-be-right-with-you finger. I took a moment to look around. The registration area opened into a large living room with a stacked stone fireplace.

Light streamed in through large arched windows, highlighting dark wooden floors, pale sofas, lavender armchairs with lightly checkered ottomans. All the tables in the room appeared to be made out of twigs. The room was darling, and absolutely perfect for a pixie.

I tried not to eavesdrop on the conversation going on behind me. The woman, late thirties, early forties, looked more like a librarian than a hotel clerk. Her hair was swept back and held with a large clip, and a pair of glasses was perched on top of her head.

"Are you sure you won't reconsider?" she was saying. She listened to the person on the other end, then added, "The village is really quite safe." A pause. "I see. No, I understand. Thank you for calling."

She hung up and rose, offering me her hand. "I'm Harmony Atchison. You're Darcy, aren't you?"

"Word gets around," I said.

"It's a small village." She wore a flowing bohemian-style skirt and a pristine white peasant blouse. Frowning at the phone, she added, "Which is sometimes unfortunate."

"Cancellations?" I asked.

Nodding, she tidied a stack of papers. "As if the murder wasn't bad enough, now these thefts . . . For the first time in the five years since I've taken over, the Pixie Cottage will have vacancies during the week of the Midsummer Dance."

I tipped my head. What did she mean she'd taken over?

"You don't happen to need a reservation?" she asked hopefully.

"Sadly, no, though I love the inn. It's absolutely charming."

Her smile seemed to light her from inside out. "It was in sad disrepair when I bought it."

"It's beautiful," I murmured. "But I'm a little confused. I thought Mrs. Pennywhistle lived here? That she owned the cottage?"

Sitting on the edge of the desk, Harmony said, "Mrs. P still lives here. Room number four. Her favorite. I bought this place five years ago from her. She just couldn't keep up with it on her own after Mr. P died. Debts mounted. It was a tough decision she made to sell it, and even at its fixer-upper bargain price, it was still out of my price range." Her eyes grew misty. "Mrs. P agreed to cut her price as long as she could live here free of charge. It was truly a bargain in my favor, and it still is. She's a sweet woman, a ball of energy. She helps me more than she knows, especially with the gardens. Greenest thumb I've ever seen."

I recalled what Mrs. P had said yesterday, about her being a poor old woman. How much had she discounted the cottage? "She's a sweetheart," I said. "Her laugh is the best, isn't it?"

"Contagious," she agreed.

"Is she around by any chance? I wanted to check on her."

A touch of sadness swept over her face. "She's been a touch . . . out of it lately, hasn't she? She's taking Alexandra Shively's death quite hard. I've never seen her so melancholy. The murder was quite shocking, especially for the old-timers in the village. That kind of thing just doesn't happen here. They're taking it personally."

"I think it's quite shocking for everyone," I said softly, thinking of Aunt Ve.

"You're right about that, though Alex . . ." She bit her lip. "I shouldn't gossip so much." She grinned. "Sometimes I just can't help myself. How is Velma holding up?"

I wondered what she was going to say about Alex. Probably nothing I hadn't heard in the past few days. That she was not well liked. Outspoken. Misleading.

"Holding steady. She's offering a reward for Alex's missing watch." I pulled a flyer out of my bag and handed it to her. "She's hoping that finding it will help clear Sylar's name."

Harmony glanced at the flyer. "Foolish business, arresting Sylar. The man is a cuddly teddy bear who'd have moral issues swatting a mosquito."

"You've known him long?" I really didn't know much about him, except what I'd read in the papers and learned from Ve this morning. Sixty-eight years old. Widower. Optometrist. Lived in the village for thirty years. Village council hoo-ha.

"Years and years. I've lived in this village my whole life. His wife was one of my favorite teachers when I was in school. He was devastated—the whole village was— when she passed away."

This news had me studying Harmony carefully. If there was one thing I'd learned in the two weeks I'd been in the village, it's that if you've lived here your whole life, then you're most likely a Crafter. Was she?

There was absolutely no way of telling. Which was starting to drive me a little crazy.

Something else she said stood out. I tried to recall what the paper had said. "That was about ten years ago that she died, right? Was she in an accident?"

I was fishing. If she died suspiciously, it might paint Sylar in a different light.

"An aneurysm." Her jaw set. "The police are barking up the wrong tree. If you ask me, they should be talking to that hairstylist, Ramona Todd. Chief Leighton ignored me when I suggested it."

"Ramona?" I said, shocked.

Harmony nodded. "The day Alexandra died, I saw her and Ramona in a heated argument in the alley behind Lotions and Potions. I thought they were going to come to blows, and that I was going to have to separate them."

"You didn't have to?"

"Ramona backed off and left, but I think the fight is fairly incriminating, don't you?"

Ramona seemed so even-keeled. I couldn't imagine her raising her voice in anger. "The police didn't think so?"

"Obviously not if they arrested Sylar." She shrugged. "I've not been impressed with the police chief's investigation. Seems premature to make an arrest this early, especially when there are clearly other suspects out there."

That seemed to be a general consensus.

But what had Ramona and Alex been arguing about? I thought about that appointment I was going to make with Ramona and decided I'd try to get in as soon as possible. I checked my watch. Time was flying by today. I still wanted to stop by Bewitching Boutique to look for new sneakers and inquire about a certain satin cape before heading back home to pick up the wombat.

"You may want to call Marcus Debrowski and talk to him. He's representing Sylar. Maybe if he has your information, it will help him build a case of reasonable doubt."

She perked up. "I will. I'm not sure why I didn't think of that." The phone rang, and she said, "If you'll excuse me?"

I'd almost forgotten why I was here. "Is Mrs. P around?"

She reached for the phone. "I actually haven't seen her this morning. You can check her room. Down the hall on the right. Number four. Hello, Pixie Cottage, Harmony speaking."

I thanked her and headed down the hallway. I knocked gently on the door, and I was surprised when it swung open, having been left slightly ajar. Worried, I peeked inside. A gorgeous, fantastical canopy bed made of twigs sat in the center of the room, and two 1940s-style mirrored nightstands flanked its sides. The bed was made; the room was neat, tidy, and empty.

I turned to go when a framed photo on the wall

caught my attention. It was a young version of Mrs. P. holding the hand of a little girl in a plain knee-length dress and a big bonnet. Mrs. P wore a tight-fitting skirt suit and a wide smile. I had to laugh—some things change over time, and other things stay the same. In the photo, Mrs. P's hair stuck out in every which direction, looking a lot like Cruella De Vil's hairdo. It hadn't changed a bit over the decades.

I closed the door, said good-bye to Harmony, and headed toward Bewitching Boutique. I was halfway there when what Harmony had said earlier struck me.

The day Alexandra died, I saw them in a heated argument in the alley behind Lotions and Potions.

But why, exactly, had Harmony been in the alley behind the shops?

"As I live and breathe!" a voice boomed. "*The* Darcy Merriweather has finally come *inside* the shop." A dapper man, dressed to the nines, rushed forward, took my hand, and kissed it.

I glanced around, as if I might spot some hidden cameras nearby.

"Godfrey Baleaux, Cloakcrafter extraordinaire, at your service." He bowed. "I've been waiting for you."

All I could do was stare at him. He was impeccably dressed in a white suit and vest, with a yellow silk tie and matching pocket square. A gold pocket-watch chain swung as he continued to hold my hand. Older, maybe late fifties, early sixties, he was short, squat, and balding. He reminded me a bit of a hoity-toity Humpty Dumpty.

"Come in, come in." He pulled me farther into the shop, to a small grouping of sumptuously covered chairs in front of a dressing room, fancily decorated with silk drapes and elaborate tiebacks. "I have your dress ready for you. I think you'll find everything in order."

"My dress?" I squeaked. "I—I came in for sneakers.

Running shoes. Do you carry them?" It was a stupid question. This shop was clearly not one that would deign to sell mere Asics or Nikes.

Wagging a finger, he said, "Ah-ah-ah! Do not practice to deceive with me, young lady."

I snapped my gaping mouth closed. Who *was* this man?

"I know, young Miss Darcy, that you've come in for that special blue dress you've been eyeing in the window. It is your dress, as if I made it, stitch by stitch, just for you. After all, any niece of Velma's is a nie— " He cut himself off, tapped his chin. "Perhaps not a niece of mine. Suffice it to say that any relative of Velma's is a relative of mine. Come, now, tell Godfrey the truth."

I couldn't help but smile as he tipped his head, waiting patiently. He oozed charming personality, and I found I liked him immediately.

Suddenly, a silky smooth man's voice with a pronounced French accent said, "You made that dress? Stitch by stitch? How *dare*"—he dragged the word out at least three seconds—"you? *I* made that dress."

I glanced around but didn't see anyone.

The voice continued, saying, "And if you'd kindly tell your *relative* to get off my tail, I'd appreciate it. Move it or lose it, *ma chère*."

I looked down and saw the tiny face of a mouse looking up at me behind the tiniest pair of glasses I'd ever seen. The mouse's thin whiskers had been braided together and curved upward at the ends to resemble a Dali mustache. He wore a tiny vest with three minuscule buttons.

"Eee!" I jumped onto the chair.

"That's better," the mouse said, shaking its tail.

Looking downward, Godfrey put his hands on his hips. "Must you always be so dramatic? You've scared the poor child half to death. Come down from there,

Darcy. You've nothing to fear from Pepe here. He's simply a cranky old familiar."

"Perhaps, not *she* has something to fear," Pepe said, "but *you*." Pepe walked over to Godfrey, bared his teeth, and chomped Godfrey's ankle.

Godfrey jumped around on one foot, swearing a blue streak. Cautiously, I stepped down off the chair and hoped Godfrey wasn't bleeding. The sight of blood usually made me pass out—and I didn't want to miss a second of this little talking mouse.

"*Ma chère*, I am Pepe. You must forgive my lout of a friend. He loves to take credit where none is due." He held out his hand.

I crouched down and took it.

"An honor," he said as he kissed my knuckles. "The dress was indeed made for you. The moment I saw you, I knew it had to be." He made a sweeping motion toward the dressing room, where the blue dress I'd seen earlier in the window now hung.

"But I don't need a dress," I said.

Godfrey had sat in one of the chairs and was dabbing his forehead with his pocket square. "Of course you do. For the Midsummer Dance."

"But I don't think I'm even going to the dance."

Pepe said, "You are going, *ma chère*, and you will look *magnifique* in the dress." He kissed his fingertips. "I am currently working on a piece for your aunt. Stunning, if I do say so myself."

I didn't dare argue that I wasn't going to the dance for fear he'd chomp my ankle, too. "You know Ve well?" I asked, looking between the two of them. She could have warned me that there were talking mice in the village.

Pepe peered up at Godfrey, whose cheeks had colored a mottled red. "You could say so. We were, at one point . . . married."

"Married?" I choked out.

"I believe"—he dabbed his forehead again—"I was her third husband."

"Mr. Rat Toad?" I said before I could stop myself.

His cheeks were now in full flush. His eyebrows rose into bristly white peaks. "I believe you forgot to add 'bottom dweller.' Ve's favorite endearment of all."

"Rat toad?" Pepe said, his dark little eyes brightening. He started laughing. Great, gusty gales of laughter. He fell on his back and started rolling back and forth. "Rat toad! Bottom dweller," he gasped, still rolling around, holding his chubby little tummy in glee.

Godfrey lifted him by the tail. "That is quite enough."

"Put me down!" Pepe swung tiny fists.

Godfrey set him on the table at the center of the four chairs. "I can't believe you bit me."

"It is but a tiny scratch. This time," Pepe warned, shaking his fist again.

Godfrey leaned down and poked Pepe's round belly. "You should watch it, or perhaps I'll decide a nice black cat would add to our store image and be good for business."

Pepe's eyes widened. "You wouldn't."

"I would," Godfrey countered.

Pepe glared for a moment, then bowed to me. "A pleasure, *ma chère*. Now, if you'll excuse me, *I* have work to do." He slid down the table leg, hit the floor, and adjusted his vest. His tail shot in the air, and there was a definite swagger in his step as he strode toward a small arched wooden door in the baseboard next to the dressing room. He opened the door, strode in, and slammed the door behind him.

"You wouldn't really get a cat, would you?" I asked Godfrey.

"I might. Perhaps. Do not frown, Miss Darcy. Pepe would be in no danger. It is very difficult to kill a familiar. However, he is not immune from being chased around. And caught."

I sat down opposite him. "Are there many familiars in the village?"

"A few," he said evasively.

My mind was reeling with questions. "How does one become a familiar, exactly?"

"There are a few ways. The most popular is dying."

"Dying?"

"Familiars, after all, are spirits inside an animal's body. Most commonly, a spell is cast when a person dies, and their spirit is brought back in the form of an animal."

"And anyone can cast this spell?"

"Any Crafter who knows it. But the person who dies must want to come back."

"And they're here forever? A pet that doesn't die?" It sounded a bit creepy to me.

"Not always. They can decide, at any time, to go back to being a free spirit and go to the place spirits dwell."

I glanced at Pepe's door. "Pepe? How old is he?"

Godfrey tipped his head side to side. "He died in 1798 and has been with my family ever since."

I was struggling to take it all in, to absorb the information. "Does the spirit get to choose its animal body?"

"Usually," Godfrey said. "It depends on the spell and who's casting it. A form must be available."

"What's that mean? A familiar doesn't come back as a newborn animal? It can be an animal that's years old?"

"Certainly."

This was all very confusing.

"The spirit has a choice," he said.

I chewed my lip, trying to make sense of what Godfrey was telling me. "So, for example," I said, racking my brain for one, "Higgins."

Godfrey laughed. "Gayle Chastain's Saint Bernard?"

I nodded. "He's a few years old, but Russ died only last year. If he was a Crafter, and knew the familiar spell, could he have taken over Higgins' body?"

"Indeed!" Godfrey exclaimed as though I was a star student. "Though to my knowledge Higgins is simply a big drooling buffoon of a dog. Not a familiar."

"Interesting. Can a familiar change bodies at will?"

"Once a form is chosen, it is usually permanent. There are rare exceptions."

"Like what?"

"If the form suffers an injury, a broken paw or some such. Or if the form is relocated unwillingly."

"Dognapped?"

"Exactly." He smiled. "And sometimes, if the spirit has a valid reason for switching forms, the Elder has the ability to grant the requested change."

"She does?"

"Indeed. Her powers are boundless."

I was taking in so much information, it was hard to process. Before I could ask anything about the Elder (I had so many questions), Godfrey said, "There are downsides to consider when becoming a familiar."

"Like what?"

"The familiar retains his spirit, but also inherits the natural traits of the form. Pepe, for example, craves cheese. A cat familiar would respond, even perhaps against her will, to scratching and start purring. A bee would search for pollen." His gaze softened. "You've much to learn, Darcy Merriweather. Velma has been re-miss."

"She's been a little busy," I defended.

"Ah yes, this murder business. Terrible." He gave me a conspiratorial smile. "Between us, I am not so sad to see that tacky Sylar Dewitt behind bars."

Tacky? I thought he dressed quite a bit like Godfrey, though I thought better about saying so. "Even if he's innocent?"

In a serious tone, he said, "The man is not who he appears to be. That will soon come to light, I should think."

"What do you mean?" What did he know?

He waved a hand. "Nothing certain. Only a feeling. An instinct."

I bit my cheek. I believed greatly in trusting instincts. What he said motivated me to learn as much about Sylar as I could.

"Now, Miss Darcy, are you ready to admit you came in to finally try on your dress?"

I smiled. "Honestly, Godfrey?"

He nodded.

"I really came in to see if you've ever made a cloak for a Vaporcrafter."

His face fell. "Really?"

"Really."

He looked so sad that I added, "But I'll try on the dress as well. I do love it."

Perking right up, he said, "I knew it! Now, what's this about a Vaporcrafter?"

I explained what had happened in Lotions and Potions.

"Velma's correct," he said. "There hasn't been a Vaporcrafter in the village in decades." He clapped twice, two short bursts. A leather-bound book appeared in his hands.

I drew in a breath.

His teeth glistened as he smiled wide. "A little razzle-dazzle meant to impress. Did it work?"

Nodding, I said, "I'm definitely impressed."

"Good, good."

Pepe's voice came from behind the door in the baseboard. "Show-off."

"He's just jealous," Godfrey said, dismissing Pepe's comment with a wave of his hand. "Now, let's see about that Vaporcrafter." He flipped pages through the old book filled with names and dates, written with meticulous penmanship. "Vaporcrafter, Vaporcrafter . . ." His finger slid down a page. "Interesting," he finally said.

"What?" I leaned in, trying to read upside down.

"In my family's history, we've made only one cloak for a Vaporcrafter." As an aside he said, "They don't really need them with the way they can dissolve into thin air and such. It was back in 1959 to Isaiah Clemson. As far as I know, there are no remaining Clemsons. The Elder would know for certain."

A half hour later, I left the shop with a lot more information than I'd hoped for, a gauzy blue dress, and a pit in my stomach.

Because if I wanted to help Sylar, I was going to have to contact the Elder.

Chapter Sixteen

I rushed home to find the dog door open. I groaned, thinking Missy had once again escaped. But no sooner was the sound out of my mouth than she came barreling into the room, full force. She yapped and barked happily. I grabbed her up, rubbing her ears. I slipped her collar back over her head. "No more losing it, okay?"

Tilda sat on the kitchen counter. I noticed a leaf caught on her fur and plucked it off. It wasn't often she ventured outside through the dog door, but when she did, she never strayed far—mostly because she liked to stare at the macaw next door, who was often in his outdoor cage. I had a feeling she was trying to figure out how to set the bird free so she could "play" with him.

I scratched her ears, too, and looked into her blue eyes. After meeting Pepe, I couldn't help but wonder. . . .

Tilda stared back at me.

"Are you a familiar?" I asked her. I had to ask. Because on my way home I'd finally realized where I'd heard the term before. It was the day after Alex had been killed. I'd heard Ve upstairs talking to a mystery woman and they'd talked about a familiar. Ve had explained the voice away as talking to herself, but after learning about familiars, I doubted that was true. "Are you?" I asked Tilda again.

She commenced taking a bath.

I looked down at Missy. "Are you?"

She tried to wiggle out of my arms to help Tilda with her bath. Tilda *rreow*ed and took off. "I guess that means no," I said as I set Missy on the floor.

After I looked around for little doors in the baseboards (there were none), I noticed that Aunt Ve had left a note on the counter.

> *Darcy dear,*
>
> *I had to run out to meet with Marcus. Can you drop this off at All That Glitters for me? Shea is expecting you.*
>
> > *Love,*
> > *Auntie Ve*

Ve's locket sat next to the note.

I glanced at the clock. I had just enough time to stuff the wombat with candy, drop off the locket, and pick up Evan. I needed to change, too. The shorts and T-shirt I was wearing weren't professional enough for Jake Carey's party.

I made sure Tilda and Missy had plenty of water, and took Missy for a quick walk before I left. On my way out, I slid the panel down over the dog door to make sure they both stayed in the house.

All That Glitters was just a half block down the road, so I loaded the wombat into the car, and decided I'd walk to the shop. As I passed the house next door, I slowed to a stop. Now that I knew one of Ve's exes lived there, I was curious. As I stood surveying the cottage, the macaw, Archie, started yelling, "Stelllaaaaaa! Stellllaaaaa!"

Mr. Goodwin had obviously watched *A Streetcar Named Desire* at some point.

I hurried on as several tourists stopped to gawk. Archie seemed to love the attention—I could hear his spot-on catcalls from down the block. There were more people roaming the village this afternoon than there had been this morning, but not nearly as many as usual. The bad press was definitely taking its toll.

All That Glitters was located between the Cauldron and the Furry Toadstool, its glittery awning an eye-catcher. Shea Carling was behind the counter when I stepped into the shop. Max Carling was helping a couple on the other side of the room. The woman was oohing and aahing over a selection of necklaces.

"Darcy, hello! I believe you have something for me?"

I smiled. Shea had a way about her that made me feel welcome. Warmth flowed from her eyes, her smile. I guessed her to be early forties, but her long blond hair and bare-minimum makeup (she truly didn't need any) made her look years younger.

I pulled the locket out of my pocket and set it on the counter. "The clasp isn't working right. The necklace keeps falling off."

She held the clasp up to the light. "It's very loose. Ve's lucky she didn't lose it." She clicked open the locket. I leaned in—I'd never seen what was in it.

"Awww," she said, turning it to face me. "That's sweet."

On one side, the locket held a photograph of Sylar. It had been trimmed to fit into the oval frame. On the other side, there was an inscription.

Journeys end in lovers meeting.

I stared at the words, trying to remember how I knew them. I repeated them over and over in my head until it clicked. I'd just seen them this morning. At the gift shop—on one of the Shakespeare quote mugs. Right next to the mug with "A Madness Most Discreet"—the inscription that had been on Alexandra's watch.

"Do you want to wait for this? It'll only take me a second," Shea said. "Darcy? Are you okay? You're white as a ghost!"

"I—I'll come back for the locket," I stammered. Turning, I hurried out of the shop. I needed fresh air.

Outside, I leaned against a streetlight. My stomach rolled, and I felt queasy.

Because if my hunch was right—and I suspected it was—then I knew who Alexandra Shively's secret boyfriend had been.

"Maybe you're wrong, Darcy," Evan said.

We were on our way to drop off the wombat and then to the Goodwins' house. I glanced over at him, hoping that Cherise could cure him. He looked like a prepubescent desperado with his loose baggy jeans, oversized sweatshirt with the hood up, big sunglasses, and bandanna tied loosely around the bottom half of his face.

I had the air-conditioning at full blast so he wouldn't overheat. I, on the other hand, was starting to shiver. Jake's marsupial-themed party in Melrose was a good half-hour drive, give or take the traffic situation, from Salem. I might be a Darcycicle by the time we arrived.

I'd told Evan about my Sylar theory. I just couldn't keep it in, and knew I could trust him. After all, as another Wishcrafter, we were practically family. I had a ton of questions about him being a Cross-Crafter, but kept them in check in light of the Sylar situation. I thought about what Evan said, that my theory might be wrong.

"Don't you think," I said, "it's just a bit too coincidental that two pieces of jewelry that are given to two local women are inscribed with Shakespeare quotes found on mugs from the local gift shop? And it would also explain why Sylar disliked Alex so much—if she was his ex."

"If I was Ve, I'd be mad that Alex got the Harry Winston."

"If I was Ve," I said, "I'd be mad that he got my inscription from a mug at the local gift shop."

Evan held the wombat steady as I turned a corner. "I never really considered Sylar to be wealthy. He certainly doesn't throw money around like he is. Lives in a brownstone down the street from me. Drives a Ford. I can't see him buying a watch like that—or having the money to."

"Everyone has their secrets."

He nodded. "True. How do we find out if they dated for sure?"

"I have a feeling the police already know." I was reading street signs as I drove along, looking for the right one.

"What makes you say so?"

"He was arrested so early on in the case, yet there isn't a lot of evidence against him. True, he was found over the body, and he was the last one to have Ve's scarf, and then how you said Alex was supposed to meet him, but all that is fairly circumstantial. Police Chief Leighton had to have something more to hand over to the state police. Something other than a grudge. Something bigger that they aren't divulging just yet. They would have had access to his bank accounts, his records. And something like a fifty-thousand-dollar watch would pop off the page."

"You might be right, but the watch wasn't on Sylar when he was arrested. It's still missing."

"He could have hidden it. Somewhere near the bookshop. He had time."

Evan whistled. "I hate to say it, but it makes sense."

It did, but I didn't want it to, and clung stubbornly to the notion that he might be innocent. If he was Alex's ex, it was pretty damning, though.

I found the right street and turned. Both sides were lined with cars, and I had to park a good bit down the block from the house with a giant inflatable bounce house in the front yard that had a big sign taped to it that said KANGAROO HOP. Balloons in the shapes of kangaroos, koalas, and possums were tied all around the yard, and kids ran and screamed.

"You need to tell Ve about the watch," Evan said.

I wasn't looking forward to the conversation. "I know. Do you want to come with me to make this delivery?" I asked Evan.

He looked at me. Hardly any of his face was showing, yet I could tell he was giving me a "Be serious" look.

"Okay, I'll be right back."

I took the wombat and threaded my way through the crowd, taking my time to let the sunshine warm me up again. A group of moms were circled under a large oak tree. I tapped a shoulder of one of them. "I'm looking for Mrs. Carey."

The woman pointed to a petite woman in a shirtwaist dress, who appeared to be trying to keep two little boys from killing each other with plastic swords.

What plastic swords were doing at a marsupial party was beyond me.

"If you can't play nice . . . ," she was saying as I walked up. When she spotted me, she ushered them off with orders to stop stabbing each other. She wiped her brow with the back of her hand.

"Mrs. Carey, I'm Darcy from As You Wish."

"You found one!" she cried, taking hold of the piñata. "I was afraid you wouldn't be able to. I tried and tried to find one online, but there was nothing out there. And Jake wouldn't settle for a kangaroo or a koala. He had to have the wombat. He'll be thrilled. Just thrilled. Thank you so much!"

Her enthusiasm had me glowing with pride. It had been worth all the hassle of making the wombat myself.

"Jake, Jake!" the woman called. "Come see your wombat!"

A little boy with a mop of unruly brown hair came running over. He stopped short when he saw the piñata.

"What's that?" he asked with much more disdain than I thought a seven-year-old could possess.

My glow started to fade.

Mrs. Carey looked nervous. "It's your wombat piñata. Isn't it great? Just what you asked for." She tittered.

He glared at her. Suddenly I wanted to take my wombat and go. He didn't deserve it.

"I asked for a real wombat!" He stomped his foot. I was reminded of the scene in *Willy Wonka* where the girl didn't get her golden egg. "That's not a real wombat!"

Everyone, I noticed, was staring. I just wanted to go. "I'll, ah—"

"Now, Jake, you know you can't have a real wombat. . . ." She tittered again and looked around at all the faces lapping up this delicious meltdown.

"But it's what I wished for!" he cried. Big tears fell from his eyes.

My senses went on alert at the word "wish." "I really should be going," I said, trying to edge backward.

"I wished for a wombat! A real one."

As long as he stayed in the past tense, I was okay. I just needed to get out of there. Fast.

"I want a real wombat! I wish I had a real wombat!"

Oh. No.

I gulped, not sure what to do. If I didn't grant the wish, I'd be in danger of losing my powers. If I did, there might possibly be a real wombat in my near future.

For the love, as Harper would say. Taking a deep breath, I mouthed the words I needed to say and blinked twice.

At first, it seemed like nothing had happened. Relief flowed through me until I heard the screams.

The crowd parted as a terrified-looking wombat came running toward me. It looked like a small brown bear cub who'd lost its mama. I was too worried about *it* to be concerned about *me* when it knocked into my legs, sweeping them out from under me.

I fell with a *whoosh* but had enough sense to grab the wombat around its middle. It wiggled and struggled until Jake dropped to the ground next to me, his eyes filled with wonder.

"Everyone needs to be quiet," he said, quite unnecessarily, since the screaming had stopped and everyone stared in shock. "Wombats are shy."

The wombat had stopped struggling and seemed to find solace with the little boy. Jake, the wombat whisperer.

"He's so scared," Jake said. "Can I take him inside, Mom? He needs to start building his burrow in the backyard. You're the best mom ever!"

Jake strode off toward the house, singing "Happy birthday to me," the wombat in his arms.

"Are you okay?" someone asked, giving me a hand up.

I yelped at the unexpected sight of Desperado Evan. "I'm fine. I thought you were staying in the car."

"I heard screaming. Was that a real wombat?"

"Don't ask." I looked around. Chatter had started up again around us as people rushed toward Mrs. Carey, who stood frozen, her hand over her mouth. "We should go," I said. "Right now."

We speed-walked toward the car.

"Stuff like this never happens to me and Starla." He slid into the passenger seat.

"Are you trying to make me feel better or worse?"

"Better, of course!"

I frowned at him. "It's not working."

Chapter Seventeen

"How is it you know Cherise Goodwin again?" Evan asked me.

"Let's just say I did some work for her." I'd rather not go into the tulle-y details. I gazed at the house. "Maybe you should stay here for a few minutes. I didn't tell her I was bringing you along, and I want to give her a little warning."

He lowered his sunglasses. "I can't imagine why."

I patted his hand. "It's almost over. Hang in there a few more minutes."

Glumly, he nodded.

I left the car running so he wouldn't overheat, and knocked on Cherise's front door. A moment later, it swung open. "Thank goodness you're here." She pulled me inside. "Maybe you can talk some sense into him."

"Him who?"

"Dennis. Because he's not listening to a word I say."

Truly, the last person I wanted to see was Dennis. I'm sure he felt the same about me.

"Ma? Who was it?" Dennis came around the corner from the kitchen and froze when he saw me. He threw his hands in the air. "Not again."

I sighed. "I'm not here to cause any trouble. I actually came to see if Cherise would wish Amanda and Laurel Grace home."

Cherise shook her head. "Dennis was just demonstrating why that's not a good idea."

By her tone, I could tell he'd been making an ass of himself. "How so?"

"He's moaning about not having had a properly cooked dinner in the past week that he's been living on his own. That he can't figure out which dry cleaner his clothes are at, that his fridge is empty."

Marital separations were hard, but hadn't he realized there would be repercussions when he moved out? "Seriously?"

She nodded.

"You make it sound like a bad thing," he said, a bit whiny.

"When was the last time you made dinner for Amanda?" I asked. "Brought her flowers or even a simple card? When was the last time you danced with her? Took a walk with her? Asked about her day, her wants, her desires?" I poked him in the chest. "Is it always all about you, you, you?"

"Hey!" he protested, pushing my hand away.

Cherise said, "When, Dennis?"

His face flamed. "I'm busy. I work. I pày the bills."

He was apparently one of those men who believed the louder he got, the more right he was.

I was starting to get a headache.

"See what I'm dealing with?" Cherise asked, exasperation clear in her high-pitched tone. "You know what?"

I didn't like where this was going.

"I really wish I was with Amanda and Laurel Grace."

Oh, jeez.

"Wish I might, wish I may," I said angrily, "grant this wish without delay."

Cherise vanished.

Great.

"Wish them back," Dennis demanded. "Enough is enough."

Since he hadn't phrased it right, I felt free to ignore him. "Are you really happy on your own?" I asked softly. "Don't you miss that warm body to wake up next to in the morning? Amanda's smile, knowing you're the only one she smiles at like that? Don't you miss cuddling with her late at night, when the house is quiet, and it's just the two of you and your thoughts and your dreams of the future? Don't you miss Laurel Grace's grin? Her exuberance for life? The way she's so curious?"

"You don't know what you're talking about."

"Sadly, I do."

There was a soft tap at the front door; then Evan's voice carried. "Hello?"

"In here," I called out.

Evan came in. He'd removed the bandanna and the glasses.

Dennis said, "What the hell happened to you?"

"Alexandra Shively," Evan said. "Where's Cherise? Did you talk to her?"

"I didn't get the chance." Nervously, I bit my lip. "But maybe Dennis can help?"

We both looked his way. He folded his arms and laughed. "You're joking. Help you? I don't think so."

"You're not helping *me*," I clarified. "You're helping *Evan*."

Evan nodded.

"No," Dennis said.

"But didn't you take the Hippocratic oath? Don't you have to help?"

"Sue me."

Evan looked even more pained than before. "But . . ."

"Look." Dennis shifted his weight. "Maybe we can make a deal."

"What kind of deal?" I didn't trust him one bit.

"You bring back my family, and I cure your friend. Simple. Darcy, I wish my family was home."

I rolled my eyes, but said the spell.

Nothing happened. No surprise there. His wish had all the passion of a pureed turnip.

Heartbroken, I looked at Evan. He appeared close to tears.

Dennis said, "Let me know when you're ready to bring them home, and I'll see to your friend. Now it's time for you both to leave."

As he ushered us to the door, I said, "You just don't get it, do you, Dennis?"

"Get what?"

"I'm not the one who can bring back your family. Only you have that power."

His eyes narrowed as he slammed the door on us.

"What now?" Evan sounded deflated.

I looked at his swollen face and made a rash (ha, ha) decision. "Plan B."

"What's that?"

"You'll see."

Plan B involved doing something I was highly against— perpetrating an illegal activity. However, I considered this an emergency and so was willing to temporarily ignore my moral compass.

For Evan, it was worth the risk.

"The key is," I said, "to look as natural as possible. We belong here. We're just going about our business. Nothing to see here, folks. Don't mind us. Nothing suspicious going on at all." I looked at Desperado Evan and realized exactly how suspicious he looked with his hood, glasses, and bandanna. "Well," I amended, "*I* don't look suspicious."

"You also don't look like something out of a sci-fi movie."

True. So true.

It was almost seven and the green was fairly quiet as we strolled along the alley behind Lotions and Potions, looking to an outsider as if we didn't have a care in the world. I'd hoped sneaking into Alex's shop wouldn't be too hard—after all, the back door was already cracked.

"Maybe you should start whistling," I said to Evan. I'd never learned how.

"With these lips?" He laughed.

"Good point."

As we passed Spellbound Bookshop's back door, we both slowed and gave it a thoughtful glance. Each shop had two metal doors leading to the alleyway; one was the residential entrance for the upstairs apartment, and the other was to the downstairs business. The alley was meticulous. No pallets or boxes anywhere. No nooks or crannies in which to hide something small and valuable. Clouds had moved in and cast the area in yawning shadows. It was a bit creepy, and I tried not to be skeeved out knowing that someone had died in this spot the other night.

"Nowhere to hide a watch," I said, glancing around.

"He could have thrown it in one of the Dumpsters."

"They were all searched." I didn't envy that job. I glanced at the fence. "I guess it's possible Sylar could have shoved it under the fencing—or thrown it over."

"Or he could have hidden it in the police car on the way to the station."

"Or even at the station, somehow," I said. "In a potted plant or something."

"It can be anywhere."

Nick's words came back to me.

If Alex was killed for another reason and the watch taken to throw suspicion on the pickpocket, then that watch is never going to surface. It's probably at the bottom of the Charles.

If that watch was the key to this murder, then finding Alex's killer might be impossible. I thought about Ve and her belief in Sylar's innocence. While I trusted her instincts, I also recognized that she'd had four husbands. Her choice in men might be lacking.

Alex's shop was the corner unit, four shops down from Spellbound. As we neared, my heart sank. The back door had been completely boarded up with plywood.

"Plan B just went down the tubes," I said.

"Why?" Evan asked.

I knew his eyes were swollen, but surely he could see the huge plywood sheets covering the door.

"No way to get in."

Evan pulled down his bandanna and smiled (I think). He pulled a key from his pocket, walked over to the residential door next to the shop, and slid the key into the lock. The door swung open.

I stared. "Where'd you get a key?"

We strolled inside, as casual as could be, and closed the door behind us. Evan flipped on a light next to the door. There was a connecting door to the retail space on my right, and a wooden staircase led upstairs.

"Alexandra gave it to me a while back. She thought someone should have a spare in case she lost hers. She trusted me," he said softly.

For a while there, I'd forgotten they had been friends, and how hard this must be for him. I put my hand on his shoulder and squeezed, but I didn't know what to say. "I'm sorry" just didn't feel like it was enough.

Evan reached up and squeezed my hand back.

After a second, I said, "What are we looking for exactly?"

Evan opened the connecting door to the retail shop. "Alexandra kept all her recipe cards in a wooden chest on the counter behind the register."

I'd seen the chest the night before. Elaborately carved, it had stood out as something special. The pink witch's hat had been atop it.

"If we can find the formula card for the lotion she gave me, then maybe we can figure out how to counteract it." Evan tiptoed along the hallway, looking left and right as though he expected someone to jump out and scream "boo" at him.

He was making me nervous.

Someone had drawn the shades on the front windows—probably the police to deter looters or gawkers—and the shop was filled with dim light that gave off an eerie glow. Goose bumps rose on my arms.

The shop still held that musky smell mixed with a strong hint of cinnamon and vanilla, and in the (muted) light of day, I could see why. Along a short wall, there were several clear bins stacked atop each other—the kind you might find at a penny-candy store. Each held a different herb or root or spice. Everything from cinnamon sticks to gingerroot. I spotted bins for milk thistle, evening primrose, ginseng, licorice root, vanilla beans, chicory root, aloe, and cayenne.

Evan had stopped short and I bumped into him. "What is it?" I asked.

"The box is gone."

"Gone?" I scooted around him. Sure enough, the box I'd seen last night was missing. I thought back. When the police came to investigate the break-in, they hadn't removed anything.

What did that mean?

Evan checked behind the counter, in the back office, in cabinets and drawers. The box was missing.

Just as we were about to leave, a crash sounded above our heads.

I jumped, my heart pounding, as I looked upward.

Evan steadied me. "Someone's upstairs." Anger flashed in his eyes. "I bet whoever it is has the formula box." He started for the stairway.

I grabbed his hood and yanked him back.

"Darcy!" he whispered fiercely.

"You just can't go storming up there. Whoever it is might be armed."

He looked around and grabbed a can of furniture polish from the storage closet. I refrained from making any jokes about polishing off the burglar, though it was tempting.

We crept up the stairs, treading softly on the steps. As we neared the top, I could hear the prowler moving around in Alex's apartment.

Evan went first into the apartment, checked to make sure it was clear, then waved me in. The place was a mess. Furniture ripped, books tossed, drawers upended. The intruder had been thorough.

The burglar was currently in Alex's bedroom, to my right. Evan took a stance next to the doorway, the furniture polish aimed strategically.

I went to stand behind him and tripped on a book.

The apartment went deathly quiet.

My breath caught and my heart hammered in my throat. I took cover behind the sofa.

Silence filled the air, creating a tension so thick I thought I was going to choke. I pressed my hands together to keep them from shaking. Still, no sound from the bedroom. Were we just going to wait each other out?

I glanced down and noticed the book that I tripped on had been a Bible. A piece of paper was sticking out of it. I slowly dragged it closer to me. I pulled on the paper, which turned out to be the corner of a photo. It was of a little girl, maybe six or seven. She looked vaguely familiar, but I couldn't place her. I flipped the photo over. "Virginia Clemson, Aged Eight" was written on the back.

Clemson. I knew the name, had just heard it that afternoon. It was the name of the Vaporcrafter family Godfrey Baleaux had told me about. Coincidence? I hardly thought so.

I tucked the photo in my pocket as the floorboards squeaked. The intruder was on the move.

Just like that, my heart was pounding again, my palms sweating, my throat tight. My whole body tingled with adrenaline.

Creak, creak. The person was being cautious, moving slowly.

I shifted and peeked out from behind the couch just as I heard Evan yell, "Stop right there!"

The sound of the furniture polish spraying filled the air along with a lemony scent. I spotted the burglar barreling forward with the wooden box in his hands. Dressed all in black, he was a dark blur hurrying toward the stairs.

I stuck out my foot. The creep went sprawling, sending the box flying. It bounced, then skidded down the stairs. In a split second, Evan ran forward and jumped on the guy's back. The man easily pushed him off and scrambled to his feet. He was down the steps and out the door in a flash.

I helped Evan up. "Did you get a good look at his face?"

Evan shook his head. "It was mostly covered with a drawstring hood, and he was moving too fast."

It had been a man, though. Tall and trim but wiry and strong. Not the same person who had broken into the shop the night before.

I tried to catch my breath. My adrenaline rush was still strong, and my hands were shaking. I wished I could remember something about the man—his shoe type, if he was wearing jeans or trousers . . . something. But the whole scene had happened so fast I didn't get a good look at anything other than the box in his hands.

We looked down the steps. There were recipe cards everywhere. Evan started gathering them up.

I looked around at the devastation. "We need to call the police."

Evan's eyes widened; then he shook his head. "We can't, unless you want to go to jail. I know I don't."

Jail wasn't exactly on my list of must-visit places, either, but we needed to do something. The police had to be involved. I needed a new plan.

Unfortunately, the only plan I could come up with involved Nick Sawyer.

Chapter Eighteen

Dark clouds had brought an early nightfall as I walked Evan oh-so casually back to my car, handed him my keys, and grabbed my purse from where I'd tucked it under the front seat.

He was going to take my car to his place, and I'd meet him there later to pick it up and to see if he'd found a miracle cure in the box of cards he clung to.

I waved good-bye, fished around in my bag, and pulled out Nick Sawyer's business card. And then did something I never thought I'd do.

I called him.

My stomach fluttered when he answered, his voice rough-and-tumble and yet at the same time smooth and promising. I shook my head at even thinking such things. Smooth and promising? Promising of what?

Then my mind flashed to a fantasy of him kissing me.

Oh. That's what.

What *was* it with me? I cleared my throat—and my thoughts. "Hi, Nick, it's Darcy Merriweather. Could you maybe meet me behind Lotions and Potions? As soon as possible?"

"Is this about the pickpocket?"

"Not quite."

"The break-in last night?"

I swallowed hard. "Not really."

He was sounding impatient. "Then what?"

"The break-in today."

Silence stretched. A second. Two. "Did you call the police?"

"No."

"Why?"

"It's complicated."

"I'll be right there," he said, and hung up.

I didn't want to loiter behind Lotions and Potions, so I took my time walking the fence line in the alley, looking for anything shiny. Most of that time was spent along the fence area behind Spellbound Books. Crouching, I searched for any disturbed areas, and didn't find so much as a weed out of place.

I was in the midst of looking when Spellbound's back door opened. Harper came out, carrying a bag of trash. She spotted me, stopped, and stared.

I stared back.

"Well?" she said.

Slowly, I stood. "Well what?"

"Are you going to tell me what you're doing back here, examining the ground?"

Kicking at a pebble, I shrugged. "I might be looking for a watch."

She shook her head and swung the garbage bag into the closest Dumpster. "Don't you think I already did that?"

Of course she would have, Ms. Forensic Investigator wannabe. I should have thought of that before I got down on my hands and knees in the alley. Because, as meticulous as it was, I could easily imagine the microscopic germs I may have picked up.

Dusting off my khaki pants, I suddenly wished I could take a bath in hand sanitizer. "Just double-checking," I said. Then I glanced at my watch. "It's late—what are you still doing here?"

"Overtime. There's been an issue," she said in a soft voice.

"Issue?"

"Gayle is freaking out, not sure what to do."

"What kind of issue?"

"A health department issue. She thinks that Evan Sullivan may have contaminated the treats he brought to the village meeting the other night." She scratched at an imaginary hive on her neck. "Vince started getting hives yesterday on his arms and back. Then today, when I was talking to Ramona Todd, I noticed she had welts on her hands and wrists. Then, I ran into Mrs. Penny-whistle at lunchtime, and she had some on her neck. They were all at the meeting the other night. They all ate the little cakes. . . ."

"I ate the cakes, too, and feel just fine." I resisted the urge to scratch my arms. The power of suggestion was intense. "Besides, Evan said he's not contagious."

She shrugged. "Just telling you what I know. Gayle has spent the afternoon with her lawyer. She's terrified she's going to be sued. And Vince has been at the hospi-tal, trying to get some relief."

I dropped my voice, leaned my head close to hers. "Is Vince a Crafter?" I hadn't thought so—not with the way he went on about witchcraft and his willingness to talk about it with reporters.

"Mortal, but he's very interested in the subject. Trust me, he goes on and on."

"You know you don't mind."

She smiled shyly and didn't deny it.

"He's a Seeker, then?" I asked.

"I—"

"Harper?" Vince's voice carried.

We jumped apart, tried to look innocent.

Vince filled the back doorway, his hand on his heart. "Oh, thank God. I just got back and couldn't find you. Then I saw the door open, and I started having flash-backs to the other night." He wiped his forehead, ran his hand through his curly hair. His bright blue shirt brought out the color in his eyes—and the bright red blisters on his forearms. He saw me looking and quickly pulled his sleeves down.

"Just taking out the trash and ran into Darcy."

I wanted to kick her.

"In the alley?" he asked.

"Shortcut," I said quickly. "To, ah, the Pixie Cottage. I was going to check on Mrs. Pennywhistle."

As the lie escaped my lips, I realized the alley *was* a shortcut from the Pixie Cottage to the neighborhoods behind the green. Was that why the Pixie Cottage owner Harmony Atchison had been in the alley the day she saw Ramona and Alex fighting?

Vince said, "Mrs. P has been acting strangely lately. When I saw her today, I was pretty sure she was still wearing the same clothes from Thursday night."

The night Alex died.

I was really beginning to suspect that there was more going on with Mrs. P than her concern about the village's future. Was she declining mentally? Other than her appearance, it didn't seem so. Yesterday, she seemed lucid. Sad but lucid. Yet wearing the same clothes—and not doing her hair—for three days was anything but normal for her. "Do you know if she has family nearby? Maybe one of us should call them and let them know what's going on. Something just doesn't feel right."

"You can't help yourself, can you?" Harper teased, but there was a softness in her eyes.

"Help what?" I asked, not sure I wanted to know.

"Getting involved. Fixing. Nurturing."

I didn't think there was anything wrong with that. I shrugged. "I'd want someone to do the same for me."

Harper's eyes filled with understanding. I mothered everyone because my mother hadn't been around very long—and because I'd taken over as Harper's pseudo mom at a young age. It was all I knew.

Suddenly, I was remembering all the arguments Troy

and I'd had about starting a family. How badly I'd wanted one. How badly he didn't.

Then he left, found a new wife, and had a baby right off. The perfect little family.

What should have been *my* family.

I bit my cheek so I wouldn't focus on the swift, stabbing pain in my chest.

It was in the past. I had to leave it there.

"It's a nice thought, Darcy, but I don't think she has any family left," Vince said. "I remember her saying once that she was the end of the line."

A raindrop fell, then another. "That's strange. I could have sworn yesterday that she said she had a granddaughter."

Vince shrugged. "She was married once before, a long time ago. I suppose it's possible a long-lost relative surfaced."

Harper laughed. "We wouldn't know anything about that."

She was half right—we'd always known about Aunt Ve. We just never really knew her until now.

As they ducked for cover inside the bookstore, I told Harper I'd be home in an hour or so. I waved and hurried off, trying to dodge raindrops.

A suspicion was growing in the pit of my stomach. About Mrs. Pennywhistle. About Alex.

I was so focused on my thoughts, I didn't even see the man reaching out to grab me until his hand closed around my arm.

I screamed and threw a punch.

He evaded it.

"Darcy!" He shook me. "It's just me."

I stopped screaming and focused. It was Nick. And I felt every kind of fool for acting the way I did—especially since I was expecting him to meet me.

He let me go. "Sorry I scared you."

Again, I silently added, willing my heartbeat to return to normal.

"I tried calling your name," he continued, "but you obviously didn't hear me."

I leaned against the brick wall. Maybe my old boring life was just fine, thankyouverymuch.

His hair was damp, and rain speckled his light blue shirt. His eyes were kind, concerned. "You okay?"

I nodded, glanced around. "I'm surprised no one's come running."

"I'm not. You don't scream very loud. It comes out as a little squeak. *Eee, eee,*" he mimicked in a strained whisper.

My face went hot. "I don't believe you." I'd been *screaming.* Loudly.

Hadn't I?

Solemnly, he said, "It's true. I can help you work on that."

I thought of some of the ways how, and my face went from hot to burning.

He must have realized how suggestive he sounded, because he quickly added, "I give self-defense seminars every few months. It might be good for you and your sister to attend one. You already have a good right hook." He jabbed the air playfully. "We just need to work on the vocals."

I turned my face up to the sky in hopes the rain would cool it. The drops were falling harder now. Faster. I didn't mind in the least. I loved rain. Hated thunder and lightning, though, so when the first crack sounded, it prompted me to remember why I'd called Nick in the first place.

When I looked at him to explain, I found him staring at me. My mouth went dry at the hungry look in his eyes. A tingle started at the base of my spine and worked its way up, one vertebra at a time. The humid air seemed even thicker, the rain warmer.

His damp hair started to curl along the ends. I curved my hands into fists to keep from reaching out and catching a raindrop as it fell from his chin, to keep from touching him. My heart beat even faster now than when he'd scared me. A quick *whump-whump-whump*, a telltale sign of attraction. I liked Nick Sawyer. A lot. And by his look, he liked me, too.

His gaze had gone to my lips, and as he took a step closer to me, my heart screamed, "GET OUT OF HERE AS FAST AS YOU CAN," while my mind screamed, "OH YEAH! GO FOR IT!" And these weren't little *eee, eee* screams, either, but earsplitting cries, almost drowning each other out.

I closed my eyes, ready to fully ignore what my heart had to say. No doubt, I'd pay for that later, but at this moment, I didn't care one little whit.

Suddenly, the sky opened. Lightning cracked nearby and I yelped as the hair on my arms rose from the electricity. My eyes popped open.

Nick was standing close. So close. He smiled. "That— that was a scream."

Thunder roared like an oncoming freight train. I grabbed his hand and ran toward Lotions and Potions, to the door leading up to Alex's apartment. His eyes went wide as I took the key out of my pocket and inserted it into the lock. I pushed him inside and closed the door behind us.

The thunder trailed into a rumble that eventually faded away.

I fumbled for the light switch on the wall.

"Darcy?" Nick said in the darkness.

"Yes?" I could feel his body heat, pulsing in waves.

"Do I want to know why you have a key?"

"Probably not." I found the light, flipped it on. "But I need your help. I don't know where else to turn."

The desire was gone from his eyes, replaced now with wariness.

I wasn't sure if I was happy or sad about that.

A little of both, I realized.

Dripping wet, I took a step away from him and explained everything as we stood in the tiny vestibule. His eyes had stopped widening after I told him about Evan's rash, and his face had begun to turn stony when I explained about the wooden box. The color in his cheeks started to rise when I mentioned the intruder, and for a second there, I thought steam might actually come out of his ears.

Thunder crashed and I flinched.

"You know the thunder can't hurt you, right?" he said kind of snidely. "The bark and the bite?"

I could tell he was trying to control his temper, but my nerves were frazzled and I wasn't in the mood. "I'm aware. Thank you, though, for the lesson."

When I saw the hurt in his eyes, I sighed, and swallowed over a lump in my throat. I'd never told anyone what I was about to tell him. "When I was seven, I went with my mother to run errands. We were driving when a summer storm popped up. Lightning hit the car, and we went off the side of the road. I was safely buckled in, but my mother hadn't been wearing her seat belt because she was pregnant and the belt didn't fit right. . . ." I swallowed hard over the tightness in my throat. "That was the day Harper was born, and my mother died. I've hated storms ever since." I felt tears puddle in my eyes. "But I love the rain."

His thumb brushed away a tear. "Why?" he asked softly.

"Because my mother loved the rain. When I was little, we'd dance in it, twirling and laughing." I smiled through my tears. "When it rains, I remember that. I'm that little girl again, so filled with love for my mother, it's like she's still here. But storms, thunder and lightning?" I shook my head.

Gently, he pulled me into his arms and held me close.

I could feel his heart beating against mine as I rested my head on his shoulder. I'd forgotten how good a hug could feel. How good being held and comforted was.

"I'm sorry for what I said about the thunder." The vibration of his voice rumbled through my whole body.

"You didn't know."

"It doesn't excuse it."

I pulled away. "I think it does."

"Arguing with me again?" he asked, teasing.

"It seems to be a thing with us."

He nodded and stared at me for a long second.

Then, as if remembering where we were, he glanced up the stairs and motioned for us to go up. "Tell me about this intruder."

My steps squeaked and my drenched shoes squished as I climbed. I was getting awfully used to tiptoeing through strange houses at night. "Tall and lean. Definitely a man—broad shoulders, narrow-waisted. Strong, too, because he threw Evan off like he was a rag doll, but not overly muscular. He was wearing gloves, but he had big hands—the box seemed tiny in them, though I know it's not."

"Height?"

"I was on the floor, so it was hard to tell. Around your height, I'd say. Six feet or so." I turned and gave him a suspicious look. "Where were you an hour ago?"

"You really want to know?"

"Yes."

"At the pound, looking at dogs with Mimi. She's enamored with yours and wants one of her own."

We'd reached the landing. The door to the apartment was closed, just as Evan and I had left it. "Did you find one?"

"If Mimi had her way, we'd have ten. We've narrowed it down to four. We need to think about it, spend more time with each one."

"That's so sweet."

"Yeah, yeah," he said. "My ex-wife was always the dog person, not me. I'm kind of out of my element."

"Ex?" I asked without thinking.

He looked at me strangely.

"It's just, ah, I thought you were a widower."

His voice echoed slightly in the stairwell. "We were divorced for about a year before she died."

"Oh." I didn't know what to say to that. I wondered about his wife, what kind of person she was. If I would have liked her. I imagined I would. Mimi was wonderful, and his wife obviously had good taste in men, though they'd divorced. I wondered why. I didn't want to sound nosy, though, so I simply said, "Judging by the way Missy acts around you, and the way you tolerate it, you'll do just fine with a dog."

I opened the door of Alex's apartment and winced at the mess. Alex hadn't had many possessions, but the intruder had left no stone unturned.

"Whoa," Nick said as he looked inside.

We wandered in, taking in the destruction. He crouched next to a desk and looked through the mail scattered on the floor. "Bills, some overdue. And lots of letters from lawyer offices."

I glanced at the stack and noticed Marcus Debrowski's firm as the return address on at least three of the letters. I read one of them. It was a bill from Marcus. I frowned. He was representing her against class action suits? And also representing Sylar for her murder? That didn't make sense—it was a clear conflict of interest. Wasn't it?

Thunder rumbled and my nerves jumped. I wished the storm would hurry up and blow through already.

"I'm not surprised," I said, "if she was selling lotions that made people go bald and blister. That's a lawsuit waiting to happen." The kitchen area was open to the rest of the apartment and looked like this was where Alex made most of her products. There were vi-

als and herbs and bottles and tubes of every size—
most scattered on the floor. I noticed a vase of pink
chrysanthemums had been knocked over onto the
counter, and the water was seeping into a set of books.
I picked my way through the mess and set the vase
right, added water, and rearranged the flowers. I found
a roll of paper towels and sopped up the rest of the
spill. The books might be able to be saved if left to dry
out properly.

"We need to call the police," Nick said.

"I know," I agreed.

"I wish I had brought gloves," he said.

My nerves danced. I turned my back to him and
mouthed my spell. I blinked twice and cast it.

When I turned back around, I fully expected him to
have stumbled across a box of latex gloves. Alex had to
have some around with all the chemistry she had going
on in the apartment.

Nick was looking at my hands. "You, too. It's going to
be hard to explain why we were in here. And how we
have a key."

Anxious, I glanced around. No gloves. "Are you sure
you don't carry around a spare pair of gloves in your
pockets?" I hoped I didn't sound desperate.

He gave me an odd look. "I'm sure."

"Can you check?" I asked with a laugh, hoping I
sounded playful and not frantic.

Again the strange look, but he stuck his hands in his
pockets. "I've got nothing except my cell phone and wallet. Neither is going to help us right now."

My stomach churned. Why hadn't my wish worked?
Was Nick a Wishcrafter? But no, he was in the picture
with me that Starla had taken. Had his wish not been
pure of heart?

He watched me as though he was waiting for an answer. I blinked innocently. "We can lie."

Did Nick have a hidden agenda? Was there some reason he wanted our prints found in Alex's apartment? I couldn't think of a single *good* reason why he would.

And suddenly, just like that, I realized how much I didn't know about him. Other than my attraction to him. And that he seemed like a great dad. And that he was really, really handsome. And that he used to be a cop.

On second thought, that was a lot of information. All the marks of a good guy.

So why hadn't the wish been granted?

He thought about it a second. "Sounds good. I'll think of something to tell them. You should go."

"Are you sure?"

"Yes. The police will have questions better left to me to answer on my own."

"Thank you," I said softly. It was the outcome I'd hoped for, and I was beyond grateful he was taking care of it.

He nodded.

I was almost out the door downstairs, using the handrail so I wouldn't fall in my rush to get out of there, when a sharp pain had me snatching my hand off the wood. I stopped, examined the splinter, and held my breath as I pulled it out. Thankfully, no blood. How something so little could cause such pain was hard to understand.

I glanced at the oak handrail and saw the rough spot, a small crack. I wondered how long it had been like that, or if it was caused earlier today by the wooden box smashing into it. I supposed it didn't really matter and was about to get a move on when something caught my eye. I leaned down for a closer look at that rough spot of oak. Something had caught, snagged. I picked it up.

It was a bit of pink fuzz.

Chapter Nineteen

The storm lingered as I ran for home—it was closer than Evan's place. I'd call when I got there and let him know I'd pick up my car in the morning. And see if he'd found an antidote.

I really hoped so. I didn't know how much more he could take. If the rash on his face didn't stop spreading soon, he might be in very real danger.

Was it possible he *was* contagious?

I'd spent a lot of time with him recently, but I hadn't had so much as an itch. But if Ramona's, Mrs. P's, and Vince's rashes didn't start showing for a couple of days, maybe there was an incubation period.

If the murder and thefts in the village hadn't already driven the tourists away, I was sure any whisper of a medical outbreak would.

Nothing like a plague to create a ghost town.

I dashed along the walkway that cut across the green, hauling along faster than I had this morning with Starla, despite the fact that I was wearing black flats and not sneakers.

Flashes of lightning lit the sky every few minutes, followed by low growls of thunder. The storm was finally starting to ebb.

Soaked to the bone, I ran up the back steps and into

the mudroom and shook myself off much like Missy probably would have done.

The kitchen was empty as I tiptoed through into the laundry room. I found a clean towel and dried off the best I could. Dry clothes were next. I kept the towel tied around my waist and climbed the back staircase. I was halfway up when I heard voices.

"Don't get snippy with me," Aunt Ve said with a strong measure of patience. "The choices you've made are yours alone. You knew the consequences of changing your previous form to this one."

"Don't remind me," a woman's voice said. It was the voice I'd heard the other day, when Ve said she'd been talking to herself. The voice I suspected belonged to a familiar. I inched upward, hoping to get a glimpse of the conversation taking place.

"Do you have regrets?"

There was a brief silence. Then the woman said, "How could I?"

Ve said, "It isn't an easy task you've taken on, but I believe the benefits outweigh the negatives."

The woman's voice sounded thready and tired. "Just remind her to leave the damn door open. I'll deal with the other stuff."

Door? What door?

"You'll go easy on her?"

The back door opened and slammed closed. "Hello!" Harper shouted. She stepped into the kitchen, looking a bit like a drowned rat. "It's pouring buckets," she said unnecessarily, slinging her backpack onto the kitchen counter. "How'd things go with Mrs. P?"

I turned and pretended I'd been coming *down* the steps. "I actually didn't get a chance to see her."

Aunt Ve appeared at the top of the steps, Missy trailing behind her. Tilda lurked in the shadows of the upstairs hallway. I eyed both the pets. Was one of them a familiar?

"Girls!" Ve said brightly. "I didn't know you were home. Harper! You're soaking wet. Let me get you a towel." Her gaze drifted to me, to the towel already wrapped around my waist.

I didn't dare look her in the eye. I was trying hard to process the conversation I heard. Either someone was hiding out upstairs, or there was a familiar in the house. Was it Missy or Tilda?

Or . . . something else. A mouse? A bee? What? And why hadn't Ve told us about it? About *her*?

"Darcy, dear, are you feeling well?" Ve asked as she passed me on the stairs. "You're looking a trifle bit pale. Shea Carling called, concerned about you. Should I be worried?"

Shea. My eyes drifted closed. I'd forgotten all about the locket and what it signified.

"Darcy? I'm beginning to worry."

"You don't have any hives, do you, Darcy?" Harper asked. "There's been an outbreak, you know," she told Ve.

Ve's eyebrows dipped. "I hadn't heard. What's going on?"

"I'm going to change while Harper explains," I announced, heading up the stairs. Missy's tail wagged and I patted her head. Tilda gave me a sideways glance and flicked her tail.

"After you're done," Ve called after me, "there's something I want to show you."

"Me?" I asked, looking back at her.

"You," she said, amusement in her eyes.

I could only imagine. "I'll be down in a minute."

As I passed Ve's bedroom, I peeked in. No sign of any wayward critters.

Strange. Very strange.

I changed quickly and towel dried my hair. The rain had almost stopped, and the worst of the storm had finally moved off. I hurried downstairs. Maybe Ve was ready to share a little more about the Craft with us. I found her and Harper in the family room connected to the kitchen, the TV on and flickering. Ve had the remote in her hand and a smile on her face.

"I thought you might want to see this, so I recorded it," she said. "Since I'm fairly certain you may have had something to do with it."

Puzzled, I tipped my head as she hit a button on the remote. It was the six o'clock newscast.

A perky anchorwoman said, "Investigators believe the wombat most likely escaped from the nearby Franklin Park Zoo. They are in touch with zoo officials."

A camera panned across the Careys' front yard. I stared, wide-eyed, at the TV as the footage played. The recording focused on the brown blur racing across the yard and knocking into a bright white light.

"We apologize to our viewers for the quality of the video, provided to us by an amateur videographer hired to film the birthday event. As you can see," the anchor said, "an unidentified bystander was knocked to the ground by the wild wombat, a normally docile animal."

Harper clamped a hand over her mouth. I glanced at her—her eyes were leaking amused tears.

Aunt Ve, too, was trying hard not to laugh.

I had to admit, it was funny, watching the partygoers scatter like confetti. The poor wombat, though. He looked scared to death—except, I noticed, when he was with Jake, the wombat whisperer.

"For now," the anchor continued, "the wombat is in the care of the animal control. However, we have just learned that the Carey family has expressed a desire to keep the animal. Perhaps the birthday boy will get his wish after all."

Aunt Ve clicked off the TV set. "I presume you had something to do with this?" She gestured to the blank screen.

"He made a wish."

Harper said, "Where did the wombat come from,

though? When someone wishes for money, that money is taken from someone else, right? So, if someone wishes for a wombat, is that wombat taken from somewhere else?"

"I don't have the answer to that. As far as I know, magic produces the wished-for object. I've never heard otherwise." Ve's hand went to her neck, to swing her locket, then dropped. "I keep forgetting I'm not wearing it," she said with a laugh.

"I can pick it up for you tomorrow," I offered. "But there's something I want to talk to you about. Do you have a minute?"

"Plenty of them. Is something the matter?"

"Possibly."

"Let's make some tea; then we'll settle in for a chat."

"But how does the magic work?" Harper persisted as we moved into the kitchen.

Ve smiled patiently as she set the kettle to boil. "It is not for us to understand, my dear, but to accept."

Harper frowned. She was used to having all the answers. This was a topic, I was quite sure, that she would bring up again.

The peal of the doorbell had the three of us looking toward the front of the house. Missy barked and took off for the front door. I glanced at the microwave clock. It was almost eight thirty. A little late for a drop-in visitor.

"Now, who could that be?" Ve asked.

Curiosity got the better of Harper and me, and we followed her toward the front door.

Ve moved the curtain on the door aside and peered out. "Oh no," she murmured.

"Who is it?" Harper asked.

My pulse pounded. Was it the police? Had they come for me? What had Nick told them, exactly? I needed to warn Evan. . . .

Ve opened the door.

Archie, the macaw, flew inside and landed on the

newel post. He was gorgeous, with a bright red hood, white eye patches, and a bold blue and yellow tail.

He bowed.

Harper's eyes widened.

"Good evening, Archie," Ve said.

"Madame, good evening to you," he said, bowing again. His voice was a deep, rich baritone that sounded oddly like that of a British James Earl Jones.

Harper's mouth dropped open.

I smiled. First Pepe, now Archie?

He pivoted slightly to face me. "Darcy Ann Merriweather, you have been found in violation of Wishcraft Law forty-three, section B, and have been hereby summoned by the Elder for your sentencing. Go now, go alone, and do not delay."

He bowed again and Ve opened the door. He flew out into the cloudy night.

I looked at Ve. "What's law forty-three, section B?" I couldn't think of what I'd done that broke any of the laws. Wishcraft Laws, that is. Breaking and entering into Lotions and Potions didn't count, did it?

"We don't have time to find out. You must go now." She opened the front closet and pulled out a satin cloak. "You can wear mine until you get one of your own." She swung it around my back, lifted the hood, and tied the string under my chin.

"But where do I go?" My heart hammered.

"To the Elder's tree. In the woods."

I tried to remember the directions. Down the path, past a rock . . . I panicked. "I don't remember!"

"Start on the path"—she pressed a small flashlight into my hand—"and the Elder will guide you the rest of the way. You need to hurry." She pushed me toward the back door.

Harper squeaked as she followed. "Is no one the least bit surprised by the talking bird?"

"Not after meeting the talking mouse earlier today,"

I said. What law could I have broken? What would my sentencing entail?

"Oh!" Ve exclaimed. "You've met Pepe? Charming little fellow, isn't he?" She shook her head. "If only I'd married him instead of Godfrey."

"Feisty, I'd say. And Godfrey is charming, too." I slipped on my sneakers.

Ve rolled her eyes and muttered, "Rat-toad."

"Mouse?" Harper repeated. "Godfrey? Someone needs to tell me what's going on!"

Ve patted her cheek. "I'll tell you all about them, after Darcy leaves." To me she said, "We'll wait up, my dear. Hurry, now. You *do not* want to keep the Elder waiting."

With that, she shoved me out the back door into the night.

I hurried through the garden gate and toward the dark woods. I flicked on the flashlight.

Low clouds clung to the treetops and my pulse raced as I followed the path. The rain had brought forth the earthy scent of the forest, of pine, loam, and moss. It was ordinarily a smell I would have enjoyed, but tonight I was too nervous to take much notice.

I swallowed hard over the fear wedged in my throat. I jumped at every twig that snapped, every raindrop that fell on my hood from a branch above. My palms sweat; my nerves were shot.

The path was narrow, barely wide enough for one person. I wished I'd thought to bring Missy for company, then remembered Archie's edict: *Go alone.* As I walked along—it was impossible to run with it being so dark—I couldn't help but feel as though I was being watched. I looked around—and upward—for Archie's beaded eyes but didn't see anything—or anyone—out of place.

However, as I went deeper into the silence of the woods, my ears clearly picked up on other movement.

Something—or someone—was nearby. I could hear the footsteps disturbing the undergrowth, and a few times I thought I could hear breathing.

I paused and swept my flashlight past trees and shrubs, mossy rocks, and tall plants. I looked behind me but saw only my own footsteps on the damp trail.

My throat was thick, my mouth dry. My heart felt like it was going to beat right out of my chest, drop to the ground, and run back home.

I didn't blame it. I wanted to turn tail and run as fast as I could, back to Ve's kitchen, to the safety of the people who loved me.

But Archie's voice echoed in my head along with Ve's warning about keeping the Elder waiting.

This was my new life. I had to live it.

Taking a deep breath, I pressed on. When I came to a split in the path, marked by a large rock that looked like a piece of cake, I hesitated. Which way to go? I looked left, then right.

Down the path to the right, I could see a faint yellow glow. To the left, I saw nothing but tree branches overhanging the path, looking like spindly arms ready to reach out and grab me.

I went right.

Soon, I found myself at the edge of a circular clearing. In its center, there was a glowing tree, not too tall, not too short. With its weeping branches, the shape reminded me of a mushroom. The warm glow of the tree illuminated the field. It was entirely filled with wildflowers, except for a narrow path leading to a door cut into the tree.

"Come closer, Darcy."

It was a woman's voice, cool, smooth, and refined. Classy. It was coming from within the tree and was amplified, as though she was using some sort of microphone. Her tone wasn't as intimidating as I'd feared, but not exactly friendly, and it was a much younger voice than I'd expected. Nothing elderly about it. Thirties, forties, maybe early fifties at the oldest. It sounded vaguely familiar, though I couldn't quite place it. I was sure, though, that I'd heard it before.

As I took a few tentative steps forward, I tried to recall all the women I'd spoken with recently. Just today, I'd talked with so many. Harmony at the Pixie Cottage, Ramona Todd, Starla, Shea Carling, Jeannette Dorsey at the gift shop. I was suddenly reminded of the line from *The Wizard of Oz*: "Pay no attention to that man behind the curtain."

Who was inside that tree?

"Sit down," the voice said.

A chair made from a tree stump materialized behind me, and I sat. I must really be getting used to this lifestyle if a chair magically appearing didn't faze me at all.

"Do you know why you've been called here?" she asked.

"No," I answered, glad my voice wasn't shaking as badly as my hands.

"You're in violation of Wishcraft Law number forty-three, section B. No Wishcrafter shall prompt, suggest, hint, evoke, prod, or elicit a wish. It is akin to Wishcrafter entrapment, and you have hereby been found guilty."

"B-but," I stammered, trying to think of when I'd done such a thing. Then I remembered. "Evan?" How did she even know?

"Correct."

"Does that count, even when he's a Wishcrafter himself?"

"Even if. It does not matter that the wish was not fulfilled, only that you violated the law in the first place. Now for your sentencing."

I gulped.

"Consider this a warning, Darcy. Your only warning. I have let you off easy this time, due to the novelty of your Craft. I suggest you study the Wishcrafter canon, for the next time you break a law, the consequences shall be more severe. You may go."

I stood and the chair vaporized into glitter that fell slowly to the ground and instantly became colorful wildflowers. Okay, that was impressive. "Elder?"

"Yes?"

"May I ask you a question?"

"Yes."

"You don't sound old."

"That," she said, "is not a question."

"How old are you?" I asked.

"That," she said, "is none of your business. I am old enough."

"But the name 'Elder' makes it seem like you're . . . old."

There was a hint of amusement in her tone when she answered. "It is an inherited title, an honor passed down through centuries from those who came before me."

I had so many questions, and I didn't know if I'd get the chance to ask them again. One, especially, was foremost in my thoughts. "Elder?"

She sighed. "Yes?"

"Are there any Vaporcrafters living in the village?"

"Yes," she answered.

"Who?" I asked.

"It is not for me to say. Good night, Darcy."

"But wait!" I had so many questions.

"What?"

"How long have you been Elder? What's your real name? Do I know you? I mean, have we met? Do you live in the village?" I felt a little like Harper, asking all these questions.

"We are finished here, Darcy. You may go now."

The tree went dark.

Chapter Twenty

Sunlight streamed in my window early the next morning. Or at least I thought it was early, but when I rubbed the sleep from my eyes and squinted at the alarm clock, I saw it was past nine already.

I sat up and stretched. Missy had abandoned me at some point. Listening carefully, I heard voices downstairs.

Looking at the perfectly made left side of my bed, I frowned in dismay. An ache started building in my chest. I squeezed my eyes shut and told myself I couldn't keep letting this happen. I was single now. I had to adjust at some point, right?

I was sure I would, but until then, I leaned over and pounded the perfectly plumped pillow a few times, mussed the covers.

Better.

I fumbled for my glasses, brushed my teeth, and pulled my hair into a sloppy bun. I slipped on my robe. I dreaded talking to Aunt Ve about Sylar, the locket, and Alex's watch. The last thing I wanted to do was hurt my aunt, but this was information she should know—before someone else figured it out.

As I headed downstairs, I noticed my muscles had mutinied overnight and ached something fierce from running yesterday morning. I headed straight for the ibuprofen bottle in the cupboard next to the sink and nearly dropped it when I heard Harper say, "But what if I want to marry him?"

My muscles protested as I dashed into the family room. Ve and Harper sat on the sofa, their legs tucked beneath them, Missy curled between the two. "Marry who?" I gasped.

"Vince," Aunt Ve said, then took a sip from her coffee. As if her pronouncement were no big deal.

I stared.

"Hypothetically," Harper added, stressing the word.

"I think I just had a heart attack." I sank into an armchair and popped two ibuprofen in my mouth and swallowed them dry.

An insulated coffee carafe sat on a silver tray on the table along with an empty mug. Ve filled it, added a little cream and sugar, and passed it my way.

"Thank you." I took it like a lifeline and breathed in the steam. My head felt fuzzy—probably from sleeping in so late.

Or from all the stress.

Or from the murder. Or thefts. Or outbreak.

I eyed the ibuprofen bottle and wondered how many I could take in a day without overdosing. "Why are you two discussing marrying Vince. Even *hypothetically*?"

Ve said, "Harper was telling me about Vince's interest in the Craft and asking what would happen if she married him. Would he become a Wishcrafter."

I recalled Aunt Ve had mentioned something before, about being able to become a Crafter through marriage. "Would he?"

"Of sorts."

"How?" I asked, "When we're not allowed to tell mortals we're Crafters?"

Tilda hopped up on the arm of my chair and swooshed her tail in my face. I plucked a leaf out of her hair and noticed her paws were a bit muddy—she must have been romping around outside this morning.

As I went in search of the towel we kept by the back door for wiping off paws, Ve said loudly, "If a Wishcrafter chooses to marry a mortal and *tells* him of her power, the Crafter forfeits the use of her powers. However, the person she marries is then adopted into the Craft family and becomes a Halfcrafter, which basically means he's half mortal, half Crafter. The new spouse is then told about the Craft legacy and treated as if he was born into the family. But he will not have any powers. Just knowledge."

The rag by the back door was already damp and muddy—most likely from Missy's morning walk—so I grabbed a wad of paper towels from the kitchen and dampened them. By the time I made it back to the chair, Tilda was gone.

There was no way I was chasing after her, so I sat down to await her return.

"What if the Halfcrafter tells a mortal what he learned?"

Ve's eyes darkened. "There are dire consequences, of which the Halfcrafter is informed."

"What kind of consequences?" Harper asked.

I imagined she was thinking about Vince and his propensity to share his witchcraft knowledge with anyone interested, including reporters.

Harper laughed. "Do you turn them into toads or something?"

Ve lifted an eyebrow, her expression dead serious. "Frogs usually."

She *was* serious.

A tension-filled minute passed.

"So," Harper said after clearing her throat, "if I marry Vince, I'd lose my powers but remain a Wishcrafter?"

"Yes," Ve said, petting Missy's head. "So you can pass

the legacy on to your children, but you will no longer be able to grant wishes yourself."

"But Vince would then become a Halfcrafter?" Harper asked, her tone dubious. "Why bother when I no longer have powers?"

"It is necessary for the legacy to continue. For if you and Vince were to have kids, those children will be full-fledged Wishcrafters, powers intact."

"Can we stop talking about Harper getting married and having kids? It's freaking me out." I refilled my coffee mug.

Harper said, "He is cute."

"So is Missy," I pointed out.

She lifted her head at the sound of her name, then put it back down.

"He does manage the bookstore, which is currently my favorite place on earth." Her eyes glazed over. "All those books. If I married him, I could probably work there the rest of my life. Nothing would make me happier."

"What about love?" Ve asked.

"Oh," Harper said solemnly, "I love books."

Aunt Ve laughed. It was good seeing her happy, even if only for a few moments.

I'd been thinking about what Aunt Ve said. "So, technically, our father was a Wishcrafter, too?"

Ve said, "A Halfcrafter—half mortal, half Wishcrafter. He chose not to share your history with you two, however. Which was fully within his rights. It is up to the parents to decide whether they want to raise their children as Crafters or mortals. You both were raised as mortals. I do fully believe, had your mother not died so young, that she would have shared your gift with you when you were older and could understand it better."

"Why do you think Dad didn't tell us?" Harper asked.

I thought of our father, of how he threw himself into his work after Mom died. "My guess is he couldn't cope with anything that reminded him of Mom." Not Crafting. Not us. Not really. He provided for us, fed us, clothed us. But he was never really there for us. A part of him died the day my mother did. Harper and I had really lost both parents that day.

"But Dad had no actual powers, right?" Harper said.

"Right," Ve affirmed.

"So if you're a Seeker looking to become a Crafter," Harper said, "you're in for a huge disappointment if you marry a witch?"

"If you're only marrying because of the Craft. Not if you're marrying out of love. This way, Seekers are discouraged from seeking only their own agendas," Ve said, her hand going to her neck, searching for her locket. She dropped it with a laugh, then said, "Darcy, you never did tell me your important news last night before you were called to see the Elder."

I hadn't. I'd been too swept up on what happened with my trip into the woods.

"What was it you wanted to talk to me about?" Ve asked.

I glanced between her and Harper, not sure how to break the news.

"Darcy?" Ve asked. "What is it?"

"Spit it out," Harper urged, leaning forward. "Is this about Alex's murder? Do you know who killed her?"

Shaking my head, I took a deep breath and decided there was no easy way to say what I needed to. "No, but I do think I know who the secret boyfriend was who gave her the fancy watch."

Harper's eyes went wide. "Who?"

"Sylar." I gulped and looked at Aunt Ve, awaiting her reaction. She'd been through so much lately—how much more could she take without breaking down completely?

Ve set her cup on the table, took a deep breath, and said, "I'm surprised it took this long to come out. Now tell me, Darcy, how many people know?"

                           *   *   *

"She already knew!" I said to Starla as we jogged, very slowly, around the green. Mrs. P, with her speed-walking, could have easily lapped us.

"No way," Starla huffed, her eyes wide and unbelieving.

I couldn't wrap my brain around why Aunt Ve hadn't told Harper and me. "Apparently, he wanted Alex to give the watch back, so Alex struck a bargain with him."

"What kind of bargain?"

"Alex was looking for some specific genealogical information, and Sylar, as the village grand hoo-ha, had easy access to the records database."

"Hoo-ha?" Starla asked.

I smiled. "It's Harper's nickname for anyone in charge."

She laughed, then said, "What kind of records?"

"Ve didn't know. But Sylar supposedly delivered his goods the day before Alex died. And she was supposed to turn over the watch as soon as she verified the information. Evidently, everything was verified, because she asked to see him after the village meeting to turn the watch over. According to Aunt Ve, Sylar insists the watch was already gone when he found Alex's body."

"How long ago did they date?"

"Over a year ago."

"And he just now asked for the watch back?" Starla asked.

"He's in debt up to his eyeballs—apparently the downturn in the economy has hit him hard. He overextended himself financially trying to help various eyesight charities, funding trips to foreign countries and buying glasses for those in need. Also, Ve admitted he enjoys the dog track a little too much. The value of that watch and the fact that he's Alex's ex makes his motive for murder that much stronger, doesn't it?"

Starla snorted. "I have a few exes I'd like to kill."

I thought of Troy. As much as he'd hurt me, I couldn't imagine killing him. Maiming, maybe.

"No wonder Ve wanted to protect him," she said. "That's pretty damaging."

It was. "I wonder why Sylar and Alex kept their relationship a secret in the first place."

"Ve didn't say?"

"No."

"I can only speculate that it's because Sylar is a community leader, and Alex wasn't exactly well liked. Or maybe it was their age difference. He was much older than her. Maybe she didn't want to be labeled a gold digger. Maybe he didn't want to be labeled a cradle robber."

I tried picturing the two together. Short, roly-poly Sylar with tall, striking Alex. I couldn't see them as a couple.

We rounded the bend, and I spotted Nick trotting ahead. Relief filled me as he turned right and headed down another path. "How much do you know about Nick?" I asked.

"Other than he's gorgeous?"

"Other than."

"Well, let's see. Used to be a state trooper; now does freelance security work around the city. He likes woodworking and sells his goods at the village shops. Loves Mimi to death. Thirty-five. Divorced about a year before his ex died."

"How did she die?"

"Cancer. One day she had a stomachache. Went to get it checked out. Two months later, she was gone. Pancreatic cancer that was too widespread to treat—no warning, really."

"How do you know all this?"

"Mimi. She's a talker."

My heart broke for her. I knew what it was like to lose a mom at such a young age.

"And then Mimi and Nick moved here?"

"A couple of years ago."

"Why?" I asked.

Starla shrugged. "I don't know."

"Is there any chance Nick's a Crafter?"

"Not that I know of, but Crafters are very secretive unless they know for certain, one hundred percent, that you're a Crafter, too. Even then, some don't discuss it at all."

I was coming to learn that.

"For example, even though Evan and I knew Ve was a Wishcrafter, we weren't sure you and Harper were, because we didn't know who your mother was. You could have been nieces from one of her husbands' sides of the family. It wasn't until that picture...."

"You took it on purpose, didn't you?"

She wiggled her eyebrows. "Guilty."

"Sneaky."

"I wanted to be sure. It was the easiest way. Why all the questions about Nick?"

I explained about his wish and how it hadn't come true.

"That's very strange," she said, slowing to a walk. "I can only figure that he wasn't pure of heart in his wish."

"But that makes no sense."

"No, it doesn't."

I shook my head. "Maybe I need to stop thinking about it so much." Or *him* so much, too.

"No, we need to figure this out."

I laughed. "No, what we need to figure out is who killed Alex. Because Aunt Ve is positive it wasn't Sylar, and now, more than ever, she needs the proof. Because once the public finds out the watch came from him, they're going to convict him without a jury."

"There certainly isn't a shortage of suspects."

"True. Did you know that Marcus Debrowski was representing Alex against her lawsuits?"

"Isn't he Sylar's lawyer?"

I nodded.

"Isn't that a conflict of interest or something?"

"I'd think so. What do you know about Marcus?"

"Not much, Darcy. He's a Lawcrafter, one of the best, especially for being so young. He's only twenty-seven. A complete workaholic—works seven days a week, all hours."

Billable hours, I was sure. "Married?" I hoped not, with the way he looked at Harper and how he'd asked her to coffee.

"No. And no girlfriend that I know of. People in the village think highly of him. Have you talked to Ve about all this?"

"I haven't had the time. Things have been . . . busy." She didn't need to know about my late-night romp through the woods. I glanced at the Bewitching Boutique across the green. I wanted to stop in and see Pepe. He'd been in the village a long time, and he might know something Godfrey didn't about the Vaporcrafter family. He might be able to confirm my hunches. . . .

"For me, too. The dance is coming up fast. Will you help me with the prep?" She blinked long lashes.

"If I say yes, I don't have to attend, do I?"

"If you don't want to."

"Then I'll definitely help with the setup."

"Good!" She looked at her watch. "I've got to get going. I'm covering for Evan at the bakery today."

"Did he have any luck with his face?"

"Not so far. Darcy, he looks worse than ever."

Chapter Twenty-one

Technically, the Bewitching Boutique wasn't yet open for business, but I could see lights on in the back of the shop. I knocked loudly on the glass door, and after a second, I saw Godfrey's head pop into the doorway of the back room.

When he spotted me, he smiled and toddled forward to open the door.

"You've come to shop," he said, eyeing my *Tom and Jerry* T-shirt with amused disdain.

"Not today."

"For shame." He *tsk*ed.

"I'll have you know, vintage tees are quite the hot trend these days."

He rubbed the fabric of my sleeve between two fingers, made a face like a skunk had just wandered by, and said, "Not in my world."

He might just cry if I told him I'd bought the shirt at a garage sale. "I actually came in to see Pepe. Is he around?"

"In the back. Come along."

I followed him into the back room, a workshop with colorful fabrics, scissors, dress forms, and a small corner office.

"Pepe, you have company," Godfrey said loudly.

A small door in the baseboard opened, and Pepe

came out wearing a tiny towel around his waist. "You do not fool me," he said, his fogged glasses slowly clearing. "We never have visitors this ear— Ay-eee!" he squealed. "Pardon!" Pivoting, he hurried back in his hole.

Godfrey's smile stretched across his whole face.

I said, "How do you explain the little doors to the mortals?"

"Ambience, my friend." He winked. "Ambience."

A second later, Pepe reappeared, dressed in a tiny pin-striped suit. He gave a little bow. "How may I be of service, *ma chère*?" He eyed me much the way Godfrey had. "Something a little more . . . formal perhaps?"

He was adorable. I wanted to take him home. Then I remembered Tilda's claws. The two might not get along. "I was hoping you could help me identify someone."

He climbed up the back of a chair, scurried across the table, and sat, his little legs dangling. "Please, *ma chère*." With a nod of his head, he motioned to the chair.

I sat. "You've been in the village a long time."

"Indeed," he said with a heavy sigh.

"I assume you know everyone who's lived here."

"A good assumption."

"There was a family who lived here decades ago. Clemson. They were Vaporcrafters."

Pepe nodded. "I remember the cloak. One of my finest pieces," he said fondly. "The family, they moved some time ago. Husband, wife, small daughter."

"Virginia?" I asked.

"Yes. Nice girl despite that she enjoyed pulling my tail. The husband . . ." He turned up his nose. "I could do without. He was a crankypuss Vaporcraftor, and not at all inclined to accept the Craft into his life—in fact he downright turned his nose up at it. It was the wife who placed the order for the cloak," Pepe said.

"Not so." Godfrey clapped his hands twice. The thick leather-bound book appeared. "No, no, it says right here it was Isaiah Clemson." He tapped the page.

Indignantly, Pepe said, "Your book is wrong." To me, he added, "My memory is impeccable. In those days the women, they ordered everything using their husband's name. It was as if they did not have identities of their own."

Godfrey huffed and threw the book into the air. It vanished. "You're still wondering about the Vaporcrafters, Miss Darcy?"

"I think I know who it is," I said, "but I wanted to see if Pepe could confirm it. He's as close to a village historian as I've met. Do you recall Mr. Clemson's wife's name?"

He twirled his whiskers. "Eugenia." With a flirtatious smile, he grinned. "As I mentioned, my memory, it is impeccable."

"Braggart," Godfrey mumbled.

"Buffoon," Pepe retorted.

They amused me to no end. "What happened to them? When did they move?"

Pepe looked deep in thought. "Nineteen sixty."

I played my hunch. "Did Mrs. Clemson ever come back?"

Godfrey shook his head. "Not that I'm aware."

Pepe grinned slyly. "She did."

"About thirty years later?"

"Oui."

"With a new name?"

"You're very astute, *ma chère*."

Godfrey's neck swiveled between the two of us. "What, perchance, am I missing?"

"The hair does not lie," I said to Godfrey.

"If only you were a mouse," Pepe said wistfully.

I smiled at him. "Do you recall what became of her daughter?"

"I do not know, for the woman returned only with her new husband."

"Will someone please tell me what's going on?" Godfrey asked, his cheeks turning red.

"Where are you going with this, *ma chère*?" Pepe asked, standing.

"Think about that hair. It's hereditary, is it not?"

Pepe's eyes widened. "Are you sure?"

"I'm having palpitations," Godfrey said in a singsong voice. "What will it take to get an answer? Must I have a coronary and die on the spot?"

"I'm fairly certain," I answered Pepe, then stood. I took hold of Godfrey's hand. "Please don't have a heart attack. I'm not up to speed on CPR, and I'm not at all sure Pepe would revive you."

Pepe chuckled. "I think he would rather stay dead than get mouth-to-mouth resuscitation from *moi*."

Godfrey shuddered. "Then please, my friend, tell me what you're talking about."

I could hardly believe I hadn't seen the resemblance before. "The Vaporcrafter is Mrs. Pennywhistle," I said. "And if I'm right, her granddaughter was Alexandra Shively."

I rushed home and once again found the house empty, except for Tilda. She was lurking in the shadows, trying her best to look disinterested.

I went straight to the office, found the number for the Pixie Cottage, and dialed.

"Pixie Cottage, this is Harmony. How may I help you?"

There was hope in her voice I hated to dash. "Hi, Harmony, it's Darcy Merriweather. Is Mrs. Pennywhistle around?" I wanted to make sure she was home before I trekked over there. I needed to make sure she was all right. Now that I knew for certain Alex had been her granddaughter, it explained why Mrs. P had been so devastated lately. She might be in need of a friend.

"Darcy, no. She went out about ten minutes ago. I'm not sure where, but she sure did look somber. Did you want to leave a message?"

"No, thank you. I'll check back later."

I hung up and stared at the computer screen. If Mrs. P was Alex's grandmother, and she was the one who claimed Alex's body from the medical examiner's office . . . she'd be planning a funeral of some sort, wouldn't she?

Glancing around, I looked for a phone book, but didn't see one in all the clutter. One day soon I was going to have to get cleaning in here. The office needed some good organizing. I pulled up a search engine on the computer and looked for local funeral homes. There were several in the area. I picked up the phone and started dialing.

I hit pay dirt on the fourth one. "Hello," I said. "I'm calling to find out the time of Alexandra Shively's viewing."

"I'm sorry," a monotone man said, "but that visitation is closed to the public."

"Oh, but Mrs. Pennywhistle told me to call and get the information," I lied. "She said there would be no problem. I suppose I'll try to get in touch with her again. In her time of sorrow." I could lay it on thick when I wanted.

"I suppose if Mrs. Pennywhistle requested you call . . ." His voice trailed off, and I could almost hear the inner debate he was having with himself. "The viewing is set for today at three p.m. with interment immediately following."

I thanked him and hung up, not exactly sure what to do with the information now that I had it.

Tilda slunk into the room, took the long way around the desk, and then hopped into my lap and began kneading my thighs. I scratched her ears, her chin, and just under her neck. The purrs began almost instantly.

I looked at her, and she looked at me, her blue eyes half-closed. "Can you talk?" I asked her. "And if so, why aren't you talking to me?"

Her eyes drifted closed and she curled up in a small furry ball. I petted her head, laughing at myself. Was I going to talk to every animal I came across now?

I had to decide what to do about Alex's viewing. My heart was aching for Mrs. P, but I was also curious to know why she hadn't told anyone Alex was her granddaughter.

And what had caused Mrs. P to storm out of the bookstore the other night, and why had she broken into Lotions and Potions? What was she looking for?

Her break-in also reminded me that someone else had broken into Alex's apartment. The man who'd tried to steal her recipe box. Who was he?

Thinking about that break-in reminded me, once again, of Nick Sawyer and his unfulfilled wish. Starla had filled in a lot of blanks, but hadn't been able to answer my biggest question. Why hadn't I been able to grant his wish?

As I was sitting there, my wrist started to itch. Absently, I scratched it. What had brought Nick and Mimi to the village? Did they have family here?

I scratched some more, and did a quick search on Nick Sawyer online. I had to narrow it down to Nick Sawyer, state trooper, to find any information at all. The link I clicked led me to a story of him at his retirement party. He'd retired young, after having been shot several times during a traffic stop gone wrong. My breath caught at the thought of Nick being wounded. Another story linked him to an obituary for his ex-wife.

It confirmed everything Starla had told me. And gave me one more piece of information: Melina Sawyer had originally been raised in Salem, Massachusetts. Was she from the village? Did Mimi have family here? Was that why Nick moved here?

Maybe Aunt Ve would know. If not, maybe Pepe.

I scratched at my arm again, disturbing Tilda. She gave me a dirty look and hopped down and ran out the door.

"You're welcome," I called after her.

Then I looked down and let out a yelp when I finally noticed what I'd been scratching. Huge welts had appeared on my hands, my wrists.

Chapter Twenty-two

Was I contagious?

It was a thought I didn't even want to think.

What was I going to do?

Besides stop scratching. Because I'd practically worn my skin raw. I'd never been so itchy in my life. Was Evan's whole face like this?

I dashed into the kitchen in search of something to soothe it. Oatmeal, milk. Anything. I settled for a damp rag pressed against my skin. It barely helped. Great.

I needed calamine. Or aloe. Or something.

I was in the mudroom when the front doorbell ding-donged. Hopping back out of my shoes, I wished I had on long sleeves. One look at my hands, and people were going to run for the hills. Very bad for business.

Then I remembered that we weren't even open today. Sundays were our only day off.

So who was at the door?

A brief flutter of panic spun through me. What if it was Archie, the macaw, again? Had I done anything to break the Wishcraft Laws today? I nibbled my lip and hurried through the kitchen, down the hallway. I hadn't thought so. But I hadn't thought so yesterday, either.

Someone stood on the front porch, his back to me as I peeped through the glass. I opened the door a crack and was shocked when Evan turned around.

His face was absolutely, perfectly clear. Not so much as a mole marred his perfect skin.

"Evan! Your face . . .".

He beamed. The bright smile stretched wide, pushing the limits of his cheeks.

"What happened? You found the cure, obviously. You look amazing!"

"I didn't find the cure."

"Who did?"

He pulled me out onto the porch and gestured to the house next door. Archie was singing Right Said Fred's "I'm Too Sexy" as Dennis Goodwin sashayed up the walkway, playing it up for the tourists lingering on the sidewalk. "I do my little turn on the catwalk," crooned Archie as Dennis implemented a spin.

It was nice to see Dennis with a little charm and personality. Up till now I'd thought him a dried-up clod.

The tourists clapped. Dennis rushed inside the house as Archie catcalled after him.

Evan shook his head. "He's so dramatic."

"Dennis?"

"No, Archie. He was once an actor at London's Adelphi Theatre. Did you know?"

"I didn't even know he was a familiar until last night." When I'd been summoned to see the Elder. I left that part out. No need to get into *that*.

"I'm surprised he didn't tell you. It's his favorite topic."

"The theater?"

"Himself. I'm sure you'll be hearing more from him now that you know his secret. Loves the sound of his own voice."

"He chose the right form, then."

Evan nodded. "Rumor is he's had a wild crush on Dennis for years now. Dennis humors him because he's such a good companion to Mr. Goodwin. Terry."

And to think this village looked so sedate, calm, and peaceful the first time I saw it. If only the tourists knew what lurked beneath the surface. "I haven't met him yet."

"He's a hermit, but he does come out every once in a while. *Interesting* guy."

"Why do people keep calling him that?"

"No reason." His lip twitched.

Between him and Ve, I was extremely curious about my neighbor.

Archie launched into a Lady Gaga song. Evan winced. "I just wish Archie would shut up once in a while. Sometimes, when the wind is blowing right, I can hear him all the way over at the bakery."

My adrenaline shot at the word "wish"; then I breathed a sigh of relief. I didn't have to worry about granting wishes around Evan.

"But enough about that," Evan said. His eyes lit with pure happiness. "I answered the door twenty minutes ago and found Dennis standing on the stoop."

The tourists dispersed, and we went inside. "I'm a little surprised."

"I was, too, but apparently he'd had an attack of the guilts. He even apologized for how long it took him to come to his senses and track me down. Hated to think I'd been suffering."

Dennis had a conscience. Who knew? Was it possible what I'd said to him sank in? Dare I hope he was having second thoughts about his family, too?

I poured us some iced tea. Evan grabbed my hand, and I almost dropped the pitcher. "What's this?" He was looking at my welts.

"Hives, best I can tell."

"From what?"

I shrugged. "You?"

"What?"

"Rumor is you're contagious. Or were."

Shaking his head, he said, "No way. I wasn't contagious at all."

"Well, there's been an outbreak in the village. I have welts; so do Ramona, Mrs. P, and even Vince. Gayle thinks you contaminated the cakes at the village meeting." I lowered my voice. "She's worried about being sued."

"Not possible. I'm always careful when baking, and use gloves. The only way to have a reaction is to have used Alex's lotion."

I held up my hands. "I didn't use her lotion. I'm not sure about Mrs. P or Ramona, but Vince said he hardly knew Alex, so I doubt he used any. Unless . . ."

"What?" he asked.

"Is it possible you had some traces of the lotion on your hands when you made the cakes for the meeting?"

It was easy to blame Alex's lotion, since it had definitely been the cause of Evan's rash. She obviously had no clue what she was doing when it came to creating her own formulas. The problem seemed to be that she had been attempting the wrong Craft.

Why had she been trying to do a Potioncrafter's job? Had she not known she was a Vaporcrafter? I thought about her remark at the bookshop the night of the village meeting.

It means that you'll finally have to accept that I'm one of you. I've finally learned the truth of my past.

She'd been a Seeker—until she finally learned the truth. And suddenly I had an idea of why Mrs. P had rushed out of the shop that night. My guess was she'd just learned the truth of her relationship to Alex as well—it would explain so much. She hadn't known she had a granddaughter until Alex sprang it on her.

I filled Evan in on what I'd found out about Mrs. P and how I thought it connected to Alex. "Crafting is hereditary—if Mrs. P is a Crafter, it was in Alex's genes, too."

"It doesn't make sense," he said. "If Alex knew she was a Vaporcrafter, why was she trying to cast spells and make potions? And why was she telling everyone she was orphaned when she had a grandmother?"

"I don't know. My guess is that she knew she was a Crafter but didn't know what kind. If her mother died young, as she's been telling everyone, maybe Alex hadn't learned all she needed to pursue the Craft. I think we need to talk to Mrs. P. She might have some of the answers we're looking for." I told him about the closed visitation later today, and how I had decided I wanted to go. He agreed to come with me. I also thought Mimi might want to attend. I'd have to check with Nick to make sure it was okay.

Evan's eyes grew misty. "I know Alex wasn't very likable—she was too hard, and too intense, for most people to see past—but I can't imagine why anyone would actually harm her."

"The guy whose hair fell out might disagree. He was plenty mad."

Evan fussed with his glass, sliding it back and forth on the countertop. "Griffin? Harmless. Full of bluster, looking for a photo op to boost his sales at the car dealership."

"His hair *did* fall out."

"I wouldn't be surprised if it was a publicity stunt. He probably saw that Alexandra had died, and decided to take advantage. Used some Nair or something on himself."

I looked at him carefully. "You know what Nair is?"

"We won't get into that," he said with a grin. "Griffin is an opportunist."

The way Evan framed it, I could picture it. Especially since Griffin had been on just about every newscast I'd seen since Alex died. "Did he know Alex before she died?"

"They'd dated briefly, back when Alexandra was new in the village, and remained friendly after the breakup. Alex isn't really his type."

Sylar, Griffin. Who else? A sudden thought occurred — and I immediately wished it hadn't.

Had she dated Nick? Suddenly queasy, I used the condensation from my glass to cool the hives on my arms. "If they were friends, would he use her death like that? Just for a little PR?"

"You haven't met Griffin, have you?"

I shook my head.

"He'd do just about anything for PR, including going bald."

"Do you think he could have been the one who broke into Alex's place yesterday?" It had been a man — a tall man. Griffin fit the bill. Right now, he was the only one who fit the bill. . . .

Evan thought about that for a second. "It's possible, I guess."

"Well, if he really did go bald from one of Alex's lotions, he may have been looking for the cure, the same way you were looking for yours."

"Do you think we should break into his place and see if he has any Nair lying around? I'm game if you are."

"I think we're done with our breaking and entering."

Evan pouted, then looked at the clock. "I need to check in with the bakery, show off my new face."

I walked him to the front door.

"You should see if you can catch Dennis before he leaves," he said. "He can cure your hands."

He hopped off the porch and waved good-bye. I glanced next door, then down at my hands.

Even if Dennis could cure me, I had to wonder — if Evan wasn't contagious — what had caused the rash in the first place.

*   *   *

I watched Tilda prowl around the backyard as I waited for Dennis to come out of his father's house, and hoped it didn't appear obvious that I was waiting for him.

It had been an hour since Evan had left, and there was still no sign of Harper, Aunt Ve, or Missy. I'd tried calling and texting, but neither had answered.

It was enough to make me start worrying.

Archie's cage was just across from me, and we'd been playing a game of name that movie. He'd recite a line, and I had five seconds to come up with a title. So far I was winning twenty-two to two.

In my couch-potato days, I'd watched a lot of movies. Mostly alone, since Troy was more interested in playing poker with his friends or hanging out at the local pub, and even when he was home, he was obsessed with shoot-'em-up video games. Right this second, I was having trouble remembering how we'd fallen in love in the first place.

"'You're gonna need a bigger boat,'" Archie quoted.

"*Jaws*." I'd just watched it a few nights ago with Harper.

"Lucky guess," he mumbled under his breath. "'Rosebud,'" he whispered in a strangled gasp.

Tilda had parked herself at the edge of the picket fence separating the yards, and watched Archie's every move through whitewashed slats.

"Archie, are you even trying anymore? *Citizen Kane*." I spotted Dennis coming out the front door. I stood up.

He chuckled. "'I think this is the beginning of a beautiful friendship.'"

"*Casablanca*, and I agree." I looked down at Tilda. "Don't get any ideas. I'm not sure he'd taste good at all."

She flicked her tail in dismissal, as if thinking he'd taste like a nice bucket of Kentucky Fried Chicken.

I jogged to meet up with Dennis as he opened the front gate. He glanced over and frowned when he recognized me.

I tried not to take it too personally. "I just wanted to say thank you for what you did for Evan."

The circles under his eyes had darkened overnight. His head hung a bit. "I acted like a jerk, and blatantly broke one of the Curecrafters' laws, all out of spite."

He sounded like he was reciting someone else's words. I assumed he'd received a summons from the Elder last night as well. If she'd done or said anything that changed his attitude, I was grateful.

He kicked at some grass that had poked out of the fence. "I apologize to you. I behaved badly."

Had the Elder told him to say that, too? "Apology accepted."

Glancing up, he squinted against the sun. "Lately, I've let my ego get the best of me. This past week has been a good reminder of what is really important. I miss them," he said softly. He looked to be on the verge of tears. "I made a huge mistake."

"You should tell them. I have a feeling they'll forgive you."

Archie screamed, "'Love means never having to say you're sorry!'"

"Not true," I said to Dennis, and gave Archie a glare.

"I know," Dennis said. "And I'll tell them as soon as they come back."

"Why wait?" I asked.

"What do you mean? I have to. I already tried calling, then realized Amanda doesn't have her phone with her. I don't even know if they're still at Disney World. They can be anywhere. What if Laurel Grace lost another tooth and I missed it?"

"You know what you could do . . . ," I said.

Archie squawked, then fluttered around his cage. "Duh-duh-duhn."

I closed my eyes and held in a groan. I realized immediately what I'd done. I'd enticed Dennis. Anxiety exploded in my stomach. I knew, without a doubt, I'd be hearing from the Elder again.

Dennis didn't pick up on the tension suddenly in the air. "But I don't want to wish them home."

I frowned. "You said . . ."

His eyes lit. "I want something else."

"What?" I asked warily.

"I wish I was with them."

Smiling, I cast the spell.

It was only after he was gone that I realized I hadn't asked him to cure my hands first.

Chapter Twenty-three

Claymore Funeral Home was a stately affair, brick with large columns. Inside, a thick carpet hushed footsteps, and I had the absurd notion it had been laid so the dead would not be disturbed.

"I hate funeral homes," Evan said, shuddering.

"Me, too." I scratched. I'd stopped at the Crone's Cupboard and bought some cortisone cream, and it seemed to be helping. If only I could wish Dennis back, *then* send him on his way again.

"May I help you?" A tall man, about my age, with a pronounced beer belly and a scruffy goatee appeared out of nowhere. He wore a shiny brass tag that had MARSHALL CLAYMORE written on it. He looked much too frat-boy to be a funeral director.

"We're here for the Shively viewing," I said.

"This way." He moved soundlessly along a wide corridor. He stopped at a doorway that had "Twilight" stenciled above its frame. Across from this doorway was another room, "Dusk." Down the hall, there was "Daybreak," "Sunset," and "Evening."

He gestured us inside and turned on his heel.

I looked at Evan. "You first."

"You."

I shoved him inside. My gaze immediately shot to the coffin at the front of the room. Letting out a breath of relief, I sagged. It was closed. Thank goodness for small favors.

"Evan? Darcy?" Mrs. Pennywhistle said. "What are you doing here?"

She sat on a folding chair in the front row.

Evan nudged me forward.

"We didn't want you to do this alone." I sat next to her. Evan sat on her other side.

Her hair had been styled, and stuck straight out, almost in points, like a starburst. Her makeup had been caked on, and she'd swapped out her pink tracksuit for a pair of leopard-print leggings and a belted black blouse.

"H-how did you know?" she asked.

Quietly, I said, "That you're a Vaporcrafter or that you're Alex's grandmother?"

I wasn't exposing myself by making the statement about her Craft, because I wasn't saying anything about *me* being a Wishcrafter. Besides, I was pretty darn sure I was right on both counts.

Her eyes went wide; her jaw dropped. "Either," she gasped.

I explained her behavior was that of someone in shock and mourning. I added the bits about the photo I'd found in Alex's apartment, the pink fuzz on the banister, and the confirmation from Pepe that Mrs. P.'s name had once been Clemson. "Your hair is very similar as well. Alex's was more curly, but the general shape is the same."

Her lower lip trembled. "I didn't know she existed. She pulled me aside at the bookshop the night she was killed and told me I was her grandmother. That her mother had been my daughter, Virginia. I was in shock—I barely knew who Alexandra was. I didn't believe her, but she said she had proof. A birth certificate—and somehow she'd gotten hold of my marriage license to Mr. P. She wanted to know about the Craft, said it was her birthright, and that before her mother died, she used to tell her about the village, and how she was a witch."

She was talking so fast she was barely breathing.

"I was in shock and accused her of lying and ran out. It wasn't until later, after I'd had some time to think about what she said, that I came to believe it might be true. By then, however, it was too late. She was dead."

Evan picked up one of her hands, held it.

I wanted to do the same, but was afraid the state of my hands might scare her. I kept them in my lap, but scooted as closely as I could to her. "I'm sorry," I whispered.

"My first husband, Isaiah, had renounced his Craft and didn't want to raise our daughter as a Crafter. When I objected we started having marital problems, and finally decided to divorce. We worked out a custody agreement that I could live with, but soon he became a superevangelical zealot, and forbade Virginia to even mention the Craft when she was with him. Then one day I went to pick up Virginia at his house and they were gone. The house was cleaned out, and there was no trace of them."

I swallowed hard, feeling the pain in her voice. I remembered the picture I'd found in the Bible in Alex's apartment. No wonder Alex knew so little of the Craft if her mother had been trained not to speak of it. I was actually surprised she knew of it at all, and wondered if Virginia had retained a little of her mother's spunk.

"Back then, there was no way to track them. I kept waiting for them to return. Over time, I met a nice man, fell in love. And finally, one day, thirty years later, I realized that my daughter wasn't ever coming back and I wanted to go home." Her gaze lingered on the coffin. "We packed up our things and moved to the village and bought the Pixie Cottage. I never wanted another man to hold that kind of power over me, so I never told my husband that I was a Crafter. I'd been gone so long no one in the village remembered me, and I had a new name. It was easy to start a new life."

"So you never knew what became of your ex and Virginia?" I asked.

"I never did," she said. "And I suppose now I never will."

"Was it the birth certificate you were looking for that night Nick and I saw you in Lotions and Potions?"

She nodded. "I'd hoped to find it, but I didn't. Then you showed up. It was the first time I'd vaporized in almost forty years. You nearly scared me to death."

I smiled. "You gave Nick quite the start. He still won't talk about it."

"He's a good boy," she said, patting my hand. Then she looked at it and snatched her hand away.

"I don't think it's contagious," I said, uneasily. "Vince mentioned that you had some hives as well. Did you use any of Alex's lotions?"

"I break out when I'm stressed. They've already healed. See?" She craned her neck. It was wrinkled, but clear of any blemishes.

I glanced at Evan. Maybe he *had* been the cause of the outbreak. It seemed strange that only Vince, Ramona, and I had welts, though. Many people ate Evan's cakes that night.

"I don't understand why it took so long for Alex to contact you," Evan said. "She'd always told me she had no living family that she knew of. Plus, she's been in the village a few years now. Why seek you out now?"

"I've been thinking about this a lot." She looked between the two of us. "I believe she knew she had roots in the village, but not with whom. The birth certificate I mentioned was not hers, but her mother's—I think she only just received it from the state. I'm still not sure how she linked Virginia to me, as no one in the village knew my former name. I have no idea how she found my marriage license."

But Pepe knew. And if he did, maybe there were others. "Something—or someone—led her to you."

Suddenly, I had an idea of who. Sylar. Had the document he'd been in charge of finding to keep his part of the bargain with Alex been the wedding certificate? It made sense. If Alex knew her mother's maiden name was Clemson, all Sylar would have to do was search all the marriage licenses with that name—very easy to do with modern technology. "Eugenia" was a fairly unique first name, so it was probably easy to link Eugenia Clemson to Eugenia Pennywhistle. From there, all it would take was a keen eye—the resemblance was strong when you knew to look for it. I'd have to ask Ve if she could find out for certain if Sylar had been involved.

Evan said, "If you didn't find the birth certificate, do you know for certain Alexandra was your granddaughter? Did you have a DNA test done during the, you know . . . ?" He trailed off instead of saying the word "autopsy."

She patted his cheek. "I don't need one. I know"—she tapped her chest—"in here. If only I'd known sooner . . ."

We sat in silence for a moment, before I finally said, "The other day at the park—the wish you'd made. You said you wanted to do something nice for your granddaughter. . . . You were talking about Alex?"

Nodding, she said, "I wanted to give her a proper burial. It's the least I could do, and I'd been worried about paying for it. My savings are meager, and my pension is pathetic. But the oddest thing happened. I was cleaning a dresser drawer and found a wad of hundred-dollar bills I must have tucked away years ago." She tapped her head. "The memory isn't what it used to be. There was just enough to pay funeral costs, plus a little extra that I was going to use to hire you."

"Me?" I asked, shocked.

"I'd like to hire As You Wish to help me clean out

Alexandra's apartment. When I figured out Alex was my granddaughter, I went and talked to Marcus Debrowski."

His name kept coming up, and it was starting to make me uneasy.

"He's handling the legal side of this revelation," Mrs. P said. "This morning he contacted Alex's landlord and gave me some options. I can't afford to carry her lease, so I can either find someone to sublease the place, or the landlord has agreed to break the lease so he can get a new renter in. Either way, I have only till the end of the month to clear things out. Will you help?"

"Of course."

"Can we start tomorrow?"

"Absolutely." I had a feeling the rush was not because of any hurry to dispose of Alex's belongings but to learn more about her from them.

She reached out her hand and took mine, hives and all. "Thank you. Thank you both for being here. I didn't realize how desperately I needed some friends."

"Well," I said, hearing voices in the hallway, "I invited two more. I hope you don't mind."

"Who?" she asked, just as Mimi and Nick stuck their heads into the room.

Her hands flew to her mouth. She stood up and Mimi ran to her and threw her arms around her waist.

Evan and I stood off to the side, giving them a little privacy. Nick approached. "Thanks for letting us know about the services."

I'd left him a brief message, explaining the bare bones of the situation.

"You're welcome," I said softly, watching Mimi and Mrs. P mourn together. My heart was full to bursting.

He leaned in, bringing his lips to my ear. My body tensed from the awareness of him being so close. "Now's not the right time, but I have a few questions for you," he whispered. "And I hope you have the answers I want to hear."

*   *   *

Two hours later, I walked into the mudroom, kicked off my shoes, and went to see if Harper and Ve were home. Alex's funeral had been brief, and I was glad Mrs. P had had some moral support during the services. She'd gone home to rest, Evan had gone back to the bakery, and Nick never did ask me any questions.

I was trying not to worry about it.

Missy bounded up and circled my legs. I scooped her up and rubbed her chin.

I could hear Harper's voice, so I followed the sound of it, up the stairs, past our bedrooms, and to the bathroom at the end of the hall. She was sitting on the edge of the tub and didn't notice me standing in the doorway.

"What's your name?" she was asking something in the palm of her hand.

What in the world? I squinted. It was a ladybug.

"Can you talk? Say something."

Missy barked.

Harper jumped up. The ladybug flew off. "I was just . . ."

I held up a hand. "No need to explain to me. I said 'sorry' to a honeybee today after swatting it away. There's no telling who's who and what's what around here."

Eyeing my black skirt, shirt, and shoes, she said, "Where have you been?"

"At Alex Shively's funeral."

"I hadn't heard of any funeral today, not that I would have gone. I didn't particularly like her." She followed me down the steps to the kitchen.

"You're not particularly alone in that. Besides, you might have known if you'd answer your phone. Where have you been? Was Ve with you all day?"

I set Missy down, filled her water dish, and scooped out some kibble.

"Well, first Missy escaped again this morning, so Ve

and I went looking for her. We found her down near Nick Sawyer's house."

I looked down at the dog. She was shameless.

"And then we got to talking about Sylar and his predicament and decided to do a little follow-up snooping on Griffin Huntley." Her voice rose in excitement. "So we staked out his house."

"Tell me you do not sell books about how to do stakeouts at the bookstore."

"No, but I watch *CSI*."

I tried really hard not to roll my eyes.

"Are you rolling your eyes at me?" she asked. "I'll have you know that Aunt Ve and I found out Griffin is a big liar."

"How so?" I asked, washing kibble dust from my hands.

"So, you know how he's been on the news every night, crying about how the lotion Alex gave him made him lose his hair"—she dropped her voice—"everywhere?"

"Unfortunately."

"Well, we followed him to New Hampshire—New Hampshire!—to a Wal-Mart, where he stocked up on—"

I gulped. "Nair?"

Her mouth dropped open. "How did you know?"

What I wanted to know was how *Evan* knew. Just how well were he and Griffin acquainted?

"Just guessed," I said weakly.

"Can you believe it?" she asked. "The little sneak. He's milking Alex's death for all it's worth, especially now that his alibi has been verified."

"It has?" This was the first I heard.

"He was at the Magic Wand at the time Alex died. Getting some manscaping done. And tanning, too. He hadn't wanted to fess up at first, but several of the salon stylists verified he was there."

Manscaping. I smiled and shook my head.

"And I didn't answer my phone because the battery

was dead, and Ve didn't answer hers because it was off, because every crackpot in a hundred-mile radius keeps calling her about that watch and the reward."

Nick had seen that one coming. "Where's Ve now?"

"At the jail visiting Sylar with Marcus. Apparently there's been some sort of big twist involving Ramona Todd. Marcus is hoping to get the whole case thrown out."

"Because of the fight Alex had with Ramona in the alley behind Lotions and Potions?"

Harper narrowed her eyes. "How do you know all this stuff? And more important, why aren't you sharing it with me?"

"Harmony Atchison, from the Pixie Cottage, is the one who saw Ramona and Alex fighting. She told me about it when I stopped by to see Mrs. P the other day."

"Did she say why they were fighting?"

I shook my head. "She couldn't really hear the conversation." And for the first time, I wondered why.

"I hope the lead pans out, for Ve's sake, if nothing else." She sat down and gave me a sheepish grin. "Vince asked me to go to the dance with him."

"Are you going to?"

She shrugged. "I don't know. You know how I feel about dances."

I knew. She hadn't gone to any in high school.

"Plus, Vince told me he had just gotten out of a serious relationship, and I don't particularly care to be a rebound."

"With who?" I asked.

"Ramona."

"He was dating Ramona?"

I couldn't keep up with the love lives of these villagers. Seemed like everyone had dated everyone else at some point.

"They broke up a while ago, but she's not letting it go so easily."

I wondered if this somehow related to the argument she'd had with Alex. "What about Marcus?" I asked. "Did you ever agree to go out to coffee with him?"

"Not yet."

I had the feeling she wouldn't until she figured out where she stood with Vince.

Missy whimpered and zigzagged before heading toward the back door. "You need to go out?" I asked her.

She barked. I took that as a yes.

I snapped on Missy's leash. No sooner did I open the back door than Archie flew in. He landed on the kitchen counter and bowed.

Harper openly stared at him as if taking mental notes.

My stomach suddenly hurt.

"Darcy Ann Merriweather, you have been found in violation of Wishcraft Law forty-three, section B, and have been hereby summoned by the Elder for your sentencing. Go tonight at nine p.m. sharp and go alone." He flew back outside without so much as a whispered movie quote in his wake.

Chapter Twenty-four

A little before nine, I found myself once again draped in Aunt Ve's cloak and on the creepy path to see the Elder.

The walk didn't take nearly as long this time, since I knew where I was going. The flashlight sliced through the dark damp night, and as I approached the clearing, the tree in its center lit up and emitted a glow.

"Darcy, Darcy, Darcy," the Elder said. "Sit down."

A tree stump appeared behind me, and obediently, I sat.

"I warned you," she said.

"I know."

"What have you to say for yourself?"

"Honestly, Elder? I have nothing. As soon as the words left my mouth, I knew what I'd done. But it was too late to take them back."

"It is imperative that you learn to control such temptations as suggesting wishes."

"I was just trying to help," I explained.

"I am aware, but you cannot help everyone. The sooner you learn that, the better."

"Then why have the power in the first place?"

She sighed. "These rules are in place to protect Wishcrafters from potential abuses. You must adhere to them. If you cannot, you might consider renouncing your gift."

It felt as though my heart had just flip-flopped in my chest. "I don't want that. I only just discovered my gift, my heritage."

"Then you must be very careful. Even the smallest infraction from here on out will be viewed as a severe violation."

"All right."

"Please rise."

I stood.

"Darcy Ann Merriweather, you have been found guilty of breaking Wishcraft Law number forty-three, section B. No Wishcrafter shall prompt, suggest, hint, evoke, prod, or elicit a wish. Your punishment is as follows: Your powers are hereby revoked for twenty-four hours, retroactive from the time of your offense. You may go now."

The tree stump fizzled into glitter and wildflowers sprouted where the sparkles fell. I was still impressed by this bit of magic.

The Elder's tree went dark.

I headed home. Although I had helped save the Goodwins' marriage, I felt a bit like a failure.

The next morning, I was up and at 'em early, cleaning out the office, sorting files, and keeping busy. This is what I knew best—office work. I'd held a job in my father's dental practice for close to ten years. After last night's scolding by the Elder, I was beginning to think I should ask Ve for a desk job at As You Wish; I was really flubbing my way as a Wishcrafter. Except being a Crafter made me happier than I'd ever been. It was fulfilling in ways I'd never imagined. I couldn't make any more mistakes—I didn't want to lose my abilities.

I'd already taken Missy for two walks, during one of which I'd practically had to drag her, as she would rather have stayed in her doggy bed, snoozing.

Harper was at work at the bookshop, and Aunt Ve was running errands before she headed to see Sylar.

I'd opted out of a morning jog with Starla because I was pretty sure my muscles wouldn't be able to move faster than a slow crawl today, and by ten o' clock I'd done two loads of laundry, washed the dishes, and made an appointment with Ramona at the Magic Wand Salon for five. I was going to have my bangs evened out, and more important, I'd have the chance to find out why Ramona and Alex had been fighting.

As soon as the clock flashed to ten thirty, I headed straight for All That Glitters, since I'd completely forgotten to pick up Ve's locket yesterday, after telling her right before Archie's initial visit that I would.

It was a picturesque June afternoon, and the village was bustling. The tourist count was up, and the green was hopping, being prepped for Saturday's dance. A pair of large banners, one on each side of the square, stretched from one side of the street to the other, fluttering in the soft sea breeze. Fancily printed on them was the Midsummer Dance information, how to attain tickets, and a Web site address for more details.

I was so busy watching the workers that I didn't notice Mimi and Nick until I'd practically bumped into them. They were standing in front of the pet store the Furry Toadstool, watching the puppies play in the window.

"They're so cute," Mimi said to me, her eyes filled with puppy love.

Inside the shop, a litter of pugs romped and played. My heart melted. Until I glanced at Nick. There was a hardness in his eyes I hadn't seen before, and suddenly I was very worried about what he'd wanted to talk to me about—he'd never had the chance to tell me yesterday after Alex's visitation.

I tried to ignore the rising dread I felt and looked away. Starla was on the green, snapping pictures of a pair of toddlers. She had Twink with her and the children were laughing and playing with the tiny dog. She spotted me and waved. I waved back and turned my attention to Mimi and the puppies. It was easy to ignore Nick's glare when looking at adorable little faces.

A couple strolled up next to us, to window-shop at All That Glitters.

"Have you decided against a shelter dog?" I asked Nick.

"Nothing's been decided yet," he said. "Mimi falls in love with every dog she sees."

She glanced over her shoulder at him and rolled her eyes.

My gaze shifted to the window-shopping couple as they ooohed and aaahed over a ring on display. It was easy to eavesdrop, as they stood only about two feet away.

The woman said, "I just have to have it. Please, honey?"

The man said, "But, pooh, I just don't have the money."

I couldn't help but wince at the endearments. Stealing a glance at Nick, I saw he was trying to hold back a smile. Mimi was openly grinning.

"But, honey bear," the woman said, "I really, really want it."

He put his arm around her and pulled her close. "But, pooh, sweetheart, I don't have the money for it."

Her lower lip jutted. "I wish you had the money, honey puddin' pie." She blinked at him.

I'd gone still, the word "wish" ringing in my thoughts. I mouthed the words to the spell. It wasn't until I blinked twice to cast it that I realized I didn't have any powers; they'd been revoked for the day.

"Be that as it may, my cuddly wuddly pooh, I don't." He pulled out his pockets to prove his point.

I was fighting a wave of queasiness—the couple was

gag-worthy—when she squealed and gave him a playful shove. "Oh! How you love to tease me!" She scooped up the wad of bills that had fallen from his pocket and quickly pulled him toward the door to the shop.

"But that's not mine." Clearly confused, he dug in his heels and stared at the ground.

"Nonsense, honey, it just fell from your pocket." She counted off the bills. "And it's just enough for that ring."

The man looked at us. "Did any of you lose some money?"

We shook our heads.

"Strange," he said, allowing himself to be pulled into the shop.

Had the Elder changed her mind and allowed me to keep my powers after all?

Nick said, "I wish I could find a wad of money like that."

I did the spell thing and cast it. Nothing happened. Not so much as a sticky penny appeared on the sidewalk.

"Maybe you need to pull out your pockets like he did," I said.

"Yeah, Dad," Mimi echoed.

He gave me a look that clearly said, "Why do you keep asking me to check my pockets?" But he did it. They were empty. "Things like that just don't happen to guys like me."

Okay, maybe I didn't have my powers back after all.

"Do you have a second?" he asked me, the hard look back in his eyes.

I glanced toward All That Glitters. It wasn't going anywhere. I still had an hour before I was to meet Mrs. P at Alex's apartment. "Yes."

"Mimi, we'll be right back," Nick said.

I'm not sure she heard him, so enamored was she with the puppies. We walked out of earshot and stood under a large tree, its outstretched branches offering shade against the bright sun. I leaned against its trunk. "What's wrong?"

Something was. I could tell by the look in his eye.

He was all business as he said, "Why didn't you tell me Harper has a record?"

A record. A criminal record. My heart pounded. He'd found out. Of course he'd found out. It was his job to be thorough.

I shrugged. "I didn't think it was that important."

"Not important? She has a history of stealing—"

Narrowing my eyes, I said, "Stop. That's exactly why I didn't tell you. Because of the way you're acting like she's now your prime suspect in the pickpocket case. There is no 'history' of anything. She made a mistake and already paid the price."

He crossed his arms over his chest. "If she stole once, then, yes, she becomes a suspect."

"That's ridiculous." It really wasn't, but I felt the need to defend her. "Besides, the thefts started the week before we moved here. Didn't you think of that?" I said, glaring. "Did you even check to see what she stole? Read about the case at all? Or did you jump to conclusions because you're desperate to solve a case?"

When he didn't say anything, I knew he hadn't fully checked her background, and had simply chosen to ignore the timeline.

"Harper is not your thief. The sooner you figure that out, the faster you'll catch the real criminal." I drew in a deep breath, wondered what I'd ever seen in him, and left him standing there. I said a quick good-bye to Mimi and hurried into All That Glitters to pick up Aunt Ve's locket. I was anxious to find Harper.

I had to warn her.

Chapter Twenty-five

Ten minutes later, I'd hotfooted it over to Spellbound Books. Harper looked up from drawing on a poster board when I rushed in. The customers in the shop all turned and looked at me. I smiled wanly and tried to pretend that I wasn't in a tizzy.

"What's wrong?" Harper asked as I rushed up to the desk.

She'd been working on a book club poster—this one for a tween reading group. I dropped my voice and said, "Nick knows about"—I coughed—"what happened in Ohio. With Missy. You know." I glanced over my shoulder to make sure no one was eavesdropping. "I'm sure he's going to come in and interrogate you."

She didn't look the least bit worried. "He already did."

I gaped. "When?"

"Earlier." She shrugged. "No big deal. I've been thinking about it, and I'd rather people just know. It's a lot of pressure keeping it secret. Besides, it's not like I did anything wrong."

I gaped some more.

"Well," she amended, "maybe a little wrong. But in the end it was mostly right." She took her poster to the front of the store and slid it into a freestanding display. It fit perfectly—and looked great. The fonts were perfect to catch the eyes of tweens, and the book Harper had chosen to start the club was a popular one about a magician's guild.

I trailed after her. "But he thinks you're the local pickpocket."

As she gazed up at me, she looked much wiser than I'd ever given her credit for. "You and I both know I'm not. He'll come around. It's his job to investigate these things." She took a step back from the poster and eyed it critically. "Do you think anyone will join?"

How could she be so calm? While I had visions of Nick throwing Harper in jail, she was worried about getting a group of tweens together to read a book. "You're not worried?"

"About the book club?" she asked. "Of course I am. It's kind of my pet project and I want to see it succeed. I really want to show Gayle that I'm serious about working here. Maybe she'll bump me up to full-time."

I was losing patience. Through clenched teeth, I said, "About Nick."

"Oh." She waved her hand in dismissal. "Not at all. Why? Are you?"

Was she just now picking up on that?

She must have finally noticed my panic, because she said, "Why?"

"Because. I don't want . . ." I trailed off. I didn't want Nick to hurt her in any way—not her reputation, not her chance at being part of this community.

And I realized I didn't want Nick to think badly of her. Because if he did . . . he might think badly of me.

My anxiety fizzled, replaced now with a touch of embarrassment. Whereas I thought I was being mother-bear protective over Harper, maybe my outrage over Nick investigating her had been about . . . me?

"Don't want what?" she asked, a faint smile on her face, as though she had already come to the conclusion I'd just reached.

She'd always been the smart one in the family.

"You like him, don't you? Really like him." Her eyes were aglow.

"I don't know."

"Darcy's got a cr-ush," she sang.

I gave her a little shove. "Stop that."

She bumped me with her hip. "I'm glad."

"I'm not."

"Why not? He's cute in an old-guy kind of way."

"He's not old! Only thirty-five."

"You *reallllly* like him."

I frowned at her. "More than I like you right now. Which isn't saying much."

She laughed, and I realized how happy she was. Here. In the village. In this bookshop. With her life. So happy, she was willing to let everyone know her past—and either side with her or judge her. Or even both.

Moving here had been a good thing. A great thing.

"Try not to worry so much, Darcy. Everything will work out."

I truly wanted to believe her.

"There is just so much stuff," Mrs. P said.

I'd come prepared with boxes, packing tape, and industrial-strength garbage bags. I had gloves (the irony wasn't lost on me) and bins to organize what little Alex had left behind.

"Where do we even start?" she asked.

This was why she hired me. To take charge. To take the emotional element out of cleaning the place. "We'll start with the books."

This morning Marcus had filed, on Mrs. P's behalf, a claim with the probate court. He also let us know that everything we packed today had to be inventoried before being stored.

"You'll need to decide if the object is something you

want to keep, whether it's trash, or if it's something you want to donate to charity. We'll separate it all when we store it, so when you get the go-ahead from the court, it will be easy to sort."

In my opinion there wasn't much here worthy of keeping. Which was just as well. Mrs. P's tiny room at the Pixie Cottage couldn't hold much clutter.

She took a deep breath and nodded. "I'm ready."

I rolled up my sleeves and started with the books on the top shelves. Most were reference books on how to make lotions, oils, scrubs, and masks. There were also books on making soaps, shower gels, and shampoos. And even more on holistic health and healing and making herbal remedies. "These might be good to donate to the local library."

"Good idea. These, too," she said, pointing to four full shelves of witchcraft-themed books. It was as if Alex were a one-woman bookstore.

We worked quietly and quickly, packing small boxes with books. Big boxes would have made the task go faster, but the boxes would have been impossible for us to lift and carry to my car.

Two hours later, we'd made progress. The bookshelves were empty, and Alex's bedroom had been cleared of everything personal, including clothes that were going to be donated to a local women's shelter.

Mrs. P went about cleaning up the mess the intruder had left behind, sweeping up shards of vases and soil from overturned potted plants.

I tackled the desk, trying to sort everyday riffraff from the important stuff. Alex didn't seem to have any sort of filing system—everything from pens and pencils, mail, and magazines was shoved in the desk's drawers and cubbies. I'd brought along a file box with hanging folders, and with each piece of mail I came across, I either shredded it or put it in a proper file for Mrs. P to go through later. She'd have to make some calls soon and cancel things like Alex's credit cards, Netflix account, and magazine subscriptions.

An hour into the task, Mrs. P said, "You didn't happen to find that birth certificate, did you? Not that I care, you know, but . . . it would be nice to have." She'd moved on to emptying the kitchen cabinets and was looking at me with hopeful eyes as she wrapped glasses in newspaper.

"Not yet." Truth be told, I'd been hoping to find the birth certificate as well. "Just lots of legal notices, bills, and copies of invoices for things she'd ordered for the shop."

I wondered if some of these vendors would take returns. Alex's apartment was fairly easy to pack up, but her shop was going to take days. I tucked a few of the notices aside to call later.

"Will those lawsuits still be binding?"

"I'm not sure. Her estate might still be held liable. You'll need to check with Marcus."

She nodded and went back to packing.

From what I could tell, there wouldn't be much of an estate. Alex's personal checkbook showed a balance of just over two thousand dollars, and her shop's account was barely in the black. It appeared she made just enough to get by every month.

There was nothing of value in the apartment. The decor had been nice, but inexpensive. The artwork was mostly cheap prints set into nicer frames. All told, Mrs. P might be able to get a couple of thousand if she sold the furniture and the kitchen items. I suspected most of Alex's worth was downstairs in the shop. I just didn't know if Mrs. P would be able to liquidate all that merchandise—or if she wanted to, considering the spate of lawsuits sitting in the file box. Maybe Marcus would have some thoughts on that as well.

I kept digging and sorting and as I was reaching into

the back of a drawer, I noticed something I hadn't seen before. Alex's purse was tucked under the desk. It was black, and nearly hidden in the shadows. I pulled it out, hoping that the birth certificate Mrs. P needed was inside.

It was a little creepy going through a dead woman's purse, I had to admit. Touching the lip balm she'd never use again, looking through receipts, and her wallet. I noticed one of the receipts was from a fancy downtown restaurant, known for its romantic ambiance, the night before she died. The bill came to just over two hundred dollars, and she'd put the tab on her credit card. Whom had she been dining with?

I tucked the credit card slip back into her purse and came across a pocket calendar. I flipped to the night she died, and written in the little square was "Vill Mtg 9:30." The day before had a notation of "9 p.m.," and also a symbol that looked like a tweaked eighth note, but the arm of the note was as long as the circle part and the circle was hollow, not shaded in.

I stood up and brought the calendar over to Mrs. P. "Does this symbol mean anything to you?"

She shook her head. "You think it means something?"

"I'm not sure." I flipped back a few pages. The little symbol appeared a lot. Usually along with a time—usually late at night. "I think this symbol might stand for a person. See here?" I showed her all the other pages, times, and dates. "I found a receipt from a fancy, romantic restaurant the night before she died, the same night she was meeting with this symbol at nine o'clock."

"Why not just write his name down?" she asked.

I shrugged. "She has a thing about keeping boyfriends secret. Maybe it was a little game with her."

Sadness filled Mrs. P's eyes. "There are just so many things I don't know. I should have known." Her jaw jutted and her lower lip trembled.

I put my arm around her. "Why don't we finish up for the day?"

She nodded. "Just let me finish with these glasses."

"Do you mind if I take this home?" I asked, holding up the calendar. "I want to see if Ve or Harper recognizes the symbol."

"Take it," she said, wrapping another glass.

I tucked the calendar in my purse and went to help in the kitchen. Mrs. P had the glasses under control, so I decided to do a quick fridge cleanout, before the perishables rotted. Alex didn't have much in the fridge. I grabbed a trash bag and started tossing items in. Brown salad, a carton of milk, a half dozen eggs, some old Chinese food. I surveyed and closed the fridge door. I emptied the trash container next to the fridge and noticed that the chrysanthemums had started to brown and wilt. I reached for them.

As I did so, Mrs. P said, "You may want to use your gloves, Darcy. Some people are very sensitive to chrysanthemums."

I recalled how Harmony Atchison at the Pixie Cottage had said Mrs. P had the greenest thumb around. If anyone would know about plant sensitivities, it would be her. "Sensitivities? Like what?" My eyes widened. "Like this?" I asked, holding up my hands. "I touched these flowers when I was here on Saturday."

Mrs. P *tsk*ed. "Just like that. Chrysanthemums can cause a bad skin reaction, especially after your skin is exposed to sunlight."

I'd touched the flowers Saturday evening, then hadn't showered until after my jog on Sunday morning, when it had been bright and sunny. I glanced at my hands. My hives were almost gone, but my skin was still red and irritated. Several jars full of pink lotion and a mortar and pestle sat on the counter. "If these flowers were ground up and put into a lotion, would they cause a reaction?"

"I'd say so, especially if the tubers and leaves were ground as well."

It all suddenly made sense. "This is probably what's

been causing the rashes around the village. Evan's going to be relieved that he didn't cause an epidemic. I wonder why he reacted so badly and I didn't."

"Some people are more sensitive than others and some people aren't sensitive at all, and if he used a large amount of lotion, he would have been more exposed than you. You should wash your hands," she said.

I washed, grabbed my gloves, and threw all the flowers—cut and dried—away. "Alex couldn't have known how dangerous these could be."

"I imagine not. She probably chose them for the color and didn't investigate the properties thoroughly. She should have consulted a botanist or herbalist, but perhaps she believed she knew what she was doing."

No wonder she had so many people suing her. "I'm going to take this trash out to the Dumpster. Then we'll wrap up for the day, okay?"

Looking around, she nodded. "We've made good progress."

We had. "Tomorrow we can bring this stuff to the storage locker, and start with the shop."

Absently, she nodded as she wrapped another glass. I stepped carefully down the narrow staircase, thinking about those chrysanthemums. Evan had used the lotion, and I had touched the flowers. But how had Vince gotten the rash? Or Ramona?

Was it possible Evan had transferred the lotion to one of his trays? He thought no, but maybe he'd been careless just that once.

Had Alex's fight with Ramona gotten physical? Had Alex laid chrysanthemum-laced hands on her?

I pushed open the back door and froze when I heard a noise coming from behind the Dumpster. My heart pounded. Probably a squirrel, I told myself, inching forward, the trash bag in front of me like a shield.

Nothing to be worried about.... I was being paranoid.

A loud clunk echoed, and I jumped back. "Who's there?" I said loudly.

No one answered, and I thought maybe a very large squirrel had gotten into the Dumpster and couldn't get out. I edged forward and was getting ready to heave the trash bag over the metal rim when suddenly someone jumped out of the Dumpster, nearly landing on me.

I screamed.

Chapter Twenty-six

"Did I scare you?" Harmony Atchison asked, dusting off her jeans.

As Nick had predicted, my scream had been barely a whisper. I was pretty sure I looked terrified, though, because Harmony came over and said, "I'm so sorry! Are you okay? I didn't realize you were out here. I guess you caught me in the act."

She stepped forward and dragged a broken window frame that had been propped on the corner of the Dumpster. Her cheeks were aflame. "I hate when people catch me. They always look at me like I'm crazy. Kind of like how you're looking at me now."

I finally found my voice. "What is it you're doing?" I still held the trash bag like a shield. My heart rate was slowly returning to normal.

"I guess you'd call it Dumpster diving. I call it Permanent Article Relocation."

I smiled at her, though I didn't get too close. She smelled. "And what do you do with the article once it's relocated?"

Her eyes lit. "I repurpose it! Picture this," she said, holding up the window frame. "I'll paint it white, maybe add a crackle glaze or a distressed finish, then add four legs." She flipped the frame so it sat horizontally. "Voilà, a beautiful table."

"Amazing." My inner Martha Stewart was impressed.

"Sometimes trash really is treasure. It's just a shame I have to climb into Dumpsters to find it. Blech."

I glanced between her and the Dumpster, the Dumpster and her, and I suddenly realized where Harmony had been the day she overhead Alex and Ramona fighting. I just needed her to confirm it.

When I asked, she blushed again and nodded. "They had no idea I was there."

I thought about those chrysanthemums. "Do you know if they got into a catfight?" I made a pawing motion. "Did it get physical?"

She was smiling at my gestures. "As soon as I spotted them, I ducked down. I didn't hear any slapping or anything, though. I couldn't really hear anything other than raised voices."

That explained a few things.

"I did follow up with Marcus Debrowski like you suggested. He thinks it will help Sylar's case."

"That's good news." For Sylar. Not so much for Ramona. I checked my watch. I had an hour before my appointment with her. Had she already been questioned by the police?

"I've got to get this back," Harmony said, holding up the window frame. "And shower."

I laughed and tossed the trash bag into the Dumpster. "I'd love to see it when it's done."

"Come by anytime."

I waved good-bye and headed back inside. I found Mrs. P downstairs, in the shop. She was holding the pink witch hat in her hands. "Think anyone would notice if this hat doesn't show up on the inventory list?"

"Hat?" I said. "What hat? I don't see any hat in this shop."

She patted my cheek and looked around. Her attention seemed focused on the plastic bins filled with herbs and roots. Walking over to them, she said, "Alexandra must have known about herbs somewhat. Or else ..."

"What?"

"Some of these are extremely dangerous. Poisonous. Can cause rashes, digestive problems, strokes, and even death. If she didn't know what she was doing, she could have killed someone."

Thank goodness she hadn't.

Mrs. P said, "Perhaps she just didn't know about the chrysanthemum, as it's so common."

Unfortunately, we'd never know.

With one final look around, she said, "Let's go. I have a little girl I want to see."

I made sure to lock up behind us. As I turned the key, shouts rang out in the alley. "Tell me!" someone yelled.

"Is that Vince?" I asked, squinting.

"Is that Evan?" she countered.

We'd just about reached them when the first punch flew.

Evan ducked and evaded. Vince struck out again. Evan high-kicked him in the stomach. Vince moaned and doubled over.

"Black belt," Evan said at our stunned glances.

Gayle Chastain came running out the back door of the bookshop. "Stop it right now!" she shouted, getting between the two. "For goodness' sake, stop acting like children. You're grown men."

"At least one of us is," Evan said.

Vince had recovered and struck out again. Evan was light on his feet, though, and the punch didn't connect.

Gayle twisted Vince's ear. "I said stop!"

Vince didn't look happy. "All right. Fine."

"What's this about?" Mrs. P asked.

"Evan brought the scourge into the bookshop with his infected little cakes," Vince sneered, "and now he won't even tell me how he cleared up his rash."

" 'Infected little cakes'?" Evan stepped forward, fists raised, but Mrs. P stopped him with a glare. "I'll sue you for libel if you spread that around!"

"Like you spread around your rash?"

"I'm calling Marcus immediately," Evan said.

"Not if I call him first," Vince sneered.

Gayle looked like she wanted to ground both and send them to their rooms without dinner. "Enough."

Everyone went silent, though anger pulsed in the air.

"Now," Gayle said calmly, turning to look at Evan. "Evan, your face looks great. What treatment did you get?" She swiveled to Vince. "Because I know Vince has been suffering and is looking for relief, and truly, I'd be relieved if I knew those cakes weren't the source of the rash."

Evan pasted on a phony smile. "As I was telling Vince, the rash cleared up on its own; it was never contagious, so you have no reason to worry."

He sounded convincing enough that I would have believed him if I hadn't known the truth about how his rash had cleared.

"He's lying," Vince said.

Evan rolled his eyes.

"Come here. Let me see your rash," Mrs. P said to Vince.

He reluctantly rolled up his sleeves and held his arms out for inspection.

She *tsk*ed and nodded.

"What?" Gayle asked. "Do you know what it is? What the cure is?"

Mrs. P looked at me. "Looks like classic dermatitis caused by the chrysanthemum." She turned her attention to Vince. "Have you been using Alex's lotions?"

He stammered. "I—no. I barely knew Alex." Color rose on his cheeks. "And why would I use a frilly pink lotion?"

"Vince?" I said.

"Yeah?"

"How did you know the lotion was pink?"

His brow furrowed. "Lucky guess. Look, I don't need this kind of aggravation." He stomped back into the bookshop.

Evan raised his eyebrows. "That was interesting."

Rather telling, I thought. Vince had obviously had contact with that lotion. How did he get it? And why was he denying it?

"Is there a treatment for the dermatitis, Mrs. P?" Gayle asked.

"Usually, it goes away on its own after a few days. It depends on how allergic the person is to the chrysanthemum. Sometimes a doctor needs to get involved and stronger medications are needed."

"Mine's almost gone," I said, showing my hands. "And the cortisone cream helped with the itching."

"I'll let Vince know," Gayle said. "And Evan, I suggest we let time cool things down. I don't think there's any need to get lawyers involved."

Evan nodded.

Gayle went back inside the shop and closed the door behind her. I looked between Mrs. P and Evan. "Someone needs to clear something up for me."

"What's that?" Mrs. P asked.

"Is Marcus the *only* lawyer in the village?"

"Pretty much," Evan said. "Why?"

It seemed to me that if that was the case, then he was privy to a lot of people's secrets.

The Magic Wand Salon was housed in an adorable storybook cottage. With its shingled exterior, steep-pitched slate roof, and huge stone chimney next to the door, I felt like Hansel and Gretel might come skipping along at any moment.

Despite the outside looking like it was built in eighteenth-century England, when I pulled open the arched doorway, I stepped into a modern world. A sleek display case held shampoos and hair creams, brushes, and expensive flatirons and hair dryers. A young woman stood at the black granite reception desk, a welcome smile on her face.

"Welcome to the Magic Wand Salon," she said. "May I help you?"

She wasn't exactly staring at my uneven bangs, but I could tell she knew they were self-inflicted. "I have an appointment with Ramona at five."

She *tap-tap*ped into a touch-screen computer system. "She'll be right along. Would you care for a beverage while you wait? Coffee, tea, tonic, wine?"

Wine sounded great after the day I'd had, but I passed with a "No, thank you." I sat on a black sofa and tapped my foot nervously on the marble floor. I kept thinking about Marcus Debrowski, and my mind was conjuring all kinds of nefarious plots.

What if Marcus killed Alex? Then, if he defended Sylar badly, and Sylar went to prison, no one would ever be the wiser.

But Marcus seemed like a nice guy. Too nice to kill someone. Besides, why would he kill Alex? She was bringing him a lot of business. Unless there was more to their relationship than met the eye.

I shook my head. I couldn't see it. At all.

Sighing, I took out Alex's calendar to distract myself from my thoughts. I flipped through its pages. I kept staring at that funky little music-note symbol. It appeared the night before she died, the Monday before, and many times before that—usually every other day or so, at varying times, late evening being the most common. I narrowed down the first time the symbol appeared to a month and a half ago.

More interesting was all the private consultation meetings she had penciled in. Alex had been a busy woman. I noted all the familiar names, including Ramona Todd's last Monday. Evan. Griffin. Marcus Debrowski—were those legal appointments or consultations? I saw Mimi's name written a few times but never spotted Nick's.

On average, Alex had three to four consults a week. Which made me wonder why she didn't have more money in her bank account.

I was flipping pages through past entries, looking for any kind of clue as to who might have killed Alex, when Ramona came strolling out from behind an opaque glass partition.

With a smile on her face, she said, "Darcy, I'm glad you made it! Come on back."

She walked me through a maze of occupied styling stations and motioned me into a cushioned chair.

I sat and looked at her in the reflection of the mirror as she examined my hair and said, "Have you thought about highlights?"

I nodded. "I thought I was ready, but the bangs were a big enough change."

We talked about various shades and finally settled on keeping my natural color but adding a gloss treatment to make my natural hair color shinier. Baby steps, I told myself.

"Nervous?" she asked.

"Terribly."

She laughed. "Don't be. You're in good hands."

I glanced around, my gaze hopping from face to face. Everyone was busy, chatting and laughing. I liked the feel of the salon. Even though it was ultramodern, it had a friendly atmosphere.

Ramona reached for a pair of gloves. It was then that I noticed the rash on her hands, arms, and neck.

"Have you tried cortisone cream?" I asked, inquiring about the rash.

"I've tried everything," she said as she started buttering my hair with what looked like a basting brush. "My doctor thinks it's just a bad case of poison ivy. Vince thinks Evan was contagious and has infected the whole village."

"I heard."

"Vince says a lot of things that aren't true, though," she added, a sad undertone in her voice. The undertone of someone who'd had her heart broken—I recognized it well.

"Are the two of you ... dating?" I didn't want to let on that I knew about their breakup.

She brushed gloss mix onto my hair. "We were. We're not now. Thanks to Alex Shively."

I tipped my head, confused. "But Vince said he didn't even know Alex that well."

"Ha!" She snorted. Her backbone seemed to melt before my eyes and she slumped, bracing her hands on the back of my chair for support. She met my eyes in the mirror. "If you call sleeping with someone barely knowing them."

Feeling a little queasy, I said, "He was dating her?"

"He's so stupid. So, so stupid."

Said like a woman still in love with Mr. Stupid.

Drawing in a deep breath, she straightened. Confession must be like a jolt of caffeine, because suddenly she was talking so fast I could barely keep up. "So, we were dating like five months, right? And I'm thinking it's getting serious. I'm ready for a big commitment. Okay, he never said he loved me, but I could tell. I just wanted to hear it. Instead all he ever talked about was witchcraft this, witchcraft that. And it's true he barely knew Alex—at first. She'd come into the shop for books. On witchcraft. My God, the conversations they'd have—for hours—over witches. Nothing flirtatious at all. At first. But *witch this*, *witch that*. Then he starts telling me all about how Alex is a witch. And he wanted to be one, too. Well, a warlock. Is that what they call them?"

I shrugged. Ve told us male witches were never called

warlocks, which was insulting. Just witches. But I didn't correct Ramona—that might steer us into another conversation, and I really wanted to hear what she had to say about Vince.

"Anyway, he says that Alex is going to teach him everything she knows. Make him her *apprentice*."

"How long ago was this?" I asked.

Her head bobbed side to side as she calculated. "Maybe a month ago? A little more? He was happier than I've ever seen him. So, I'm starting to get nervous, right? I mean, Alex is way older than I am, but she's still a knockout, and he's still a man."

I smiled. Alex was probably only ten years older or so.

"Plus, she's a witch. Or at least that's what stupid-head thinks, and he finds that more attractive than how pretty she is. Was."

More gloss on my hair.

"So, I'm trying to think fast. What can I do? How do I get him to turn his attention back to me?"

At this point I was wondering why she wanted to.

"I decided to go on the offensive. So, a week ago I make an appointment with Alex. She is absolutely clueless as to who I am. Vince hasn't mentioned me at all, of course, so I make sure I drop his name a time or two or twenty. I'm there trying to find out if she's a real witch or not. If I can prove she's a fake, then maybe, just maybe, I can get Vince to see reason. So, I ask her for a love potion. Explain how I've been waiting for Vince to say 'I love you.' The whole time I'm talking, I'm giving off warning vibes. You know what I mean? Like, you-better-keep-your-shiny-fingernails-off-my-man kind of thing, right?"

I nodded and thanked my lucky stars she'd run out of gloss. I could only imagine if there'd been an endless pot. Was there a fine line between glossy and greasy?

She set a timer and carried on. "She says she has the perfect thing—something she'd been working on. She gives me this lotion, a love lotion. It's pink; it smells good. I'm game. But of course Vince is busy that night. With her. Apprenticing. So I don't get a chance to use the lotion until the next night. I'm supposed to use the lotion on just me, but I think it might be stronger if I use it on both of us." She waggled her eyebrows. "I gave him the best massage he's ever had."

Vince was keeping lots of secrets. I'd bet money he was *covered* in that rash—not just his arms and back. No wonder he was going out of his mind, looking for a cure.

Looking for a cure . . . enough to break into Lotions and Potions to steal the recipe box? He was the right size and had a very good motivation. I also recalled that Harper said he hadn't been at work that afternoon— he'd supposedly been at the hospital seeking treatment. I'd bet every last hair on my glossy head that he was the one who'd broken into Alex's building the day Evan and I had. He'd been seeking treatment, all right, but not from a hospital.

"After, I'm waiting patiently. And waiting. And waiting. No 'I love you.' I'm getting madder and madder. Still nothing. The next morning, he gets up, leaves, suddenly in a hurry to get to work. Then he calls and tells me he'll be with Alex that night, *apprenticing*. So I decide I need to find out what this apprentice thing is all about."

I nodded again. Sounded perfectly rational to me.

"And just so you know, I'm not really proud of this next part. I should be stronger, more secure, blah, blah. . . . Let's just say I'm not proud. I parked down the street from the bookshop and waited for him to leave work. I followed him to Lotions and Potions and parked so I could see inside the shop. Imagine my surprise when they didn't stay. When I saw them walking toward Vince's car, I was stunned. I followed them into the city. And when I saw them go into this adorable little restaurant and sit there and cuddle and kiss and coo at each other,

I thought I was going to throw up. I couldn't even make myself confront them—I felt so sick. I ended up going home and crying myself to sleep. The next day, though, whoa! I was ticked. I went to see Alex at her shop, and we end up having this huge fight in the back alley." She shook her head. "It got pretty nasty. Basically, she told me she loved him, and that he would be hers, and that I just better back off now or I'd get more hurt in the process."

I bit my lip. I wondered if Ramona knew how incriminating all this sounded.

"And you know what? I decided right then and there she could have him. Now, I'm not saying it didn't hurt, but who needs a creep like that in their life? I don't. I just can't believe how long it took me to see it. I figured I'd just sit back and see how long it took her to realize that he didn't love her. He loved what she could teach him."

"About witchcraft?"

She nodded, deflating again. "I don't think he loves anyone or anything more. At the village meeting, he tried to act like nothing had happened at all, like everything was status quo. I set him straight, and I even tried to warn him about how Alex was a fake. But he wouldn't listen."

I said, "If he really thought he'd been tricked by her, would he be mad?"

"Oh, definitely. He was—he is—obsessed with witchcraft."

My gaze met hers. "Do you think he'd be mad enough to kill her?"

Her mouth dropped open. Her throat bobbed as she swallowed. "I . . . I don't know. You don't think Sylar did it?"

I shook my head.

"Or the thief killed her? Stole her watch?"

"I doubt it."

She let out a whoosh of air. "I just don't know, Darcy. But I have to say I wish I could find that watch. I saw the reward Velma posted for it—that's a lot of cash."

My nerves tingled. I surreptitiously covered my mouth, faked a yawn, and cast the spell. Ramona was lucky—my penalty for breaking the Wishcraft Law had expired a couple of hours ago.

The timer dinged. As she led me back to the wash-bowl, she said, "This is so crazy, but suddenly I have this vision of where that watch might be. So weird."

"Really?" I asked, hopeful.

"Yeah, but it doesn't make sense."

"Why?" I asked.

She frowned. "I keep seeing it in the bookshop. In a box on Vince's desk." She laughed. "Isn't that silly? I mean, why on earth would it be there?"

My heart pounded. I could think of a reason. A deadly one.

Chapter Twenty-seven

An hour later, my hair looked better than it had in years, and I still didn't know what to do with the information I'd learned from Ramona. Antsy, I was jittery and couldn't make a decision.

I started for home, then spun around and headed for the bookstore. It couldn't hurt to look, could it?

One little peek to see if granting Ramona's wish had caused her to see the vision of the watch.

I bit my fingernail, lingering near Mrs. P's bench on the green. What if someone caught me? What if Vince caught me? If he had Alex's watch, he was most likely Alex's killer. Would he kill me, too? To keep his secret?

I should call the police.

But no. What if Vince was perfectly innocent? And there was a really good reason why he was hiding Alex's watch in his office?

I tried to think of a single good one but failed.

I bit another nail. I sat on the bench. Stood. Sat. I realized now that the little awkward music-note symbol had to relate to Vince. Pulling out the calendar, I looked at it again. And as if a lightbulb went off, I turned the book upside down. The symbol was a melding of a *V* and a *P*. Vincent Paxton.

Why, I wondered, had she been so secretive about her meetings with him?

I tucked the calendar back into my purse and stared at the bookshop. Harper was still working—I could see her moving about inside the store. Gayle, too. I didn't see Vince, however, and that made me more nervous for some reason. Where was he? What was he doing?

Had he killed Alex?

If so, why?

"Darcy?"

I let out a little *"eee!"* and scrambled to my feet.

With a smile Nick said, "We definitely need to work on that."

I told myself not to be charmed by his smile. I was still upset with him for suspecting Harper was a pickpocket, even though Harper was right—he'd only been doing his job. Besides, the anger was a good way to put distance between us. "If you'd stop scaring me, it wouldn't be an issue."

His tucked his hands into his pockets and rocked on his heels. He was dressed for work—dark jeans, spiffy shoes, button-down shirt. He was on the job. Was he here to rehash the conversation we'd had this morning? If so, I really wasn't in the mood. I looked back to the bookstore. I had more important things on my mind.

"I want to apologize," he said.

"For?" I asked.

He fidgeted. "This morning."

"Why? You were just doing your job," I stated.

His eyebrows dipped, and the faint lines around his eyes deepened. "True."

I kind of enjoyed watching him squirm. It was rather cute.

"But I went about it the wrong way. I let personal issues get mixed up with business. It won't happen again."

"What do you mean, personal issues?"

He looked away, over my shoulder, not really focusing on anything. Again his eyebrows dipped. "I, ah . . ."

He had my full attention now. "What?"

Finally, he looked me in the eye. My stomach did that weird little gushy thing again.

"You know some about my wife. . . ."

I nodded.

"Melina was an amazing mother," he said, "but we had problems. She hated my job, the long hours, the danger. She was alone a lot and resented me for it. She'd given up a lot to be with me, and felt I should have done the same. But I loved my job and at that point, I didn't know how to be anything else."

I wasn't sure where he was going with this, so I let him continue.

"We fought. All the time. And it got to the point where we didn't even like each other very much. I left after she had her first affair. She wanted to find someone who'd give her everything she needed, and I wasn't that person—not anymore. Not by a long shot. We'd grown too far apart over the years. We wanted different things. She wanted the socialite lifestyle, whereas I wanted a nice, quiet suburban life. She wanted parties and champagne, and I wanted family movie night and popcorn."

The mushy feeling in my stomach threatened to overtake my heart.

"The divorce proceedings were filled with animosity, though we tried to shelter Mimi as much as possible. Then Melina got sick."

"And you went back to her?"

"I had to. There was no one else. Besides, I wanted to." He shrugged. "She needed me. Mimi needed me."

He was definitely the honorable sort.

"We at least became friends again before she died, but the emotional scars . . . they're still there."

Oh, I knew all about emotional scars. I tipped my head to the side. "Why are you telling me all this?"

He took a deep breath. "It's been over two years

since Mel died. Three since we'd separated." His eyes
locked on mine. "You're the first woman I've had any
interest in for years and years."

My eyes widened. My heart hammered.

"And I guess, I'm just trying to explain, I overreacted
this morning because of that."

"Because you like me?" Oh Lordy, Lordy. He liked
me. I felt giddy. And nauseated. And like a teenager all
of a sudden.

"I guess I didn't expect you to have a past. Or secrets.
You just seem so normal. And nice. It caught me by surprise is all, and I took it out on you. And I shouldn't
have. We all keep secrets."

Normal. Ha! If he only knew what secrets I was lug-
ging around.

"So, I'm sorry. Still friends?" he asked.

I was sorry, too. Because I'd never be able to tell him
I was a Wishcrafter. And not telling him would feel like
a betrayal after everything he'd just revealed. Which
meant only one thing.

There could never be anything between us—nothing
too deep, anyway. No matter how much we liked each
other. I put my hand out to shake. "Friends." And that
was all it could ever be.

"So," he said casually. "Your dog, Missy. Is that the
one Harper stole?"

"Her real name is Miss Demeanor. You've been doing your research."

"Sometimes I can be very thorough."

And just like that, the gushy feeling was back. I ignored it for the sake of my mental health.

"Can I ask you a question?" he said.

"Sure."

"Why do you keep looking over at the bookshop like
the bogeyman is in there?"

I didn't know what to say. Or how to say it. I couldn't
exactly explain my theory, but I could use his help. And

he did help me cover up the break-in at Alex's place. Though his wish about the gloves hadn't come true, so maybe he was covering something up, too. . . .

"Darcy, stop."

I blinked. "Stop what?"

"Thinking so hard."

"It shows, huh?"

"You'd never make a good poker player. Your emotions don't hide."

Well, that was good to know.

"What are you so worried about?"

I had to make a split decision. Trust him or not. I looked into his eyes and said, "I think I know who killed Alex."

"Ramona had this vision," I explained as we walked toward Spellbound Books. "That the watch was in Vince's office." I'd already told him about Ramona and Alex's catfight, both of their relationships with Vince, and my theory that Vince had been the one who tried to steal the recipe box from Lotions and Potions.

"A vision?" he repeated, a trace of skepticism in his voice.

"I know it sounds strange, but she's convinced."

He put his hand on my arm. "Darcy, did you stop to think that anyone could have planted that watch in Vince's office?"

"Anyone meaning Ramona?"

"She is a woman scorned."

"But Vince lied. About his relationship with Alex. Why would he cover that up?"

"Why would Ramona suddenly have a 'vision'?" he said, using air quotes.

I couldn't explain about the wish being granted, so I said, "It's possible. Anything's possible in this village, right?"

Heck, just a few nights ago, we saw someone vanish

before our eyes. He must have been thinking the same thing, because he said, "Do you think she's psychic?"

"I don't know. All I know is that she said she saw a vision clear as day as to where the watch was."

He shook his head. "I just don't buy it. I'd lay odds she put it there. She has more of a motive than anyone at this point. Vince may have lied, but he doesn't have a motive."

"If he thought Alex was a real witch, then found out she wasn't, he might be upset enough to kill her. He's obsessed with the Craft."

He studied me. "The Craft?"

Me and my big mouth. No one around here referred to witchcraft as the Craft except Crafters. "Witchcraft," I said as though he were the dense one for not picking up on that.

"Do you believe in witches?" His tone, his body language, his intent eyes, all told me he wanted a serious answer.

"Since moving here," I said in all honesty, "I've come to believe anything is possible."

"That's not really an answer," he pointed out.

Why was he pushing so hard?

It was then that we heard the shouting coming from inside the bookshop, then a loud crash . . . and, *oh my God*, was that a gunshot?

He yanked open the door, and we rushed inside.

The bookshop was empty and still with an eerie silence; then suddenly the shouting started once again. It was coming from the back office

"Don't make me fire again," Gayle was shouting from the doorway. She raised the gun in the air. "Next time will not be a warning."

Nick stepped up behind her. He plucked the gun out of her hand. "I'll take that."

She said, "Fine by me! It was the only way to get them to stop."

The screaming started again.

"Go, go!" She motioned him inside. "Before they kill each other."

He looked at the chaos, handed me the gun, and dove into the fracas.

I stared at the weapon, holding it with two fingers. "Maybe we should call the police?" I asked loudly, to be heard over the shouting.

Gayle yelled, "I already did."

Ramona was on Vince's back, pulling his hair, and screaming at the top of her lungs. Vince was grunting and moaning and cursing and trying to heave her off. Harper was trying to separate the two, a tiny little tennis ball in between two mighty rackets.

Nick yanked Ramona off Vince's back and put her on the ground.

Vince spun on her, his eyes blazing with fury. He lurched forward. Nick stepped in his way, held him back.

Ramona let out a cry and rushed forward, hands flailing. Harper stuck out her foot and tripped her. She fell on the floor.

"That's enough!" Nick boomed.

Everyone quieted.

I surveyed the damage. A big bookcase had toppled over; several frames had been knocked off the wall. Vince's face was scratched up, and he rubbed his scalp. Ramona rose and looked none the worse for wear.

"You," Nick said sternly to Ramona, "tell me what's going on."

"He killed Alex!" she cried, pointing at Vince.

"I did not!" Vince exclaimed. "You did!"

My head was starting to hurt.

Nick turned to Harper.

"It's all about this," she said, handing him Alex's diamond watch. "Ramona found it in Vince's desk."

"I didn't put it there!" Vince said in a panic. "Ramona had to have planted it!"

"Oh, you!" Ramona rushed forward again.

Nick lifted her off her feet and she struck out at empty air. After a second, she stopped wiggling and he set her back down—and made sure she stayed back an arm's length.

"How else would you have known where it was?" Vince asked.

"I had a vision," she said, then colored, as if only now realizing how lame that sounded. "You're the one who was having an affair with Alex!"

Harper gasped, her big eyes wounded.

"I can explain," Vince said to her.

Ramona said sarcastically, "Please do. I'm sure she'd love to hear all about how you were sleeping with Alex on Wednesday, then had asked Harper out by Sunday. Nice mourning period. Never mind that you were two-timing *me* with Alex!"

Harper stepped toward Vince and kicked him in the shin. He hopped around, crying out in pain.

"You go, girl!" Ramona said.

Gayle and I stood back, taking it all in and staying far out of the way.

Sirens grew louder and louder, and I spotted a village cruiser screech to a halt in front of the shop, lights flashing.

"You should probably put that gun down, Darcy," Nick said, "before they come in."

I quickly set it on the floor.

"Who called the cops?" Vince asked in a high, scared voice.

"I did," Gayle said. Her eyes blazed, and her lips had thinned. "And in case the gunshot warning wasn't enough of a hint, you're fired."

His eyes hardened. "I don't need this place anyway."

"Why's that?" Nick asked.

"I have something else lined up." He puffed with bravado. "Something bigger. Better."

Ramona snorted. "The only thing you have lined up is prison. Where you'll be staying for the rest of your life."

His fists clenched. "There's no proof I did anything to Alex. You're the one with the motive!"

What a jerk. I can't believe I'd been fooled by his puppy-dog eyes.

More shouting erupted; then it abruptly stopped as the police burst into the shop.

Nick looked between Ramona and Vince. "I hate to break it to you, but you're both going to jail."

Chapter Twenty-eight

Later that night, I lay in Ve's bed, Missy between us, as we watched the nightly news. I sipped my tea and watched as the Very Serious news anchor reported the new developments in Alex's murder and seemed to take great satisfaction that there were now two more viable suspects.

Harper came in and sat on the edge of the bed just as the news anchor was saying, "Marcus Debrowski, lawyer for the currently incarcerated Sylar Dewitt, maintains his client's innocence and feels his client will now be fully exonerated. The lawyer plans to approach the court tomorrow to reconsider bail."

Ve said, "He'll get it, won't he? Bail?"

"I can't imagine he wouldn't," I said. "Between Ramona and Vince, there is plenty of reasonable doubt. The judge will take that into consideration. He has to."

The pair were still being held for questioning. The state police were trying to sort out stories, alibis, and motives. Vince and Ramona were still accusing the other. The watch had been labeled evidence. Their houses were being searched, their names tarnished along with Sylar's.

Not surprising, Vince hadn't confessed to breaking and entering into Lotions and Potions. For which I was actually grateful—he may not have seen *me* in the apartment that afternoon, but he'd definitely seen *Evan*. Vince could have easily incriminated Evan but hadn't. I knew it wasn't out of the goodness of his own heart — pointing the finger at Evan would also cause Vince to incriminate himself — but still . . . I was grateful for his silence.

Ve took hold of her locket and swung it back and forth along its gold chain. "Which of the two do you think did it?"

Harper stared dully at the TV.

"Vince," I said, "though I doubt the police are going to get a confession. The only reason Ramona knew where that watch was is because of me. If I hadn't granted her wish, she never would have had the vision. It's hard to explain that." I wanted to believe that the police would thoroughly investigate. That justice would be served. But I also knew Sylar had been locked up for a few days on circumstantial evidence at best.

"He incriminated himself by not telling the police he was having a relationship with Alex," Ve said. "He should have owned up to that right off."

"I wonder why he didn't," I said.

Harper said, "He probably wanted to keep his job at Spellbound."

"What do you mean?" Ve asked.

"Ever since her husband died, Gayle won't tolerate any talk of witchcraft in the store, so Vince only talks about it when she's not around. He even told me that, about six months ago, she went so far as to have all the witchcraft books removed from the shelves and thrown out. He took them home."

"Isn't Gayle a Spellcrafter?" I asked Ve.

She nodded. "A Halfcrafter. Her husband was a Spellcrafter, may he rest in peace."

I bit my lip. "Is there any chance he's not resting in peace?"

Ve's eyebrows dipped. "Whatever do you mean?"

I smiled at the censure in her voice. "I was only wondering if Russ came back as a familiar. Is Higgins really Russ? Godfrey told me how Crafters can come back as familiars." He had also told me he didn't think Russ had come back, but I wanted Ve's take on it.

Ve started laughing. "Higgins? That big hulking dog? No, no." She giggled. "Russ would have been more a greyhound. *Higgins.* That's so funny."

"While we're on the subject," Harper said, "is there a familiar in this house?"

I glanced down at Missy. She lifted a sleepy eye. Tilda was in hiding.

Ve said, "Not for me to say."

Harper and I groaned in unison. We weren't going to get any answers from Ve, but Harper tried.

"Why not?" she asked.

"Darling girl, you must trust that what you need to know will be revealed in due time."

Harper huffed.

Ve started laughing again. "I'm still picturing Russ as a Saint Bernard."

I didn't think it was that funny.

I remembered the pain in Gayle's voice when she spoke about him. She was still grieving. Then I thought about Isaiah Clemson. How he'd reacted after leaving Mrs. P. He'd banished the Craft from his life—and their daughter's. "Is Gayle very religious?"

Harper shrugged. "Not to speak of. We don't talk about religion much, or the Craft, and I don't dare bring it up. I like my job. But Gayle's probably why Vince hadn't owned up to having a relationship with Alex. I don't think she would have stood for it."

It didn't matter now that he'd been fired. And was under suspicion for Alex's murder.

"I'm going to do a little reading and then go to bed," she said, bidding us good night.

She probably wasn't reading her forensics manual,

not tonight. Instead she'd turn to *Jane Eyre*, the classic
that always provided her comfort when she needed it.
And tonight, she needed it. This mess with Vince had hit
her hard.

A few minutes after she left, Ve said, "I feel for Mrs.
P, but Alexandra Shively brought nothing to this village
but discontent."

"I don't know about that," I said.

She looked sharply at me. "You disagree?"

I smiled at her tone. "I do. She was a good friend to
Evan, and Mimi Sawyer really cared for her. There was
some good there. I think, as you said last week, she was
complex. Part of that may have stemmed from the fact
that she knew she was a Crafter, but had no proof and
didn't know which kind. Think of how that made her feel.
She was an outcast in the only place she truly belonged."

Ve frowned. "Perhaps you're right."

"She also brought something else to the village," I
said, watching as the meteorologist pointed to a large
green mass off to the west. Rain would be here for the
weekend. "And I didn't realize it until I spoke with Ramona."

"What's that?" Ve asked.

"Hope."

Missy lifted her head, looked around, and set it back
down. I scratched her ears.

"How do you mean?" Ve asked.

"Look at the people who sought her help. They all
wanted, needed, something from her. They needed
hope that their lives would become fuller, richer, better.
Hope that they'd find the one they loved, that they'd get
rich, that they'd be happy. That they'd lose weight, get
healthy, have great skin. Little hopes, big hopes. She fed
those hopes, and even though sometimes she went
about it the wrong way"—I thought about Evan's
face—"or made grievous errors, she was trying to make
people's lives better."

"Complex," Ve said again, swinging her locket. "But I still didn't like her."

"That wouldn't have anything to do with her being Sylar's ex, would it?" Ve had confirmed with Sylar that he'd been the one to uncover Mrs. P's marriage license. To some, it might not seem a fair trade. A fifty-thousand-dollar watch for a piece of paper, but to Alex that paper—and the knowledge that came with it—was priceless.

"Maybe," she said coyly.

I glanced at the screen. "Oh, brother."

"In related news," the anchor said, "local business-man Griffin Huntley is now claiming Alexandra Shively, the victim in a local murder case, poisoned him."

"Just look at me," he said on-screen. "I'll be scarred for life."

The camera zoomed in on his face, which was covered with a now-familiar rash. The picture flashed to the news desk, where the normally staid anchor recoiled in horror.

The reporter went on to explain again how Griffin had been arrested for disturbing the peace after he'd been found pounding on the door of the victim's place of business the morning after she was found murdered. "Investigators have confirmed Mr. Huntley's alibi and never considered him a person of interest."

"Well," I said, "he may have been faking the baldness for fifteen minutes of fame, but that rash is very real."

"How do you suppose he got it?"

I had a good idea of how and knew whom to ask—someone who seemed to know just a little too much about Griffin Huntley's life. I just had to confirm it.

"Oh, look!" She pointed at the TV screen.

I sat up. A reporter was standing in front of Jake Carey's house. "A happy ending for this Melrose family. The Franklin Park Zoo has accepted the mysterious wombat with open arms, and has provided seven-year-old Jake with a lifetime membership, allowing him to visit the wombat, now named Ozzie, whenever he wants. As a reminder to our viewers, please check local codes before buying exotic pets. Most are endangered and illegal to own." The camera panned to Jake playing with the wombat in a secure area of the zoo. It then cut to footage of the wombat in a pen as it played with other wombats as Jake looked on. "Including wombats."

The newscast cut to a commercial.

Ve smiled at me.

"You'd think there'd be a Wishcraft Law about granting wishes for illegal pets."

She laughed. "It will probably be amended in."

I stood and stretched, ready for bed. "Just as long as I don't earn another trip to see the Elder."

"Try your best to stay on her good side."

I laughed. That was easier said than done.

A few days later, I was up early, ready to run with Starla. Mist was clinging stubbornly to the morning, and there was a hint of a chill in the air.

The green had almost been completely transformed for Saturday night's dance. Tents had been erected, a dance floor laid, and dozens of service trucks were arriving to complete last-minute tasks.

The week had passed in a blur. As You Wish had been busy, I'd finished helping Mrs. P pack up Alex's shop, and I'd been helping Starla prep for the dance. Gayle Chastain had offered Harper the managerial job at Spellbound Books—and she had eagerly accepted. Sylar had been released from jail on bail, and Ramona, though a suspect, had collected her reward from Ve. Which was gladly paid out, as Sylar was currently free because the watch had been found.

Alex's case was still open, and the state police presence in the village, including undercover officers, had increased now that they were undertaking a proper investigation. Village officers had been scarce, including the police chief. Their absence was quite obvious to the villagers, who were taking note and making plans for a complete overhaul of the police force.

The presence of the state police may have deterred the pickpocket, as there hadn't been reports of any thefts since Monday, when two hundred dollars had gone missing from a tourist the morning I picked up Ve's locket from All That Glitters.

Neither Vince nor Ramona had been arrested, though the police had named both as persons of interest. Neither had been seen much in the village since the outburst in the bookshop. There seemed to be a profound lack of evidence to arrest either of them, and it looked like Sylar would be off the hook as well.

Which all left a big pit in my stomach. I wanted justice for Alex. It didn't seem right that someone was going to get off scot-free. There had to be more evidence . . . somewhere. Someone had to know something more.

At the sound of running footsteps, I looked up and was surprised to see Evan headed my way. Usually he was in the bakery by this time every morning, and I knew for a fact that he didn't like to sweat.

He slowed to a stop at the bench and gave me a big smile. I hadn't seen him much in the past few days, except in passing. He'd been busy getting caught up at the bakery.

"Do my eyes deceive me?" I joked. "Evan Sullivan jogging?"

"I lost a bet with Starla."

I laughed. "What kind of bet?"

"I bet she couldn't convince you to cover for her today, and she bet that I couldn't keep up with the two of you this morning. This is essentially all your fault." He smiled. "Thanks a lot."

Starla actually hadn't convinced me of anything—she'd hired me through As You Wish. From noon to four today I'd be roaming around the green, snapping pictures of tourists. She'd given me a crash course in digital photography yesterday, and I hoped I would remember the basics, including Starla's dire warning to never use the phrase "Say cheese," simply because it drove her crazy.

I kept the whole hiring thing mum, though, because I had a feeling Evan would use it against her. And frankly, he could use a little exercise.

"Is she not coming this morning?" I asked.

"She's on her way. She didn't expect that I'd run faster than her." I wondered how long that would last. With newbie runners, the tortoise usually beat the hare in the long run.

"Nice shoes," he said, bending down to admire my sneakers. "What brand are they?"

They were blue, high-tech, and decorated with tiny rhinestones. "Custom-made," I said.

"Ooh la la!"

"And a gift."

He waggled his eyebrows. "From a boyfriend?"

"What boyfriend do you know would give running shoes as a gift?"

"I had one once. . . . No wonder he's an ex."

I laughed. "They were a gift from Pepe."

His eyes lit. "He's sweet on you. That's so cute."

"Nothing cute about it. The sneakers were a thank-you gift because I talked Godfrey out of getting a cat. Again."

"I'm surprised those two haven't killed each other yet."

"Give it time," I joked. "Speaking of boyfriends . . . anyone new in your life?"

"Oh no. I'm not currently on the market. My last date was enough to swear me off dating for a year."

"Your date with Griffin Huntley?"

His jaw dropped. "How'd you know?"

"I saw him on the news the other night with a rash on his face . . . and something Ramona said clicked. About how she thought if she used the love lotion on both she *and* Vince, it would work better. Your face, Griffin's face. Your comment the other day that Alex wasn't Griffin's type . . ."

"I can't believe I ever dated him." He hung his head.

"He is cute, especially now that all that horrible hair is gone."

He cracked a smile. "Alex introduced us. She knew I'd been looking for Mr. Right. A matchmaker she was not. I tried to salvage the date by pulling out the lotion. We both used it—to see if it would work. It didn't. It *really* didn't. I left the lotion at his place that night—that's where I lost it."

Ah, so he hadn't been telling me everything.

"When I called to see if he'd had a reaction, he said no. I warned him not to use any more of it, though, and told him to throw it out. But I don't think he did that at all."

"No?"

"I think he's been using gobs and gobs of it to get a reaction like mine. And therefore get more press."

Mrs. P did say that the more exposure, the worse the reaction would be.

"He got his wish. The media has been clamoring for interviews with him."

I stretched my calf muscle. "My guess is he's finally stopped using it, because the last time I saw him on the news, his face looked much better. Maybe he's learned his lesson?"

"I doubt it. He probably just ran out. It wasn't a very big tube." He sighed. "One of these days I'd like to kiss a frog and get a prince instead of just a plain old toad."

It sounded good to me, too. Which immediately had me thinking about Nick. I hadn't seen much of him, either, these last few days—Mimi was at day camp and he was busy with the pickpocketing case and avoiding me.

At least it felt as though he was avoiding me.

Even Missy had stopped escaping so much to see him.

Friends, we had said. It was better that way. At least that was what I kept telling myself. "Did I tell you I got a postcard from the Goodwins a couple days ago?"

He shook his head. "When are they coming back?"

"They'll be at the dance."

"Will you be?" he asked.

I spotted Starla coming through the mist, her ponytail slashing the air, and smiled. "I think so." Starla had kinda-sorta talked me into it. And I figured if I didn't wear that dress Pepe had made for me, he might chomp my ankle.

"With a date?" he asked, his eyes wide and hopeful.

"Nope. You're not the only one who has trouble with frogs."

"Well," he said, "as you recall, you promised me a dance."

"As I recall, you promised to save *me* a dance."

"Then it's settled!" He poked me with his elbow. "And I promise not to *ribbit*. Not even once."

Chapter Twenty-nine

"Okay, say cheese," I said, aiming the camera at a cute family crowded together. What Starla didn't know wouldn't hurt her.

They smiled, I clicked a picture, and I handed them a claim ticket. "You can purchase the photo at Hocus-Pocus Photography in an hour." I pointed toward the storefront next to the Gingerbread Shack. "Enjoy your visit to the village."

It was just after two, and I'd already taken nearly fifty pictures. Tourists had come back in droves over the past two days. The media attention had drawn out the curiosity seekers—who obviously had no worries about being pickpocketed.

Smiling, I clicked a few pictures of Higgins walking Gayle Chastain.

"Print me a copy!" she yelled as he dragged her down the block.

"Will do!" I called back, laughing as I checked the camera's display. The dog was huge. I still wondered if he was a familiar ... and realized the romantic in me wished it to be true. There was just something so sweet about Russ wanting to come back to be with his wife for a while longer. I could only imagine how hard it was for her to lose the love of her life.

Actually, I kind of knew. I'd seen my father go through

it. If my mother had been around, someway, somehow, maybe he'd have led a different life. A happier life.

Just as I was walking toward a young couple picnicking on the green, I caught a flash of bright pink. It was Mrs. P and she was with Marcus Debrowski—she was speed-walking and he was trying to keep up. They looked serious, but when Mrs. P spotted me, she beamed. She patted him on the back and turned in my direction.

I noticed Marcus took a second to catch his breath. He waved to me before heading off in the direction of his office.

I returned his wave and wondered if now that Vince was out of the picture, Harper would give the lawyer a chance. I'd just keep it to myself that I once considered him a murder suspect.

"Darcy! Just the woman I wanted to see. I need your help."

It was nice to see her bubbly again. Grief lingered in the dark circles under her eyes—she still wasn't sleeping well—but she'd come a long way from the glazed-over look she'd been walking around with after Alex's death. Grief affected people in such different ways. Mrs. P. had shut down, my father had stopped living life, Gayle had thrown herself into work, and Nick Sawyer had turned animosity into an ill-fated friendship.

"What kind of help?"

"Brute strength."

"You may have picked the wrong girl." I jiggled my flaccid arm. Less jiggly now than a week ago, but not nearly as toned as I'd hoped.

"Marcus just propositioned me."

"Mrs. P," I said in mock seriousness, "isn't he a little young for you?"

She threw her head back and laughed—the Phyllis Diller cackle I loved so much.

She winked. "I think I might be too experienced for

the likes of him. He needs someone a touch more . . . innocent."

Suddenly I was wondering what kind of life she had
led. She'd only been married twice for goodness' sake.

"Someone," she continued, "like *you*."

I started coughing. She pounded on my back.

"Oh, I don't think so," I squeaked.

"Just one little date."

"Um . . . no."

"Give it some thought."

I pretended to think. "No."

Arching an eyebrow, she studied me. "Ah, do you
have your heart set on another? Someone in particular,
who you've gotten to know well in the last week?"

"If you're talking about Evan, I don't think he's interested."

She laughed again, and tourists stopped, stared. Her
laugh was that outrageous. "All right," she said. "I'll let it
go. For now."

"What was the proposition?" I asked.

She linked arms with me and we strolled along the
path around the green. It was just about eighty degrees
and sunny with a light breeze that kept it from getting
too hot.

"He was approached by someone who wants to sublet Alex's apartment." Marcus had pulled some strings
(and, I suspected, used some magic) to fast-track having
Mrs. P named as the estate's administrator.

"That's great."

"Yes, but more interesting is that this person also
wants to buy Alex's entire inventory, lock, stock, lotions,
potions, and all. The buyer wants to keep the store open.
Marcus says it's not quite legal at this point, but as long
as all parties involved agree, he can make it happen. So
I said yes. The amount will allow me to settle Alex's remaining lawsuits."

I stopped in my tracks. "We're going to have to move

all the stuff back into the shop?" All the stuff we'd just moved out.

Nodding, she said, "Yes, but think of what great exercise it is." She jiggled my arm. "And of course, I'll fill out all the proper paperwork through As You Wish. The buyer wants to take possession at the end of next week. Are you available Monday?"

"I'll check the schedule, but I'm fairly sure it's open."

"Good!" She clapped her hands. "I'm so glad that's settled." Quietly, she added, "And I'm relieved that a little bit of Alex will live on, through that store."

I just hoped whoever was taking over was creating all new products. Or the newcomer risked more lawsuits. "Do you know who's buying it?"

She gazed at me. "I didn't think to ask. I don't suppose it matters."

I supposed not, but I still wanted to know.

"Mrs. P!" a voice shouted. "Mrs. P!"

We turned to find Mimi Sawyer running toward us, her pink witch hat in one hand, papers in the other. She was waving madly, a huge smile on her face.

Breathing hard, she caught up to us. She was so excited she was bouncing.

"What's going on?" Mrs. P asked her. "I thought you had camp today, little one."

"Half day." She gasped for air. "Today. And tomorrow. Found. These." She shoved the papers toward Mrs. P "In my hat." Turning the hat upside down, she pointed to a seam that revealed a hidden pocket.

Mrs. P smoothed out the papers and held them at arm's length so she could read them. "Can't read a damned thing without my glasses." She handed the papers to me.

"Oh!" My eyes filled with sudden tears, and I felt like such a sap.

"Tell me it's not more lawsuits," Mrs. P said.

Mimi bounced. "Tell her!"

"They're two birth certificates. For Virginia and for Alexandra. And your marriage license to Mr. Pennywhistle." The one that listed her former name as Eugenia Clemson. "Raised seals and everything. They're official."

"Is your middle name really Bartholomew?" Mimi asked.

Mrs. P laughed. She had grabbed the papers back and was trying her best to read the print. Instead, she ran her fingers over the seals. "It really is. Just don't let it get around, okay? Might ruin my reputation." She fluffed her hair. Well, she tried to. It was already poufed to the max.

"Thank you, little one, for finding these. I didn't think they were important, but now that I have them . . ." She held them to her chest and tears filled her eyes.

Mimi wrapped her arms around her.

"Snap a picture for me, will you, Darcy?" Mrs. P asked. "I want to remember this moment forever."

"I never turn out good in pictures," Mimi said, trying to wiggle away.

"Nonsense." Mrs. P latched on to her. "You're beautiful."

I'd almost forgotten about the camera around my neck. I backed up from them a few paces, took a quick look around to make sure Starla wasn't nearby, and said, "Say cheese."

"Cheese!" they echoed.

I clicked the button and looked at the display.

My chest squeezed when I looked at the photo. My skin tingled.

"What's wrong?" Mrs. P asked.

"It didn't come out," I said softly.

"Told you," Mimi said.

"Take another, then!" They posed.

I took another picture. And another. They always turned out the same.

Mrs. P's happiness exuded on the screen. But Mimi . . .

Mimi wasn't visible. Instead, there was a sunburst of bright white light in her place.

Which could mean only one thing.

Mimi was a Wishcrafter.

I quickly made up a lame excuse that I had to leave, and ran all the way home at a dead sprint.

"'Run, Forrest, run!'" Archie squawked as I passed Mr. Goodwin's house.

"*Forrest Gump*," I yelled as I shoved open the gate and ran up the back steps.

"That was a gimme," he called after me.

Inside, Missy barked. I quickly patted her head. I carefully set Starla's camera on the counter. "Ve!" I shouted. "Aunt Ve!"

I ran up the back staircase two steps at a time. "Ve!"

No one was home. I ran into my room, grabbed my purse, and dumped it onto the bed, looking for my cell phone. With shaking hands, I dialed Ve's cell. Her voice mailbox was full. I called Harper at work. It went to voice mail.

Missy was still barking. Tilda came to investigate the sound. Missy took her presence as an opportunity to play and pounced.

Tilda shot off the floor like she'd just been launched from a cannon and landed on the bed next to me. Missy came after her. Everything that had been in my purse went flying in all directions as paws searched for footing.

Tilda streaked from the room, Missy following behind, yapping. For all her maturity lately, I had a feeling that she would never learn her limits when it came to Tilda.

I sat on the edge of the bed and started picking up the mess. I didn't know what to do about what I'd learned. Mimi was a Wishcrafter. But Nick wasn't—he photographed just fine.

Then I remembered something he'd said to me. About how his wife had given up so much for him. She had been the Wishcrafter—it's the only thing that made sense. Which also explained why his wishes hadn't come true! He was a Halfcrafter. He knew about the Craft. How much, I didn't know, but he cared enough to bring his Crafter daughter back here to the village. . . .

Did Ve know? Had Nick told anyone? Did Mimi know? Or was she growing up just like Harper and I had?

As I paced, I gathered up my wallet, my comb, and two receipts from the floor.

I had to find out. And I knew of only one person who could tell me for certain.

The Elder.

I needed to meet with her.

Quickly, I gathered up the rest of my stuff and shoved it back into my purse. The last thing I picked up was Alex's pocket calendar. It had fallen open to a page from last December, and a name jumped out at me. Alex had a series of appointments with one person for a week straight.

I blinked, bits falling into place.

My stomach knotted and filled with dread.

Suddenly, I had a feeling I knew who had really killed Alex.

And hoped I wasn't right, but grief really did make people do crazy things.

Chapter Thirty

I'd commissioned Archie to deliver my note to the El-der's tree. In return I had to promise to play a game of Trivial Pursuit, the *Lord of the Rings* version, with him.

He didn't stand a chance at that one.

He promised me that he'd deliver the message and get back to me as soon as possible with an arranged time to meet with the Elder.

I walked across the green to the bookshop. My stomach hurt.

Pulling open the door, I took a deep breath. I wasn't sure why I was here. Why I hadn't simply called the police to deal with it.

I supposed I wanted to be sure. Before I turned some-one's life upside down on a hunch.

Harper frowned when she saw me. "Someone steal your magic wand?"

I smiled at what was becoming a familiar greeting from her. "Long day. Illuminating, as Starla would say."

"Are you talking in riddles on purpose?"

I didn't want to get into it with her about Mimi. Not yet. Not before I talked to the Elder.

Glancing around, I noticed that there was only one other person in the shop. A man browsing the mystery section.

I motioned her closer. She leaned in. "I think I know who killed Alex."

Gayle rose from behind the counter. "Oh?" she asked.

My cheeks heated. "I, ah, didn't see you there."

She held up a tiny screwdriver. "Just fixing the printer."

"Who?" Harper said, leaning forward, resting her elbows on the counter. Her eyes were rounded with curiosity. "I keep going over it in my head. And though Vince is a front-runner, I really can't see him killing his golden goose. And Ramona? She's just too nice."

"Sometimes niceness has nothing to do with it. Does it, Gayle?" I asked.

"Of course it does," Harper said. "Nice people just don't go around killing other people."

The man from the mystery section had moved closer to us. Clearly eavesdropping.

"Well," I said, trying to choose my words carefully. "Let me present this scenario to you."

Harper nodded eagerly. Gayle had gone pale.

"Imagine you're living your dream life, happy as a clam. You and your husband just opened your own shop, and business is good. Life is good."

"Okay," Harper said quietly, stealing glances at Gayle.

"Imagine your husband, who has heart problems to begin with, gets sick. The flu. It was bad last year, remember?"

"How could I forget? I was sick as a dog for a week."

I remembered, too—I'd been the one to take care of her.

"Well, your husband's been sick for a while. He's just not getting better as quick as he would like, but he hates doctors and refuses to see one. But he's heard of a woman in the village who sells medicinal offerings, homeopathic treatments. All-natural. Completely safe and proven to work. He thinks maybe she might be able to help him." I was filling in blanks with conjecture, but by the look on Gayle's face, I knew I wasn't far from the truth. "So he goes to see her every day for a week, swallows whatever she tells him to. But instead of getting better, he dies suddenly. A heart attack, the medical examiner says—from heart disease. But you blame her. Wait months for your revenge . . ."

Harper's head turned side to side, looking between me and Gayle. "This is all hypothetical, right?"

Softly, Gayle said, "I went and confronted her after he died. She told me all she did was give him herbal tea and wasn't responsible. When I asked what kind, she told me. She gave him licorice tea. Licorice! Any numskull herbalist knows you shouldn't give licorice root to someone who has high blood pressure. That tea killed him. It caused his heart attack sure as I'm standing here. I figured out what a fraud she was too late to help Russ, but I could sure as hell stop her from hurting someone else. I just needed time to figure out how."

Harper looked stunned. Her mouth had fallen open, and her eyes were shiny with tears. "Were you just going to let Sylar take the blame? Vince? Ramona?"

Gayle set the tiny screwdriver on the counter. "I believed the police would eventually clear Sylar—I mean, come on. Sylar wouldn't hurt anyone. Ramona, too. My plan was that Vince would be arrested. That he'd get locked up and stay there. All his talk about witchcraft. He's just as bad as Alex was and maybe more dangerous because he doesn't know how deadly it can be."

"You planted the watch on his desk?" I asked.

"Of course I did," she said. "I thought the police would search the shop." She shook her head. "They didn't search thoroughly enough." In one quick motion, she reached under the counter and pulled out a handgun. The same one that had fired the warning shots a few days ago.

"Whoa!" Harper said, backing up.

"I did everyone a favor," Gayle said, waving the gun.

I'm not sure Mrs. P, Evan, or Mimi would agree. Never mind Sylar, Vince, and Ramona.

"Put the gun down, Gayle," I said. My heart hammered, my palms dampening.

I wanted to jump the counter, protect Harper. But I was scared to death that any sudden move might make Gayle fire.

"No." She raised the gun, but didn't take aim at me, or Harper, either. She raised it to her temple. "It's time for me to go, to be with Russ."

The man from the mystery section stepped forward, a gun drawn. "Police. Lower your weapon."

Harper slid around the counter, toward me.

Gayle shook her head, closed her eyes.

I picked up the closest thing I could find—a Spanish-English pocket dictionary—and threw it at her hand just as the gun went off. The bullet barely grazed the side of her head. She screamed. Harper screamed. I screamed.

The undercover state policeman jumped the counter and tried to wrestle the gun from her hand, but she was holding on tight. Determined.

Suddenly, the gun went off again. I felt a searing pain in my arm. I looked down. Blood seeped through the sleeve of my white T-shirt and dripped down my arm.

Blood. So much blood. I *hated* the sight of blood. My knees went weak. My vision swam. The last thing I remembered was Harper screaming.

Her screams were much better than mine.

"You really don't have to do that," I said two days later. I was sitting on my bed, propped up, my arm kept close to my body so as not to pop any stitches.

"I want to."

I persisted. "It's not necessary."

"I beg to differ, *ma chère*. My glorious creation could not, and shall not, be debased by such, such . . . mediocrity." Pepe twitched his nose at me as he fingered my hospital-issued sling with a shudder.

He was busy bedazzling my new sling, and would probably have a stroke if he knew I was calling it bedazzling. He'd spent the last two hours hand-beading an intricate design on a sling he'd custom-made to match my dress.

"Well, I appreciate it. And the house call." I was trying to save my energy (doctor's orders) for the dance tonight and was limiting trips outside my bedroom. The bullet that struck me had passed cleanly through my upper right arm. Lots of stitches, pain medicine, antibiotics, and an overnight stay at the hospital later, and I was well on the road to a full recovery.

I really didn't need the bed rest, but Aunt Ve had insisted, and I had little willpower where she was concerned.

Pepe gave a little nod. "And I am grateful you have locked that furry beast out of the room."

Tilda had been trying her best to get inside since she sniffed his arrival. Every few minutes her paw would slip under the door and swipe empty air. I admired her persistence.

Missy, on the other hand, stared at Pepe with adoration, not making a single move to eat him for lunch. He even allowed her a few kisses. Nick might have some serious competition for Missy's affection.

I unfolded the note that Archie had delivered to me after I got home from the hospital yesterday. I reread it for the hundredth time, still wondering what I should do about Mimi.

You have the answers, Darcy. Trust yourself. Trust your knowledge. This is your biggest test so far. Do not fail.

I bit my fingernail. I didn't know why the Elder denied me the answers I needed. Or why she thought I already possessed them. I didn't know what to do about Nick and Mimi, and the harder I pressed Aunt Ve for help, the more mum she became. She had been given the order not to help me with this assignment. Though I did get the admission from her that she knew all along Mimi was a Wishcrafter.

I sighed.

"Are you in pain, *ma chère*?"

Not that kind. "No, the pain medication works wonders." Pepe finished sewing his last bead. The sling was a work of art. I admired it. "It's beautiful."

He tucked his tiny needle into a pouch. "Fitting for one such as yourself."

I smiled. "Thank you, Pepe."

He bowed again. "I must go now. Appointments all afternoon."

I bent down and kissed the top of his head. His cheeks reddened.

"You'll get back safely?" I asked.

"Not to worry. I have a ride." He gave a sharp whistle and Archie appeared at my open window. Pepe lifted a corner of the screen, climbed on Archie's neck, and waved good-bye. Missy barked as Archie said, "I want a rematch!"

Tilda's paw swept under the door.

Just another day in the Enchanted Village.

Where magic lived.

I dropped my head back against my pillows and scratched Missy's ears with my good hand. My room was filled with balloon arrangements and vases of flowers. I'd already had several visitors today. Starla and Evan. Ramona. Godfrey. Sylar.

After being taken to the hospital, Gayle had been arrested for the murder of Alexandra Shively. Her wound had been treated and she'd been taken to jail, where she was currently under a suicide watch. She'd been completely desolate that she'd injured me.

Complex. Ve had used the word to describe Alex, but it fit Gayle, too. On one hand, she was a grief-stricken widow, a nice person, one who cared deeply that she'd hurt me. On the other, she had no remorse for killing Alex. Or for trying to frame Vince.

It created a chasm within me, because on one hand, I could understand why she did what she did. Yet on the other, there's no excuse for her behavior. The courts would sort it out, but personally I hoped they would be lenient. She needed counseling more than prison time.

My gaze dropped to the note on my bed.

Trust yourself.

Trust myself.

I looked at Missy. "Do you want to go see Nick and Mimi?"

She bounced up, her tail wagging.

"You're shameless," I said.

She barked.

I quickly slipped my arm into my sling of mediocrity.

"Don't get too excited," I told her. "He's not going to be happy with what I have to say, especially not that his daughter is technically a criminal."

Chapter Thirty-one

I had a vague idea of where Nick and Mimi lived, but I didn't need directions when I had Missy. She led the whole way there. We walked slowly, and took the long way around the green to avoid seeing anyone I knew. There would be time enough later for questions, comments, and sympathies.

Right now, I really just wanted to see Nick, talk to him about Mimi, and get back for a nap before the dance tonight.

Gray clouds hovered overhead, and I felt a raindrop as Missy guided me toward Old Forest Lane. It was sprinkling now, but the forecast promised heavier showers for tonight. Starla was beside herself with worry that the dance would be ruined, so she'd ordered more tents. The green was covered with them. But instead of it looking like a tent city from the aftermath of a natural disaster, she'd gone to great lengths to make them pretty.

Colorful swags of tulle (acceptable in this case), fairy lights, and beautiful lanterns hung from the tent eaves, making them look like something out of a fairy-tale wedding reception. A catering truck rumbled by as Missy and I crossed the street. The treelined Old Forest Lane was paved in cobblestones and its serpentine sidewalk had a flower border. Houses were modest, with decent lots. Kids were playing kickball in the street and their laughter echoed. Farther down the street, houses spread out. Driveways were longer, houses bigger, lots larger. By the time we reached the last house, it felt as though it were the only home on the street.

The front yard was contained by a picket fence, and the driveway was gravel, not paved. The yellow farmhouse was charming with its white shutters, big front porch, and window boxes crammed full with pink petunias and cascading ivy. Behind the house, there was a large detached garage that had been designed to look like a carriage house. Its wide doors were open, and I heard the whir of a power saw.

I dragged Missy away from the hole under the fence and headed toward the noise. She had her nose to the ground and sniffed like crazy, taking in all the new scents. Gravel crunched under my feet as I approached the doorway, and my eyes slowly adjusted to the dim light inside. To the right, Nick's truck sat in a garage bay, and the rest of the space had been converted into a woodwork shop.

The smell of freshly cut wood hung in the air, and I breathed it in, loving it. Nick's back was to me as he sliced a piece of wood on a fierce-looking saw table. The saw went through the piece of wood like butter. Nick examined the edges of the board, then pushed a button on the saw, silencing it.

Suddenly, there was a booming *woof, woof,* and a coppery and white blur hurtled toward us. I was envisioning another trip to the emergency room when Nick spun around.

"Higgins, heel!" he commanded.

The Saint Bernard slowed to a stop, but kept sniffing in my direction.

I went over to pat the big dog. "Hello there, Higgins." He slobbered on my hand. Missy sniffed to her heart's content.

I bent down. "Russ, is that you?"

A little bit of drool fell from Higgins's lips.

Okay, maybe Godfrey and Ve were right about this dog not being a familiar.

Nick's look of surprise dissolved into a smile. "Look what the dog dragged in," he said, taking off his safety glasses and setting the wood aside. He wiped his hands on his jeans as he came toward me.

My chest squeezed. I looked at Nick and motioned to the dog. "How did you get Higgins?"

"Animal control brought him to the shelter when Mimi and I were there revisiting potential dogs. She recognized him right away, and he didn't want to leave her side. We couldn't come home without him."

"No," I said, my chest so tight it ached, "you couldn't."

Missy barked and danced, and Nick crouched down to give her love and attention before standing and looking at me. There was such tenderness in his eyes when he said, "Are you okay?"

I lifted the sling. "It's but a mere flesh wound." Archie would appreciate the quote.

He smiled. "No gunshot is a mere flesh wound. Trust me, I know."

"I'll be good as new in no time." I reached out and touched his cheek. His eyes flashed with the heat I'd seen the other day, and it made me want to melt. A fleck balanced on my fingertip. "Sawdust."

"Not as pretty as glitter."

I smiled.

He said, "Mimi's been dying to come see you, but I thought you might want to rest." Higgins nudged his hand, and Nick patted his head.

"A visit would have been nice. Is she home?"

He shook his head. "She's with Mrs. P and Starla, helping out with preparations for tonight."

Maybe it was just as well she wasn't here.

"Something wrong?" he asked.

"I need to talk to you about something."

"Sounds serious," he said.

"It is."

He folded his arms across his chest. They were covered in more sawdust. I kept my hands to myself.

"What?" he asked.

"I know who your pickpocket is."

"He's still in the village? I thought he'd moved on—we haven't had any reports in a week."

I smiled. "Not moved on. She's been at camp."

He looked puzzled.

I spelled it out. "Nick, Mimi is the pickpocket."

His eyes darkened. "Let's sit down. I think you'd better explain."

A few minutes later, we sat on his front-porch swing. He'd brought out some lemonade, and I clutched my glass as I tried to explain.

Trust yourself.

He was being more patient than I imagined possible, considering I'd just accused his daughter of a crime.

We swayed back and forth.

I took a deep breath and said, "Tell me what you know about the Craft. Tell me what you know about Mimi being a Wishcrafter."

He glanced down, stared at the ice cubes bobbing in his lemonade. His gaze shifted to me. "Is that what she is? A Wishcrafter?"

"You don't know?"

"I knew she was a Crafter, but Melina never told me what kind she was. We never really talked about it much at all, and hardly ever once she decided to marry me and raise Mimi as a mortal."

"What changed?" I asked. "Why did you bring Mimi back to the village?"

We swung. Missy and Higgins were busy sniffing the front yard, stem to stern.

"I'd seen how unhappy it had made Melina, not being part of her Craft. She lost her powers when she married me. Did you know that?"

"I know Wishcrafters lose their powers when they tell a mortal about their abilities, yes."

My heart was beating hard. *Trust yourself.*

"After she died, I realized I didn't want Mimi to grow up not knowing who she is, how special she is. I brought her back here. I didn't know what kind of Crafter she was, or who to approach about helping her. It's not just something you can ask out of the blue. I haven't even told Mimi that she's a Crafter yet. I don't know how to open a conversation like that. I know there's someone in this village who could help her. I just don't know who."

"Nick, she already knows."

"Why do you say that?"

"She's been practicing her wishing spells. That's how she was pickpocketing."

He stood up, paced the porch. "I don't understand."

"When someone wishes for money, and a Wishcrafter grants the wish, it has to come from someone else. Someone loses the money, usually someone who won't miss it or who has plenty to spare. So, when Mrs. P wished she had enough money to do something nice for her granddaughter, Mimi granted the wish. Later, Mrs. P inexplicably found a thousand dollars in her dresser drawer. If you add up the amount 'stolen'"—I used air quotes—"from the tourists that day by the pickpocket, it adds up to a thousand dollars."

His eyes went wide. "So the other day, in front of All That Glitters, when the man suddenly found that money in his pocket . . ."

"The woman had made a wish, remember? Mimi granted it. I expect, if you ask her, she'll admit to granting wishes all over the village the last couple of weeks. When did school let out for the summer?"

He suddenly laughed. "A little over a month ago."

Right when the pickpocketing started.

"Just so I'm clear, she's not actually sticking her hands in someone's pockets...."

Smiling, I said, "No. It's all done magically."

"That explains a lot."

I stood up. "You need to talk to her. Explain as best you can. Tell her as much as you know. The rest, she can come to me."

He rose. "You?"

I smiled. *Trust yourself.* "I'm a Wishcrafter, too."

Shaking his head, he said, "I thought Crafters couldn't tell mortals about their powers without losing them? At least that's what Melina said."

"She was right. Kind of." I explained about Halfcrafters. And how he was, by marriage, now half mortal, half Wishcrafter. My powers were safe.

He said, "Can I ask you something that's been bothering me?"

"Sure."

"The night of the break-in at Alex's shop, the person who vanished. That was a Crafter, right? I mean, I figured it had to be...."

"Mrs. Pennywhistle, looking for the birth certificate Mimi found."

His eyes widened. "What kind of Crafter is she?"

"Vapor."

Shaking his head, he said, "I have a lot to learn."

We both did.

It was still only sprinkling, but it looked like the skies were going to open any minute now. "I should go. I promised Harper I'd help her get ready for the dance."

Somehow I'd talked her into going. I'd played on her gunshot-wound sympathies a bit to help me.

"You're going, too, aren't you?" he asked.

"Yes. You?"

"Yes."

A second passed. Two.

"You'll save me a dance, won't you?" he finally said.

I nodded, and as Missy and I made our way home, all I kept thinking about were princes and frogs.

The dance was in full swing later that night as I stood with Mrs. P and Starla in the far corner of the massive tent.

"If you didn't want to help with moving Alex's things back to the shop, you just had to say so. You didn't have to go get yourself shot."

Mrs. P cackled at her own joke. She wore a fire engine red flamenco dress. Her hair had reached new heights.

"Anything to get out of manual labor," I said. I glanced across the green to Lotions and Potions. It turned out that Vince was the one who'd sublet the shop from Mrs. P.

When I'd asked her how she felt about that, she said she was okay with it. In fact, she was going to work for him, helping him replenish the stock. "Best to have someone who knows what they're doing in charge," she said.

My gaze shifted to the bookshop, lingered on the CLOSED sign in the window. No one knew what was going to happen to it.

"Come on," Starla said. "Admit that it was your own form of liposuction. You just couldn't stand that flaccid arm a moment longer."

I laughed. "Guilty."

We stood on the edge of the dance floor. Rain poured down beyond the safety of the tent. No one seemed to notice it. Or care. It seemed to only add to the magic in the air. The rain made me miss my mother something fierce, but in a strange way I also felt as though she were here with me tonight . . . almost as if the rain were her gift to me.

Harper danced by, looking slightly terrified and intrigued at the same time. Her partner was Abel Buchanan, the young undercover policeman who'd been in the bookstore the day I was shot.

I wondered if I was the only one who noticed the way Marcus Debrowski, who stood on the other side of the dance floor, closely watched them. Mimi and Nick danced by, and Sylar and Aunt Ve were practically glued together at the center of the floor.

He'd proposed last night. And she'd accepted.

I didn't know how I felt about the engagement quite yet. Time would help sort things out, I supposed.

"I'll be right back," I said, heading for the punch bowl.

It was getting late and the crowd was thinning. The dance had been a huge success.

As I was trying to ladle punch into a cup one-handed, Harper appeared at my side and took over. Her cheeks were flushed, her eyes bright.

"You're having fun," I said.

"You don't have to make it sound like an accusation."

We walked to the edge of the tent. The dinner tables here had been long abandoned, and it was relatively quiet in this corner.

"Not an accusation. Merely an observation."

"I'm having fun," she admitted. "Abel's cute, isn't he?"

"You liiike him," I sang.

She gave me a wry smile. "I suppose I deserved that."

"Absolutely."

"Have you danced with Nick?" she asked.

"Not yet."

"He better get a move on. The night's almost over."

I glanced over her head, toward the dance floor where I'd last seen him. He wasn't there. Instead, I spotted him and Mimi standing with Starla and Mrs. P. He was looking straight at me.

I smiled and looked away, thinking about the note I'd received from the Elder late this afternoon.

Well done.

"Darcy, I need your help," Harper said, her tone . . . wistful.

"With what?" I asked. "Abel?"

She laughed. "No, I think I can handle him on my own."

"Then what?"

"That."

I followed her gaze to Spellbound Books.

She looked at me, her eyes filled with excitement. "I want to buy it. I have enough from our inheritance to put down a good chunk of a down payment, but I'll need a loan for the rest. Will you cosign for me?"

I thought about what that would mean. "So you wouldn't work at As You Wish?"

"I don't think the Wishcrafter thing is for me."

"And you'd live . . ."

"Over the bookshop."

My stomach started aching.

She put her hand on my arm. "It's what I want, Darcy. It's what I've always wanted. I just didn't realize it until I worked there. Will you help me? Please?"

I searched her eyes and could feel her determination. And as always when she asked nicely, I couldn't say no. "Of course."

Her smile stretched wide. "Thank you."

"Am I interrupting?" a voice asked.

We turned. Marcus stood there, wringing his hands. He looked sheepish. And he only had eyes for Harper.

"Just finished," I said.

"Good, good. Harper, I was wondering . . ."

If he was ever going to have a chance with Harper, he had to overcome this shyness.

"If you wanted to dance. With me." He coughed. "Over there." He pointed to the dance floor.

I held in a laugh.

Harper nodded.

As they headed off, I leaned against a tent support

and stared out at the rain. A minute later, I felt a tug on the hem of my dress. At first I thought it must be Pepe, but when I looked down, I saw the face of a child staring up at me from beneath the tablecloth.

I moved a chair aside and crouched down. "Laurel Grace?"

She whispered, "Where are your wings?"

I smiled. "I had to leave them at home. I hurt my arm in a flying accident, see?"

Solemnly, she nodded. "When I broked my arm, my sling wasn't that pretty."

"I'm pretty lucky. A friend made it for me. Did you have a nice vacation?"

Her face lit up and she bobbed her head. "The best."

"Good." I heard Amanda calling for her. "I think your mom is looking for you. You better go."

She scrambled back under the table; then a second later she reappeared. "Tooth fairy?"

"Yes?"

"I think you look even prettier tonight."

Then she was gone, rushing back to her mother. I stood and Amanda waved. Dennis, too, before he wrapped his arm around his wife and took his daughter's hand.

I turned and found Nick standing off to the side. "I agree with her."

"Thank you," I murmured.

"Though I still want to see those wings someday."

"Maybe. If you're lucky. I don't show them to just anyone. Did you talk to Mimi?" I asked.

He nodded. "You were right about the wishing spell. She found one of Mel's old diaries and the spell was written in it."

I was pretty sure that was a big Wishcraft Law no-no, but didn't say anything.

A second passed. Two. He shifted from foot to foot. "Sylar paid me a visit after I saw you this afternoon."

"Oh?"

"He wanted to tell me Chief Leighton resigned today."

I tipped my head. "What does that have to do with you?"

"Sylar asked me if I wanted the chief's job."

I felt my eyes widen. "What did you say?"

"That I'd think about it. Being on the pickpocket case made me realize how much I missed police work."

"But?" I sensed there was one.

"It's a big decision. I have to think about Mimi, too. I can't ignore that it's a dangerous job."

The band announced the last song.

"But," he said, "there's enough time to think about that tomorrow. For now, would you like to dance?"

Smiling, I said, "I'd love to." I started for the dance floor.

He grabbed my hand. "Not there, Darcy. Out there." He motioned outside the tent.

The rain fell in a steady sheet, its sweet scent filling me with emotion, reminding me of my mom. Telling me just how much Nick cared for me to remember what I'd told him about my childhood.

Mushy gushiness spread throughout my whole body. My nerves tingled; my senses swirled. I couldn't stop the huge smile spreading across my face.

I kicked off my shoes and accepted his hand. We stepped out into the rain. He carefully held me with one arm, making room for my sling, and with the other, he took hold of my free hand and held it tightly.

It had been a long, interesting week. It was easy to forget about gunshots and murder when wrapped in Nick's arms. I'd be quite happy if I could wish to never be involved in another murder case for as long as I lived, but I knew it was pointless. I couldn't grant my own wishes.

But as he held me close, I thought again about princes

and frogs. And also about the wish I'd made on the four-leaf clover Mimi had given me.

As he twirled me, and I caught a glimpse of the look in his eyes, I had to wonder if sometimes, just out of pure luck or by beating the odds, my wishes could come true.

Later that night, as Darcy slept, she had no idea how closely she was being watched.

Or by whom. Which was for the best at this point, the observer reflected.

Darcy stirred, rolled. She was a restless sleeper. How long until she settled down? Settled in? Let the past remain in the past? Let her heart heal and embraced destiny?

A while, she figured. But with her help and Ve's help, Darcy would come through just fine. She was sure of it.

Mimi needed someone like Darcy in her life. And Nick deserved happiness, too.

She just wished she'd been the one to provide it. But, alas, she couldn't grant her own wishes, either. And besides, life had other plans for her. Important plans.

She'd had to pull some strings to get into this form, but at least this way she could still be part of their lives.

Darcy rolled again, reaching out and patting her observer's head. And damn if she didn't like it. She had only been in this body a few weeks, but she wondered if she'd ever get used to it, or to having animal instincts.

Or if she'd ever get used to seeing her ex-husband with someone else.

Time would tell.

"Good night, Missy," Darcy murmured.

Or if she'd ever get used to *that* name.

Melina Sawyer yawned, stretched, and turned three times in a circle before curling into a ball next to Darcy.

Again, only time would tell. . . .

Read on for a sneak peek at the next
Wishcraft Mystery,

A Witch Before Dying

Coming in August 2012 from Obsidian

"It's going to be a horrible job, Darcy."

Elodie Keaton's voice was loud, clear, and completely distraught. She really needed to learn that a warning was never the best way to describe a potential job.

And, if I'd known what was ahead for me, I would have listened to that warning. Unfortunately, that morning I was too distracted to heed anything as I met with Elodie, As You Wish's newest client, at her shop.

I was so enchanted by my surroundings that it was easy to say, "I'm sure the job's not that bad."

I wasn't much of a glitzy-glam person, but even I was charmed inside the Charmory as I stood in the midst of bright, shiny, sparkling, colorful bliss. Everywhere I looked there were gems of every cut and hue. In fanciful cases, handcrafted loose beads waited to be strung into custom bracelets and necklaces. Displays held vintage jewelry including pendants, charms, talismans, and amulets. Whimsical tableaus of stunning natural stones and minerals of various sizes, shapes, and colors. Like a magpie, I wanted to pick everything up and bring it home.

As You Wish, my aunt Ve's personal concierge service, had received a phone call that morning from Elodie, wanting to hire the company to help clean out a cluttered house. Now that my sister, Harper, was no longer an employee, and Aunt Ve was currently bedridden with a summer flu, tackling this job fell to me. And as I was desperate to escape Ve's germs, I'd volunteered to walk over to Elodie's shop right away to talk with her about the details.

It was a short walk. The Charmory was just a block away from As You Wish, where I worked and lived with Ve. Both businesses were located in the Enchanted Village, a themed neighborhood of Salem, Massachusetts. The village was a tourist hotspot for those who came to see for themselves if the village slogan of "Where Magic Lives" was true.

It was, not that mortals knew it. The Enchanted Village offered a safe haven to hundreds of witches, or, as we called ourselves, Crafters. Here, we hid in plain sight among the mortals with whom we lived and worked.

There were many types of Crafters, such as Curecrafters (healing witches), Vaporcrafters (who had the ability to vaporize in thin air), Cloakcrafters (master clothiers), and even several like me, my sister, Harper, and Aunt Ve: Wishcrafters, witches who could grant wishes using a special spell.

And as I'd come to find out, Elodie was a Wishcrafter, too.

Well, partly. Elodie was technically a Cross-Crafter (a Crafter hybrid). Elodie's wish-granting abilities, inherited from her father, were practically nonexistent. Her predominate Craft was Geocrafting—her mother's Craft. Rarely were a Cross-Crafter's abilities split equally—one gift was always stronger than the other.

Everywhere I looked inside the shop a bauble or glitzy trinket caught my eye. Elodie's Geocrafting skills with clay, gemstones, rocks, and minerals were obvious. Tiny price tags hung from ribbons. Some of the merchandise was quite affordable, and some was out-of-this-world expensive. Undoubtedly, there was something in this store that would appeal to everyone, tourist, villager, mortal, or Crafter.

A frown pulled on the corners of Elodie's mouth. "Not bad?" She echoed my words. "No, Darcy, not *bad*. It's *worse*. Much, much worse."

Her tone was starting to make me nervous. "How much worse?"

Short and thin with shoulder-length curly blond hair, a long, narrow face, wide-set blue eyes, and a shy but somewhat sad smile, Elodie was younger than me. I placed her to be more my sister, Harper's, age—early to mid-twenties. Fairly young to own her own shop—just like Harper, who'd recently taken over Spellbound Bookshop. Tapping the countertop that separated us with short fingernails painted a sparkly blue, she said, "Have you ever seen that TV show about people who hoard?"

I had seen it. And immediately afterward started cleaning and throwing clutter away. "This is your house you're talking about?" She didn't look the type to live in squalor.

Crystals hung in the big bay window overlooking the village green, and every time the sun peeked out from behind fluffy white clouds, rainbows streaked across the room, spilling color on the already vibrant collection of goods in the shop.

"No," she said. "Well, maybe." Then she looked at me, her eyes pained. "I don't know."

"If it's your house?" Seemed like a fairly straightforward question.

"Technically, it's my mother, Patrice's, as is this shop, but I've been taking care of both." Her forehead wrinkled and her voice dropped. "Mom's been missing for a year and a half, and there's just not enough money to keep up payments on both places. I'm going to have to sell her house."

I didn't know much about Patrice Keaton's disappearance. Only what Aunt Ve, in her feverish state this morning, had told me: Patrice had vanished without a trace.

"Can you do that?" I asked.

"As her trustee, I can. I don't want to, but I can't see any other option. I don't have enough savings to pay her bills and mine, and there's no one else to turn to for financial help."

I had many questions, mostly about her mother and the circumstances surrounding her disappearance, but I didn't think now was the right time to ask them. "Are you living there, in your mother's house?"

She shuddered. "No. It's really not livable. My fiancé, Connor, and I live here—upstairs."

Village shops were either side-by-side shared storefronts or detached homes that doubled as businesses. Aunt Ve's business, As You Wish, was in a gorgeous Victorian on a large corner lot at the west end of the square. The Charmory was also a Victorian. Though it was much smaller than Ve's place, it had a similar layout. On the first floor was a front parlor, a wide hallway leading to a private office space, and a small powder room. In the back of the house would be a big kitchen and family room. Upstairs, there were probably only two bedrooms (instead of Ve's three)—plenty of room for two people.

Surprisingly, I noticed Elodie wore only a modest diamond engagement ring— I would have thought a Geocrafter would have had an outrageous stone. And now that I was looking, I saw that she didn't wear any other jewelry. Not even a dainty pair of earrings. I wasn't a big jewelry wearer either, but if I had been surrounded by all those crystals and beads every day, I would have been tempted.

"In order to sell Mom's house," she was saying, "it needs to be cleaned out. Really cleaned out. I can't hire just anyone. Mom didn't collect just junk. She also collected treasures and her house is full of them, mixed in between twenty-year-old newspapers, cardboard boxes filled with flea market finds, and even some wedding presents that were never opened."

A feeling of dread was beginning to take root in my stomach. "When was her wedding?"

"Nineteen eighty-five."

I gulped. What was I in for?

Elodie's mention of a wedding suddenly reminded me of my aunt Ve, who'd recently become engaged to potential husband number five, Sylar Dewitt. After two months, I still wasn't sure about the upcoming nuptials, mostly because I didn't have a good feeling about them. The wedding was this coming Sunday. And unfortunately, Ve had come down with a nasty virus. One that had terrible timing, as she was the one in charge of the preparations for the ceremony and reception. Preparations that now fell on me to complete, since Sylar was too busy running his optometry office, the village (he was the village council chairman), and the upcoming theater production of *Cabaret* (he was a producer *and* had a supporting role). First up for me as Darcy Merriweather, wedding planner, was a menu tasting later that day. Then I had to try to figure out why there was a surprising lack of RSVPs coming in.

"My dad tried to keep her collecting in check," Elodie said, "but after he died, my mother's hoarding escalated. I was talking to Mrs. Pennywhistle the other day when she was in here shopping, and she gave you the highest of recommendations. I need someone I can trust. Someone who's not going to find an uncut gem amid the trash and stick it in a pocket."

Mrs. Pennywhistle, or as most everyone called her, Mrs. P, was the village's geriatric spitfire. I'd helped her clean out her granddaughter's apartment a couple of months ago, after she'd been murdered. Since then Mrs. P had become like family.

"Can I trust you?" Elodie asked me.

For some strange reason I had a feeling she was asking about something beyond nicking a few trinkets. It made me nervous, which immediately gave me second thoughts even as I said, "Absolutely."

"Then, you'll take on this task?" Her hands gripped the edge of the counter.

Suddenly she seemed anxious, and a little bit desperate. Which made me *really* nervous. Was there something she wasn't telling me?

Traces of panic lined her eyes. "Darcy?"

Cleaning a hoarder's house sounded like a nightmare, but I had little choice. "As You Wish's motto is that no request is too big or too small and no job impossible. I'll do it."

I didn't break my word, ever. So now that I'd given it, I was all-in on this job, for better or worse.

She smiled her sad smile. "You might come to regret that motto, especially after seeing the house."

I gazed at her. "Are you trying to scare me?"

"Just giving you fair warning."

I ignored the growing unease in the pit of my stomach. "You do know we charge by the hour, right?"

She laughed. "You'll earn every penny, Darcy. Every penny."

* * *

"What do you know about the disappearance of Patrice Keaton?" I asked village lawyer Marcus Debrowski as I filled my plate with appetizers. He'd joined me for the menu tasting at the Sorcerer's Stove, a local family restaurant.

A stuffed apricot slipped from Marcus's fingers and landed with a splat on the table. His face had gone as pale as the crème fraîche on the salmon cucumber cups. "Where'd you hear that name?" he said softly, looking around as if afraid to be overheard.

I dropped my voice, too, just because he was making me so nervous. "Her daughter, Elodie, hired As You Wish to clean out Patrice's house. She's planning on selling it."

Letting out a deep breath, he said, "You may want to turn down the job."

What was with all the warnings? "What am I missing? What happened to Patrice?"

He looked around. "Stop saying her name!"

"You're freaking me out!" I could barely eat the tomato, bacon, and cheese crostini I was holding.

"You should be freaked."

"Why? What happened to her?"

"No one knows," he said.

"You're not telling me everything," I accused. "Spill it."

ALSO AVAILABLE

Juliet Blackwell

Secondhand Spirits
A Witchcraft Mystery

Lily Ivory feels that she can finally fit in somewhere and conceal her "witchiness" in San Francisco. It's there that she opens her vintage clothing shop, outfitting customers both spiritually and stylistically.

Just when things seem normal, a client is murdered and children start disappearing from the Bay Area. Lily has a good idea that some bad phantoms are behind it. Can she keep her identity secret, or will her witchy ways be forced out of the closet as she attempts to stop the phantom?

Available wherever books are sold or at
penguin.com